A FEELING LIKE HOME

HALEIGH WENGER

Haleigh Wenger

sword
&silk
books

A FEELING LIKE Home

HALEIGH WENGER

For Vivian.

Sword and Silk Books
105 Viewpoint Circle Pell City, AL 35128
Visit our website at SwordandSilkBooks.com

To request permissions contact the publisher at
admin@swordandsilkbooks.com.

First Edition: August 2021

The characters and events in this book are fictitious. Any similarity to real
persons, living or dead, is coincidental and not intended by the author.

Ebook: 978-1-7364300-2-6

CHAPTER One

I'm having second thoughts.

We're driving down my sister Allison's driveway, the one that makes a loop in front of her house. Judging by how slow she's driving her roomy Lexus down said driveway, she's having second thoughts about this, too.

Not that anyone cared to ask for my opinion before exiling me for the entire summer.

Not that I deserve to be consulted.

Allison sucks in one of her cheeks as she ekes the car farther down the drive, headlights marking our path in the waning sunlight. The painfully slow drive mimics my hesitation. Texas wildflowers sway against the orange skyline in the summer night. From inside the car, I can just barely make out the familiar scent of tall grass and weeds that cling to the tiny, wealthy city of Old Oak, Texas.

"Justin moved all the boys' toys out of the guest bedroom, so it's not a playroom anymore. And we told Cam he's not supposed to bother you. So, you know, hopefully he won't."

I snort, a smile springing to my face despite my nerves. No chance my five-year-old nephew is going to listen to that rule. He'll be bounding onto my bed by 6 A.M. no matter what, just like he did the whole week I stayed here last spring break. But with his wide brown eyes and fuzzy crop of black hair, it's hard to stay mad at him. He's the only one I let call me by my old nickname, Piggy, instead of my real name, Paige.

When we reach the end of the driveway, my sister the garage door opener attached to the roof of her car, and the white garage door slides open. After parking inside, she pulls the keys from the ignition and turns to me.

"Should we talk about it?"

And there it is. I lift one shoulder and give my head a small shake, stomach uneasy. It's always uneasy lately. "Mom already told you everything."

I heard her on the phone, huddled in a corner of the dining room early one morning, whispering loudly like she always does when she thinks she's being discrete. Mom told Allison *everything*. My face grows hot just thinking about what she knows. That night with Griffin, the police, what it did to Dad...

She nods, a faint pink creeping along her ears. "But you could tell me too. It might be nice to hear your side."

My teeth tug at my bottom lip. I swore I would not spend all my time here rehashing the events that led to this, to my punishment.

"I messed up, Ally. It was stupid, but I didn't think..." Something catches in my throat and I can't finish. What was I going to say, anyway? That I didn't think I'd get caught?

That's true.

But really—I never thought Mom would take things this far. That she'd send me thousands of miles away to teach me a lesson. When Dad got sick the first time this year, what did I do? Sneak out in the middle of the night to meet Griffin. And when Mom grounded me for it? I spray-painted her name on the underside of a bridge in bold, drippy letters.

My eyes blink shut for a second before I release a deep breath. "Can we talk about this later?"

Allison nods a little too eagerly, her long brown hair cascading back and forth. "Absolutely. We'll talk once you're settled in."

I lift my suitcase from the trunk and follow her inside through the door that leads to the kitchen. Her flip-flops make a *swish-swish* sound across the grey tiled floors. Even with all the lights dimmed, her house is beautiful. It's one of those shiny white and grey modernist designs, but it's not cold and lifeless. Alongside the sleek lines and stainless-steel appliances are upward of one hundred framed pictures. Allison doesn't have much time for her photography business now that she has two kids, but she still takes a ton of pictures of her own family. From where I stand in the kitchen, gazing out across the open floor plan to the living room and dining room, a dozen photographed versions of my two nephews grin back at me.

My sister holds up a finger and walks through the living room and then through a door at the far corner of the first floor. "Hold on," she says.

I blink, one hand still squeezing my suitcase handle, the other skimming across the cool, black granite countertops. Five seconds later, she reappears with my brother-in-law, Justin. Even though I have older brothers of my own, Justin is one of my favorite people. When Allison brought him home to meet everyone for the first time over Christmas break, he spent the entire week teaching me how to play Phase 10. And even though I can't prove it, and he vehemently denies it, I'm almost positive he lets me win half the time—just to be nice. It would never occur to any of my older siblings to do something like that, even though I was still a little kid that Christmas. So, yeah. Justin is kind of special.

He strides toward me now, lips stretched wide in a familiar smile, and long arms outstretched. I let my bag drop and slip one arm around his waist and squeeze. He steps back to look at me, his thick black eyebrows lowering.

"I heard you've had an interesting couple of months. What's up with that?"

My heart zooms up from its normal place to an uncomfortable position in my throat. I can't forget about what I did for a minute, not even here.

From behind him, Allison shakes her head, making a growling sound. "She just got here."

He nods slowly, still sizing me up. I shift under his stare while Allison sighs deeply. She hooks an arm around her husband's waist and moves her gaze toward the shiny black clock hanging above the dining room table. "It's past our bedtime. Do you need help with your bags?"

My eyes follow hers. It's not even ten. This is where I'd usually tease them for being incredibly old and boring, but I chew on the inside of my cheek and force a grin. Better not to rock the boat the first day I'm here. I shake my head and sling my duffel bag up, tucking it under one arm. "I've got it. See you guys in the morning."

They head off to their bedroom, and I walk to the staircase on the other side of the floor. Up the stairs, past the bathroom and two other bedrooms, where yellow flickers from nightlights peep under the doors. The guest room door is slightly open and the bed's made sheets tucked in tight—just like Mom taught us.

The door firmly closed behind me, I lower myself to the bed and unzip the small bag at my side, sweeping past my newest romance book and pulling out the letter Mom sent with me with explicit directions to open it once I arrived. My eyes glaze over the first half—it's all boring sentimental stuff that sounds like she copied it from a generic parenting book. Instead I skip to the end where what she's written sends icy shivers down my spine.

With Dad's health, we can't afford to spend all our time afraid the police will show up at the house. I'll email you a link to Hopkin's Boarding School later this week. It's the same place your Aunt Sarah attended when she was having trouble in high school, and it did wonders for her attitude. Remember how much we love you. This is all for your own good. I hope you know that.

XO-Mom and Dad

At the last line, my lip involuntarily curls. "For your own good" is code for "we're the bosses, so do what we say or else." Or else boarding school.

My stomach flips over and over, like it's bobbing in deep water and struggling to stay afloat.

I appreciate space from my parents as much as the next sixteen-year-old, but still. Boarding school is not my idea of a good time. Most of the time I actually *like* my family. And Dad...

It's hard to ignore Mom's not-so-thinly veiled suggestion that *I'm* the cause of his recent bout of sickness. Crohn's disease can be exasperated by stress, but have I really been that bad?

My hand tightens around the letter, crumpling it in my fist. Probably.

A big reason I'm in this mess is because after twenty-nine years and five kids, Mom and Dad got too tired of parenting to pay attention to me. Neither of them has the energy to deal with what Dad deemed my "wild streak," especially with his worsening health. Something tells me Hopkin's Boarding School is full of the youngest children with wild streaks. I'd be one of many. Again.

I slip a pen from the front pocket of my bag and flip over Mom's letter. Numbering one through three for every month I'll be here, I start at the top. For June, I can write apology letters to everyone back home, starting with my parents. I'm surprised apologies weren't Mom's first requirement. Letters will definitely impress her. In July, I can work on myself somehow. Mom's letter says I need to change my behavior, so how about a big change? I write *change* down with a question mark after it. I can come back to that. And for the last month, August, I know what I have to do. Something big to prove that I'm not a lost cause. Some trick or easy lie that will make them sure I'm the good little girl they need me to be. We're past the point for authentic grand gestures, and I think deep down even Mom knows that. Really, there's only one thing my list should include, and it's the only thing I'm not sure I'm capable of doing: Don't. Self. Sabotage.

I slide my hand across the cool cotton sheets, lean back on the bed, and lay against the silky white pillow. I made some huge mistakes, but all I have to do is lie low this summer and do my community service, and then I can fly back to Washington in time for school in the fall. I'm *not* going to boarding school. I'll fix this.

I have to.

CHAPTER
Two

I'm going to die.

The sun isn't even up and there's this loud rapping against the guest bedroom door. It's got to be five or six in the morning based on previous nephew wake-up calls, which is a full four hours earlier than I can be bothered to wake up in the summer. Loud whispers sound from the hallway, and a tiny screechy cry pierces through the crack between the door and the carpeted floor. I'm never going to survive if this is the normal wake-up time.

Eyes blind with sleep, I fumble in the dark for my phone, which I plugged in before I crashed last night. Instead of the time at the top of the screen, my eyes focus on the unread text alerts littering my home screen.

All from Griffin.

Warm, sticky shame washes over me at the words. *I miss you so much. Call me when you get there.*

I haven't thought about him once.

The cries outside my door intensify, sounding more like what I'd imagine from a wounded raptor than an infant.

Bang!

My door shudders open and hits against the wall, a scruffy little boy with a tuft of jet-black hair and wide eyes somersaulting toward me.

Allison's right there, too, with her eyes narrowed and baby Mattie on her hip.

"Cameron Woods! I asked you to leave Aunt Paige's door alone. Now you woke her up and almost gave yourself a concussion."

She does such a spot-on impression of Mom, and my heart beats erratically in my chest. And I'm not the one in trouble.

I swipe the back of my hand over my half-opened eyes and roll to the ground. Grabbing Cam with one hand and scooping him into my lap, I blink back at my sister.

"Don't worry about it. I've been up for a while, anyway."

She gives me a sidelong glance. "It's five-thirty."

I shrug. "Guess I'm a morning person now."

Cam smooshes his head against my arm and squeals so loud I'm tempted to reach for the headphones in my duffel bag.

"Auntie Piggy!"

Ugh, that name. Mom says I originally got the nickname because I was such a fat baby. I guess she expected me to grow up as stick-thin and tall as her and Allison, or else she might have thought twice about it. Still, the corners of my mouth curve upward at his squeaky voice and his sweaty little body.

From my doorway, Allison sighs and lowers a squirming baby Mattie to the ground, where he crawls toward Cam and me like a trained infant assassin. He goes for the kill, grabbing two chubby fistfuls of my hair and pulling my head close enough for his mouth to make contact. There's slobber everywhere. I duck my head and wipe the drool on the shoulder of my t-shirt. Long, frizzy dark hairs from my head float to the floor as he releases his grasp. *Ouch.*

I snap the thick black hair tie from my wrist and wrap it around my hair. Mattie's full cheeks quiver as he watches me pull away from his entertainment. Allison walks into the room and sits on the edge of the bed, observing as I balance both of her kids on my lap.

"You'll be okay with them, right?"

Her hands wring in front of her, and she lets her feet dangle off the side of the bed.

Part of the deal is that I'll stay here and watch the kids a few days a week while Allison reopens her photography business. A pretty easy setup compared to the summer job my parents first threatened to sign me up for: picking up highway litter with convicts. I nod my head toward my lapful of kids like, "What do you think?"

Baby Mattie, all white-blond fuzz and milky skin, lunges forward to find my hair again and tumbles over on unsteady knees. Forming a cradle with one arm, I catch him before he lands upside down on the rug. He coos against my elbow, soft baby hairs tickling my skin.

Allison chews her lip. All moms are supposed to be protective of their kids, but she worries a lot. Maybe more than normal since she wasn't able to get pregnant, and they decided to adopt. It's like she's afraid if she doesn't watch closely enough, her babies will disappear in a puff of smoke.

I tuck one little boy under each arm and smash them toward me until Cam squeals in my ear so loud I'm afraid he might set a car alarm off.

"I promise to take good care of them. Go get ready. I can handle breakfast."

I mean, as long as breakfast is a bowl of cereal.

She stands and stares at the door. I look up as Justin stops in the doorframe, eyebrows raised. Allison wordlessly answers him back with a tiny nod. Glancing between them, it's obvious there's something they're not telling me.

Justin ducks through the door. "Mind if I come in and talk for a minute?"

I blink back at him, shoulders lifting as he squats down on the carpet next to me. Allison does the same, and Mattie immediately crawls to her, then stops, his arms outstretched for his mom.

Whatever this is, it can't be good. It's eerily similar to Mom and Dad's ambush when they sprang their summer plans on me. But I don't know what could be worse than your own parents exiling you. I suck in a stuttering breath just the same.

Allison tucks her hair behind her ears. First one side, then the other. "Paige, we just want to make sure we lay down some rules."

Heat splatters my cheeks. Great. Not even my sister trusts me.

"Um. What you did in Washington—the destructive stuff—you can't do that here. You know?"

She runs fingers through Mattie's tiny collection of hair, watching me.

There's a tight dryness in my throat, but I manage to squeak out a response. "I know. I wasn't planning on it." Especially not with the threat of boarding school breathing down my neck.

I turn to Justin, too, since he's here to support Allison while she plays at authoritarian.

"No destructive stuff, no graffiti, no breaking windows. I promise." My fingernails curve into my palm as I list my past nefarious activities. Maybe I should reach out and cover Cam's ears so he doesn't get any ideas. But he's snaked my phone off the bed and his eyes are glassy as he scrolls through who-knows-what.

Allison sighs, a tiny gasp of a breath. "Look—we're not planning on being spies for Mom and Dad, but if you get into trouble like that again..."

"She won't," Justin butts in. "Right, Paige?"

Cam hums to himself as he snaps a blurry picture of his foot. I press my chin against his hair and inhale that fruity, floral smell only little kids seem to possess. It's like the world's most delicious shampoo mixed with a scent all their own.

"Right." My stomach hurts so bad that saliva pools in my mouth. I was hoping my sudden onset of stomach pain was something I could leave back in Seattle too. Apparently, not so much.

THE SECOND MATTIE CLOSES HIS EYES FOR HIS AFTERNOON NAP and I've successfully tiptoed out of his bedroom with Cam's hand clutched in mine, my phone rings.

The sound probably isn't loud enough to wake him up, but after forty minutes of attempting to rock him to sleep, I'm ready to throw my phone against a wall if it'll keep him down.

My hand fumbles inside my pocket until I've felt my way to the button to silence it. Then Cam and I scurry downstairs to pillage the pantry. Turns out watching two kids might be more exhausting than collecting trash off the side of the road.

While Cam shovels Goldfish into his mouth at the table, I press my phone to my ear and play the voicemail from Griffin.

More about how much he misses me. More asking me to call him so we can talk about what happened.

I don't think I can handle talking to him so soon after our break-up. Maybe tomorrow.

Instead, I scoot into the chair next to Cam's and snag a handful of crackers from his pile. I flip over my book from where it sits face down on the table, ready to use the quiet time to dive back into relationship drama that's *not* my own. Cam's little face folds into a frown, and his nose wrinkles as he whips his arms into a folded position and shrieks, "Hey! Those are mine, Piggy!"

I press a finger to his lips to remind him we have to be quiet while the baby naps, and then I drag a hand through his silky hair.

"Sorry, bud. Piggies get hungry too."

I unload a handful of Goldfish crackers into my mouth. Salt and my childhood—that's what they taste like. Cam goes back to eating his snack, eyeing me after each bite to make sure I'm not planning on stealing any more.

Ding-dong. The chime rings through the entire house, echoing against the walls and sending me scraping backward out of my chair, book flying, and heart beating out of my chest. Whoever's on the other side of the front door better hope their doorbell ringing didn't wake up Mattie. Or else they're about to deal with one angry aunt-slash-babysitter.

I grip the knob so tightly that white streaks my knuckles, and I whip the door open. A guy around my age blinks into the sun on the front porch.

I narrow my eyes. "Can I help you?"

He shakes a mop of dark hair out of his face. "Yeah, I guess so. I'm supposed to deliver this to Allison Woods. Is that you?"

Unlike most of the residents of Old Oak, his southern accent is barely there. I'd miss it if it weren't for the way he slips the 's' of 'is' into a 'z' sound. With one hand, he extends a flat manila envelope with the words Prince Prints in bold at the top. Underneath that, Allison's name is written in black ink.

"No, but I can take it. I'm her sister."

He points to his white collared shirt bearing a matching Prince Prints logo on the left side. "Joey" is embroidered on the right in loopy black lettering.

"My boss told me to put it directly into the hands of the person with the name on the envelope. Is your last name Woods, too?"

A wail spirals down the stairs. It's Mattie, awake already thanks to Mr. Prince Prints over here.

I shake my head, my neck warming. "Nope. But like I said, I'm her sister, and I'm in charge while she's gone, so this will be safe with me."

I tug on the envelope and his grip loosens, but not before his light brown fingers slide against mine, all warm and awkward and slightly sweaty, no doubt a result of the early summer humidity.

He pulls back his hand like I have scalded him. "What's your name?"

I frown. He can't be serious. Mattie's cries pick up, and this guy *has* to hear them. I narrow my eyes, wondering if he's really that oblivious or just plain rude.

Still staring at the envelope I've wrangled from his grasp, he knits his eyebrows together. "I need to know so my boss can tell your sister who her pictures were delivered to if she asks."

"Mama! Mama!" Mattie screams like he's being tortured, which would worry me, but Ally swears that's what he always sounds like when he fights his naps.

I press a hand to the envelope, apparently full of prints Ally ordered. "I can tell her myself when she gets home. But if it makes you feel better, I'm Paige, and sorry, but I'm kind of busy."

He nods. "Paige...?"

Unbelievable. He's staring me down like I'm some kind of criminal, which makes my heartbeat pound in my head and my breath come out short and fast. It's not like telling him my full name matters, and I can't figure out why he's being such a freak about it. I gesture up the stairs behind me to the sound of pitiful baby cries and Joey Prince shifts, but has the guts to *not* leave the front porch.

"Look, *Joey*, I'm busy here, okay. I'm babysitting, and I don't have time to stand out here being interrogated. Or flirted with. Or *whatever* you think this is." I wave the envelope in front of his face. "You delivered the pictures, everything's good, so thank you. I'm going inside now."

He takes a giant step backward. "Excuse me? I'm not flirting —I'm not..." His hand grazes his hair before it sweeps down his face. "Look. Just give your sister the pictures, okay?"

I level a wordless glare at him and step inside the house, ready to close the door, but not before he calls back, his voice impossibly calm, "I'll see you this time next week for the next delivery."

The door slams shut while I lean against it and exhale. What was with the third degree? Ally's definitely going to hear about that kid when she gets home because there's no way I'm dealing with him every week for the rest of the summer. Not if he's going to talk to me like *that*. And what's the point of a photo delivery service, anyway? Isn't that the entire point of this babysitting gig—so my sister can do work stuff like take pictures and print them? Palms pressed to my now-aching temples, I walk back toward the kitchen to check on Cam just in time for a spiral of increasing wails to a crescendo from upstairs. Guess naptime's over.

Perfect.

CHAPTER *Three*

T he day before the house-building project that Mom signed me up for begins, Allison rustles through her purse before throwing a fistful of quarters on the kitchen countertop. They *clink* down as she motions to me.

"If you're feeling adventurous, there's an arcade a few blocks over that Cam's kind of obsessed with." She sneaks a look at Cam, who's busy swirling his spoon through his cereal bowl to create a milk tornado. Mattie watches him from his highchair, his face sticky with banana goop and awe.

I smirk. "Sounds fun."

She laughs, shaking her head. "Yeah, I forgot who I was talking to for a minute. Everything's an adventure to you, right, Piggy?"

I stab my cereal spoon at her, cool and metallic in my grip. "Hey. You're not allowed to call me that anymore."

Her low laugh echoes behind her as she heads to the garage.

I watch her go, spooning sugar-sweetened milk leftover from my cereal bowl into my mouth. Allison and I used to talk every day, despite the twelve years between us. When she turned eighteen and moved out, I'd call her on Mom's phone after school every day while Mom navigated the carpool lane. Then it progressed to texting her and crying over middle school drama. But now—especially with my reason for being here, hanging over us—our relationship is *off*. Like the kind of off-centered feeling you get when you jump out of bed too quickly in the morning and the world is hazy at the edges and your feet are still half-asleep. I know we'll regain our balance; it's just a question of how to prove to her I'm not the monster Mom says I am. If I'm lucky, maybe I can get Ally to explain to Mom how crazy the whole boarding school idea is.

The kids finish a breakfast buffet of every kind of fruit and cereal available in the pantry, and then it's time for us to go. I'm learning the trick is to keep so busy they don't even have time to get into trouble. I'm basically a kid whisperer, and it's only day two of my summer gig.

Allison's bulky double-stroller is parked in the garage. It's black and grey with these enormous wheels that look like they belong on a motorcycle instead of something for lugging around little kids. But it's better than the time during spring break when I volunteered to take Cam to the park and ended up carrying him on my shoulders for a solid mile. If I sleep wrong, the place where his bony butt rested still burns. The cool black rubber on the stroller handles forms to my hands when I squeeze it. After buckling Cam and Mattie in, I flex my fingers and navigate out of the garage and down the never-ending driveway toward the neighborhood gate. Because of course Allison lives in a gated neighborhood full of shiny new cars and designer dogs on rhinestone-encrusted leashes. Ally's always been the most lavish in our family. Mom never fails to remind me of the fact that Ally got her first job the same day she got her license. What Mom conveniently forgets is that Ally used all the money she earned at that job to buy piles of clothes that were still hanging in the closet the day she moved out for college.

The air here is so thick with sticky moisture—clinging to my skin and leaving warm drops of perspiration along my neck, coiling around my hair and pulling it higher and frizzier—it's harder to breathe than back home. Mom warned me Texas summer would be different than in Washington, but now I wish she would have better prepared me. Shoved me under a blazing hot showerhead in all my clothes or forced me into a hot yoga class. Something.

Nestled under the stroller's canopy in front of me, Cam exhales loudly, his arms stretching out toward the street. "It's hot."

Mattie's raspy voice echoes Cam's as he lets out a string of unintelligible babbles.

Tipping my head back toward the cloudless sky, I force myself to swallow. "Yeah, it is Cammy. But the arcade's only a few minutes away, okay?"

He answers with another sigh and folds himself back into the shaded seat. Sweat streams down the small of my back, tickling my skin and no doubt staining the back of my baby blue cotton sundress. Pushing all my weight against the stroller handle at the bottom of a sweeping cement hill, I consider my strappy leather sandals.

Apparently, fashion and function don't go hand-in-hand when strollers are involved. It's all Ally's fault for not warning me to wear running clothes to go out. Or maybe she did, but I had already tuned her out. It would have been a good time to listen, considering how hard it is to get over this hill.

Admittedly, it wouldn't be the first time.

Either way, this arcade better have AC and ice cream. Drool pools in the corners of my mouth at the thought of creamy frozen chocolate sliding its way down my throat as I collapse onto a sticky multi-colored carpet corner and watch Cam play.

Oh wow. Is this what it feels like to hit rock bottom?

From exiled almost-juvenile delinquent to faux teen mom in under a week. Talk about a heart-pounding adventure. And all thanks to my parents for sending me away to sweat to death in hell.

By the time we've reached the top of the hill where the

arcade's located, my clothes are more soaked through with sweat than not, and my vision is blurred because of the sweat dripping down from my forehead. Baby Mattie's asleep in the stroller—his head rolled onto one shoulder, his cheeks spotted red and lips slightly parted.

I could go for a nap right now, too.

Cam, on the other hand, is wide awake. Not only that, he's bouncing on the edge of the stroller seat, hands tucked underneath his legs and being used as springs to launch himself at me as soon as I stop and circle to the front. Wheezing and clutching my likely bruised ribcage after the unexpected takedown, I instruct Cam to hold on to the side of the stroller while I maneuver a still-sleeping Mattie through the arcade's front doors.

The inside's just as I pictured. Under my feet, blue-, red-, and yellow-swirled carpet spans the entire place. Framed posters of Mario, Luigi, and the gang mixed with a bunch of other familiar-looking video game characters I don't know the names of decorate the space.

It smells like plastic and glass cleaner.

Pac-Man machines line the walls near the back, across from an area labeled clearly with a floating sign as the designated space for kids. I make a beeline for it.

Stroller parked against the wall and Cam already glassy-eyed in front of a ride-on blue plastic elephant, I collapse into a toddler-sized lounge chair next to a block table. Cramped butt and all, it's still infinitely better than hiking up that hill while pushing the stroller. My heartbeat pounds in my ears, but at least the AC blasts from a giant vent overhead, just like I hoped it would.

The kid's area is empty, leaving us with room to spread out. I lean my head against the bright yellow wall and let my eyes slide shut while Cam fiddles with a game controller connected to a kid-sized machine.

"Hey, bud. You're holding that upside-down. Do you want some help?"

I squint open one eye to see someone with a swoop of dark hair pointing to the controller in Cam's hand.

And because I ranted to Ally and Justin about that voice and that hair all last night during dinner, I know exactly who it is. I've barely caught my breath from the walk here, and now I'm sucking air into my lungs at a too-rapid pace.

"A-hem."

Joey from Prince Prints straightens, runs one hand through the crop of hair falling into his eyes, and then scowls.

"Oh. Hey." His mouth twists into a polite smile. A customer service smile, even though he's not wearing an arcade uniform. He must be one of those guys that hangs out in arcades just for the fun of it, and the smile must be a reflex from working at the photo shop.

As I stand, the kiddie chair rises with me, stuck to my butt. Heat washes over me, spotting my chest and face with red splotches I'm sure to see if I dare look down.

I yank on the chair and, freeing myself, toss it to the ground, where it rolls over like a mistreated rag doll. "Um. I guess these chairs really are only for kids, huh?"

A dry laugh chokes out of me, but Joey keeps staring with that fake, too-wide smile plastered on.

Cam looks up, his eyes roving between us. Please, please, for the love of all things holy and good in this world, don't let him say anything embarrassing.

His wide brown eyes fully focused on me, Cam lowers his eyebrows and asks in a dramatic and *loud* whisper, "Aunt Piggy, is he your boyfriend?"

My stomach sinks down to the floor.

Joey's smile drops.

"Ha. Ha," I say. "Nope. He is *not* my boyfriend." It takes a lot of effort to not jab my finger too forcefully in Joey's direction and to keep my voice light.

Cam squints. "So he's just your friend?"

"Umm. Hm."

They both blink at me. If Cam weren't so freaking obser-vant of everything I do and say, I'd take this moment to rehash the first time Joey and I met and remind him it was too awkward to turn into even the barest of friendships. But seeing as there's a chance every minute of our day together will get reported back to Justin and Ally, all I can do is mumble some non-answers and hope the games distract Cam sooner rather than later.

Finally, Cam turns back to his upside-down controller and mashes a string of buttons. Joey's eyebrows knit together. He crosses his arms over his plain blue V-neck, veins bulging like Cam's ineptitude physically pains him. When he turns back to glance at me and points at Cam's controller, I raise a shoulder. Better him than me. And anyway, I have to keep an eye on Mattie while he sleeps.

"I could show you how, if you want." Crouching next to Cam, Joey rests his hand over the buttons and motions for Cam to copy him.

Three minutes into the tutelage and Cam's gazing up at his new friend like he's Mickey Mouse, a giant robot, and the ice cream truck all rolled into one.

Green waves roll through my chest, but I bite them down. Cam can't help if he's too easily impressed.

"Aunt Piggy, can we play more games?"

I fish the quarters from my purse and drop them in his sweaty hand. "Here. Knock yourselves out."

He jingles the money, showing it off to Joey, who grins and produces a pocketful of his own change.

Behind me, Mattie hiccups in his sleep. I slump against the wall and slide to the floor next to the stroller, careful not to bump it. My phone buzzes from in my purse. I peek inside to see Griffin's name flash on the screen, causing me to exhale through my nose.

Stupid, persistent Griffin. Stupid Griffin and his beautiful art and his sweet blue eyes.

Part of me should feel bad for ignoring him, I know. And part of me—a tiny, miniscule speck of me—does, but there's a much bigger part of me that understands he's better off without me whether or not he knows it. He'd have followed me anywhere, without question. At first his unquestioning loyalty made my heart pound and my blood surge with exhilarating power. Power I'd thought might be love.

I broke his heart. And now, every time he calls, my heart breaks a little, too.

Once I silence my phone and tuck it back into my purse, I retrieve the letter from a different pocket. I unfold it slowly, bending the creased squares carefully so the paper doesn't make any noise. Not that a little rusting paper could shake those two from their arcade game euphoria. Both of their shoulders are tight, eyes narrowed at the dimly lit screen. It would take an earthquake to get their attention at this point.

But still. The contents of this letter reveal stuff I'd rather not share with the general public. And that includes Joey from Prince Prints.

I re-read the words and angle my body away from their line of vision. Something in my chest pulls as I picture Mom and Dad bent over the kitchen table writing these words late one night while I was out with Griffin building a bonfire in an abandoned house or tagging the underside of a bridge with smiley faces glistening in iridescent green spray paint. I like to assume that Mom wrote this letter long before things got as bad as they did. She was probably just waiting for an excuse to get rid of me. To pull out this letter and send me on a plane. She barely gave me any warning—just a week to pack up my life. But even if she wrote it right before I left for Texas, it still stings.

At first, the stuff Griffin and I did was harmless.

But still stupid. More so considering what it cost me.

And what it cost Dad.

An ache, dull and constant, tugs at the thought of my parents' disappointment. At remembering Dad's pale face when my actions caused him physical pain. At Griffin's blank expression when I let him take the blame. And Ally and Justin's speech the other night, warning me not to mess up again.

As if I want to be a screw-up. As if I want to go to *boarding school.*

Neon blue paper blurs my vision as Cam barrels toward me, a string of tickets clutched in his hand. "Look at this. Look. *Look!*" He dangles the rectangular stubs under my nose, tickling my face with the edges.

"Wow, look at all those tickets, Cammy." I snake an arm around his toothpick waist, where his t-shirt plays peek-a-boo with his belly button, and wiggle my fingers against his ribs. He spasms, high-pitched giggles bursting from his mouth.

"Joey helped me win them. He shared his monies."

A glance at Joey, who stands a few feet away, hands stuffed in the pockets of his tan shorts, confirms Cam's story. He shrugs, a boyish grin playing at the corners of his mouth.

While Cam flops onto the tacky floor to closer inspect his tickets, I stand up and step next to Joey. I slide my letter back into my purse.

"Hey. Um. Thanks. It was nice of you to hang out with him."

He pulls a hand from his pocket and rubs his fingers through the back of his hair, eyes landing on Cam. "He's cool. It was fun."

Neither of us makes eye contact. It's like that game where you try to see who will blink first, but the total opposite. Who will stop avoiding the other first?

Obviously, I win.

"Hem." He drags his eyes to mine. Out of my peripheral vision, I note his clenched jaw. "I guess I'll see you around."

I turn my head a half-inch and nod. "Sure. For the next delivery, right?"

He nods. "Well that, and I live a few houses down from your sister. So I'm sure we'll run into each other."

Huh. That's news to me. He knows Ally, and he still gave me crap. My eye twitches at the revelation.

"Why are you guys staring at each other?" Cam's voice sends a surge of heat through my body. Joey's eyes snap from mine to the floor.

And that's my cue to go.

After I convince Cam to buckle into the stroller, I march out the arcade doors and back down the hill toward home. One glance backward is all I allow myself, but there's no sign of anything but the tinted arcade windows.

"Who's Joey?"

My lips clamp around the metal spoon heavy with yogurt I'm trying to force down my throat. I cough as I spin to face Ally, who's standing in the shadows of the darkened kitchen, hands on her hips.

"Um. What?"

"Cameron interrupted his bedtime story three different times to talk about him. He was at the arcade with you?" Clearly, she's already made up her mind about this. Allison's lips are tight, her eyes narrowed on mine.

I sigh. "What's with the interrogation? I thought you trusted me." I set my spoon down on the edge of my bowl full of yogurt, then cross my arms over my chest, hugging tight.

"And I thought we had a deal. I have a right to know who you bring my kids around."

Tears sting the corners of my eyes, but I bite them back, my teeth finding the fleshy bits on the inside of my cheek. She's no different from Mom. I'm the big bad wolf to my family, and nothing I do will change that. "You know him, too, Ally. It's the anal-retentive guy from the photo delivery service. Prince Prints?"

She steps toward me, her lips forming a tiny circle. "Oh."

"And there was no secret meeting. He just happened to be at the arcade today too."

She walks to the table and sinks into a chair next to me. "Whenever I go into the store or see them around the neighborhood, his dad calls him 'Joseph.'"

I gulp down more yogurt, deepening my silence.

Her sigh echoes between us. The point of her elbow jabs into my side. "I'm sorry."

Looking sideways at her, I shrug. "I know I've been stupid lately, but I would never..." The words stick in my throat. A shiver runs down the length of my neck, shaking my head along with it. She thinks I'll ruin things exactly like I ruined Dad's health. "I would never put your kids in danger," I manage to finish.

Her hand slips forward to find mine. She squeezes her fingers against my palm, leaning closer. "I know you wouldn't. I shouldn't have attacked you like that."

I shrug again.

"I'll stay home with the boys tomorrow morning, and you can go out and find something fun to do before you have to volunteer."

My teeth nibble at my bottom lip. "What about the deal with Mom? No fun allowed this summer, remember?"

"She doesn't have to know, as long as you swear you forgive me."

My cheeks curve upward into a smile. "Consider yourself forgiven."

Upstairs, I pee, brush my teeth, and crawl into bed. I let myself think about the sting of disappointment from Ally's doubt. How her mind immediately went to not trusting me.

My phone chimes with a text from Griffin.

I miss you...

I miss being with someone who understands me. Someone who doesn't jump to conclusions and thinks the worst of me. Griffin seems to be the only one left who sees me. And I've spent the last week pushing him away, but right now I need him. I flip my camera into reverse, tousle my hair, and find an angle that's mostly bare skin.

Miss you too ;)

I hit send and throw my phone as far away from me as possible. Then I curl onto my side and cry myself to sleep.

CHAPTER Four

W hen my phone alarm goes off, I slam a hand numb from sleeping against the screen, swiping as fast as I can to stop the ringing noise.

Only after my eyes slide closed again does the faint voice coming from my bedside table register.

It feels like a frog the size of the entire state of Texas is hopping on my chest. I press the phone to my ear. "Griffin?"

"Paige? Are you there? Did I wake you up?"

Shoot. This isn't the first time I've mistaken an incoming phone call for my alarm. Why is this happening to me? Why now?

Griffin waits on the other end, as infuriatingly patient as always. If he were an animal, he'd hands-down be a golden retriever.

Loyal.

Sun-kissed hair.

Really slobbery kisses.

I sigh into my phone. "Yes. You woke me up. Why are you awake? Isn't it even earlier there?"

A split-second pause lingers between us.

"Huh? Oh, yeah. I couldn't sleep."

His voice is deep, steady, and smooth as honey.

I wish, more than anything, I could find it in me to hate him.

But I don't.

He's the perfect boyfriend.

Or ex-boyfriend, now that I'm here and he's there. Not to mention the fact that I got him into a lot of trouble.

I guess he's the one who should hate me. And that's what makes it so hard to talk to him. I thought, stupidly, that I'd arrive in Texas with no feelings left for Griffin, and he'd forget about me and we could both pretend our breakup, our relationship, all of it, never happened. But, obviously, it doesn't work like that. For better or worse, I can't quite let him go. Griffin is reliable. That's why I sent him the pictures in a moment of weakness, because I knew he'd care. And sometimes it's nice to have someone care, to have someone see you.

Propping myself up on one elbow, I blink at the bedroom ceiling. Pristine white paint, of course. Back home my ceiling's smattered with incredibly sticky glow-in-the-dark stars that originally belonged to Allison. Those, and random splashes of paint in a rainbow of colors left over from all the different facelifts the walls have gotten over the years.

"What is it, Griff?" My voice comes out sharper than I mean it to, so I bite down on my tongue and force out some patience. He deserves my patience and more, but it's all I can offer right now.

His voice dips several octaves lower. "I got your pictures."

My thumbs needle the spot in between my eyes. I should feel bad about sending several shots of myself with the blanket draped across only a small portion of my body, eyes wide, lips pouty. I needed a distraction after my misunderstanding with Allison last night, and Griffin usually responds immediately when I send pictures. Plus, it's not like I have many options here in Middle of Nowhere, Texas. But in this sleep-deprived groggy state, aggravation courses along my clenched jaw. Why can't we both pretend like it didn't happen?

I let out a deep groan.

His voice changes back to normal. "Is everything okay?"

My hands cover my eyes. "Yeah. I'm just tired. So, why'd you call?"

He breathes into the phone, faint and slow. It's so like him to take his time, even though he can tell I'm annoyed. At one point, it didn't bother me. I thought it was cute how he takes his time thinking up the exact right thing to say instead of spitting something out.

My eyes slip shut. Like a slideshow, pictures of Griffin and me zoom past the backs of my eyelids. Walking down the hill from our middle school to our neighborhood while eating Twizzlers from the school vending machine. Flirting in chemistry while Mr. Jones obsessed over the periodic table, making out behind the school instead of eating in the cafeteria at lunch, sneaking out at night to tag the underside of all the bridges... His voice, deep and decisive, cuts my memories short.

"You said we should take a break."

Even though he can't see me, I cover my warm and flushed cheeks. "Yes," I confirm.

"Well, I don't agree. I'm going to wait until you come back at the end of the summer. Then I'll prove to you we should be together."

I turn my head and exhale into the cool, airy fabric of the pillowcase. This is exactly why I've been avoiding his calls. What is even the point of this conversation? Why can't he see how hard this is for me?

"Griffin," I start, my voice full of all the venom I can muster at seven a.m. "We broke up. I don't think you should call me anymore, okay?"

Silence.

While my finger hovers over the button to end the call, his voice surfaces.

"Please, give me a chance. We're good for each other, even if you want to pretend we aren't. And just so you know—I love the pictures." His words are pleading, but his tone is as even and calm as ever.

"Goodbye, Griffin."

I jab my finger against the screen to end the call. Then I bury my phone underneath my pillow.

After five minutes of sighing and rolling around the bed, I drag my feet to the floor and slink downstairs. The smell of cinnamon wafts toward me. Homemade cinnamon rolls are a family apology tradition. My mouth waters at the idea of cramming as many of them in my stomach as I possibly can.

"Sugar. I need sugar." I prop my elbows against the counter, leaning my forehead against the cold granite.

When I lift my head, Allison and Justin watch me, eyebrows raised. Justin slides me a porcelain-white plate with a giant golden-brown cinnamon roll in the center. Allison dangles a fork in front of me.

"Are you still mad at me for last night?"

I shake my head. After my early wake-up call, the last thing I'm worrying about is my fight with my sister.

"I accept this peace offering," I say, snatching the fork and digging into the soft cinnamon-specked layers.

A corner of her mouth turns up. "It is. And I'm sorry. Again."

With my mouth full of warm, sweet bread, I shake my head. "It's fine. We're good, Ally."

As good as we're going to get, at least. I'll add my sister to the list of people who blame me for Dad, who blame me for this summer, who blames me for everything.

It's fine.

She nods. "Good. I'll still be home today with the kids if you want to go out exploring. Justin's about to leave for work, but he can drop you off somewhere before your *thing*, if you want." My thing. The service project Mom insisted I sign up for and that I've been pretending isn't happening. Me and a pile of tools building an actual, real-life house all summer?

Justin grins at me, white teeth gleaming, his eyes wide.

Ally glances up at him, then smacks him with the back of her hand. "Stop laughing at me. I was just offering."

He rubs his chest where she made contact, still laughing softly at the thought of driving me around. "Paige doesn't want me dropping her off places. It's embarrassing, right?"

I quirk my mouth to the side, pretending to think. "It's a little embarrassing, yeah. But I don't have any other way to get around, so..." I shrug. My sister and her husband always tease each other like this. It's nice.

Ally nods, pointing at me like, "See?"

But Justin holds up a finger, his eyes bright. "Okay. Presenting option B." He disappears through the kitchen into the garage. Allison's hands slide to her hips. When he enters a few seconds later, wheeling in a pink and purple beach bike, my cheeks twitch.

He nudges the kickstand with his foot and holds his arms out in front of the bike like he's presenting a prize. "Huh? What do you think?"

Ally rolls her eyes and makes a noise between her teeth.

I clasp my hands together and lean forward. "Ooooh. I *love* it." And I do. It's not something I'd ever be caught dead on back home, but here I'm carving out a new, cleaner identity. Might as well start it off with the shiny girly bike of my five-year-old self's dreams.

Justin steps aside while I run my hands across the smooth metal and rubber handlebars. "I knew you would," he says.

Allison shakes her head. "This is my old bike. Like, from back in college. You'd rather ride this thing around than be seen in the car with one of us?"

"Sorry, but yes. I've always wanted a bike this cool. And look at this basket." Skimming a palm across the white wicker basket perched above the back wheel, I raise my eyebrows at my sister.

She sighs, clearly disappointed. I briefly wonder if I could take the bike with me to boarding school, and then I hate myself for even thinking it.

After Justin leaves for work and Allison and the kids wander upstairs to take their morning baths, I wind my hair into a messy bun near the top of my head, text Ally to let her know I'm leaving, and set off. No plan in mind, just the shaky feeling the world might pass me by if I don't step away from the safety of Allison and Justin's house. Plus, I need to find some way to convince my Mom to stop considering boarding school, and I haven't thought of anything while sitting around at Ally's.

Like yesterday, it's unbearably hot.

Humidity is a constant here as much as the mist and drizzly rain are back in Washington. Except sprinkling rain during the daytime doesn't leave everyone and everything smelling like wet dog the way the weather does here.

It hits me as I'm pedaling out the gate that separates their neighborhood from the quaint downtown area that I don't know where I'm going. Unless I want to go on some serious trails, nothing else besides the downtown area I've already seen exists within biking distance. My leather sandals probably will not cut it on the trails. And who am I kidding—I don't have the stamina for that. So I scrape back sweaty strands of hair from my eyes and turn in the arcade's direction.

I've never understood video games. Especially the old-school ones. Staring blankly at a giant blinking box while you mash buttons repeatedly in order to maybe win at something that doesn't matter all that much, anyway?

Boring.

But, like I said, all I'm familiar with is Mario. Probably because that's all my older brothers would let me play.

Even if the arcade has Mario games, I'm not going back there. Pools of warm sweat accumulating on my neck, and calves aching, I slowly make my way up the stupid hill. I thought I'd die when I had to mount it while pushing the stroller, but riding a bike is one billion times worse. Pressure beats against my chest until the only way to get air into my lungs is by sucking in ragged, thin breaths.

Zooming around town on this stylish beach cruiser is cute in theory, but so, so much harder in execution. Beside the fact I'm out of breath and my lungs might explode at any second—and the agonizing ache in my legs—the bike ride has taken my hair from perfectly messy bun to bridge troll in under thirty minutes. I plan to avoid reflective surfaces altogether so I don't have to see what the exercise has done to my already reddish skin.

Once I've made my way to the front of the arcade, I park at the empty rack next to the street. Justin didn't give me a lock, and I totally forgot bike locks are a thing. I'll have to cross my fingers extra tight no one comes by and decides my newest vehicle of choice is also the bike of their childhood heart. I use the rack as a point of reference for the rest of the miniature downtown of Old Oak, which is a set of old-timey business fronts for the surrounding wealthy neighborhoods. Along the storefront are half a dozen other stores. The arcade is sandwiched between a health food store and a vet clinic. Next to the clinic is a bakery that smells like carb heaven and whose "We're Closed" sign sends actual pangs of disappointment through me, even with Ally's cinnamon roll sitting in my stomach. A local bank sits next to the bakery, and then comes a sandwich shop, which is also closed.

Last in the row, its logo in bold blue lettering above the door, is Prince Prints.

Shoot.

After how kind Joey was to Cam at the arcade, maybe I shouldn't feel so skeevy about him anymore. But, for all I know, that day could have been an anomaly. It's hard to forget how obnoxious he was during the picture delivery when he made me out to be some kind of liar. What kind of person goes through all the trouble of lying just to get a few lousy pictures?

Thankfully, most of the shops aren't open this early, and the lights inside Prince Prints are off, so I speed-walk past it before turning the corner on to the next street.

Except the next street doesn't exist.

Not anymore, anyway.

Bright orange traffic cones and workers in matching vests

line the street, mingled amongst piles of brick rubble that used to be buildings. I step toward the nearest construction worker— a lady with bright red hair pulled into a tight ponytail with a clipboard in her hands.

"Hi. Can you tell me what happened to all the stores?"

She arches a red-penciled eyebrow. "You new?"

I make a *hmm* sound, which is easier than telling the whole truth. "Yeah, I moved here for the summer. Did something happen?"

I wave a hand to the ruined street where something *obviously* went down.

She shakes her head, her mouth twisted in dismay. "It was the tornado a few months back. Took out the whole street. All of the stores have to be torn down and rebuilt."

My tongue sticks to the roof of my mouth, but I nod, backing away as I do. I remember Ally saying something about a bad storm right after I visited for spring break. "Sorry to hear that. Do you know where I can find stationery nearby?"

She jabs a thumb behind us, in the direction I've just come from. "Prince Prints is the only place I know of that's got that kind of stuff."

I bite my lip. "Thanks."

If I'm ever going to cross off the first step in my repentance tour, I need that stationery. And I need to get away from the ruined street, which is practically begging me to purge my stress by cracking some already broken windows. No one would even notice, right?

But no. Stationery. I already came up empty raiding Ally and Justin's office after she mentioned there might be some envelopes and paper tucked away. All I found were stacks and stacks of photo negatives, some of which I recognized as my baby pictures. I might have slipped those to the bottom of the pile where they'll hopefully sit unbothered for another sixteen years.

So.

Prince Prints. After one last glance at the destroyed street, I steel my shoulders and march around the corner. The inside of the store's still dark, but the sign posted to the front door tells me they open at 8:30. Slumping to the ground with my back against a red brick wall, I sit on the pavement outside the shop.

Fifteen minutes. That's how long I have to wait.

Then I can run in and get out. And probably not see Joey at all. I mean, he can't work here *all* the time, right?

Aside from the construction workers, I have seen no one else all morning, so when voices carry down the street, I whip my head in their direction.

Outside the bakery, an old lady with short black hair and blunt bangs covering her forehead beams up at someone inside holding the door open. She throws her head back, laughing, and then hands over a white bag. Joey from Prince Prints steps outside, grasping the bag in one hand and waving goodbye with the other. As the old lady disappears inside, Joey turns to make his way in my direction.

Crap.

How is this fair? Is it actually impossible to do anything in this town without running into him? I *am* currently sitting outside his place of employment, but this totally doesn't count.

Maybe if I curl up into a ball, I'll blend into the brick and he won't be able to see me. Or I can roll down the rest of the street, round the corner, and hide behind some construction trucks. In my peripheral vision, his khaki shorts creep closer.

It's too late to run.

My stomach flip-flops. Joey pauses a few feet away from the store entrance, his mouth crooked and his eyes locked on mine.

Deer, meet headlights.

I scramble to my feet and lift my chin in the air. "I'm only here for stationery."

His eyebrows raise, and he bobs his head slowly. "Sure. Yeah. We have that." He pulls a phone from his shorts pocket and glances down at it. "It's almost time, so we might as well go in now."

Another search through his pocket yields an overfilled key chain. He grasps a small gold key and unlocks the door in front of us. Apparently, I'm standing here gaping because he waves a hand at me. "Come on in. I'll look for stationery."

I scramble behind him while he wanders through the store flipping light switches and powering on machines.

"Your boss lets you in here alone?"

Joey's mouth twists and he clears his throat. "Yeah, well, the boss is my dad. So."

Oh. That explains a lot.

I screw up my face into what I hope is a politely interested expression. "Will you take over for him someday? Become the new Prince Prints boss?"

He's busy poking in a code on a box attached to the wall. At my question, he jerks toward me, brows lowered. His eyes flash darkly. "Not if I can help it."

Oops. Guess I hit on a touchy subject.

But, hey, I get it. Parents have certain expectations. And sometimes they're hard to live up to.

I pretend to be engrossed in a wall near the back, which features a corkboard full of pinned wallet-sized pictures. Behind me, Joey sighs.

"It's just—it's not what I want to do forever, you know? I'm not even good at this kind of thing."

The urge to remind him how intensely he questioned me over a simple picture delivery niggles at me until I bite down on my tongue to stop the jab from slipping out.

I turn until he's in my line of sight. "Well, what do you want to do?"

Wide deep brown eyes blink back at me as he lifts a shoulder. "I don't know yet. I know a bunch of things I *don't* want to do." His jaw tightens like he's steadying himself for an argument.

"Maybe an interrogator?" I offer, unable to help myself.

His forehead wrinkles. "What?"

I'm not looking for a fight. It doesn't matter to me. Besides, I'm the last person who should judge. I let my silence speak for itself.

After a minute, he walks toward the other corner of the store, where a small sign advertising paper goods dangles from the ceiling on a thin, clear wire. I follow him, hands on hips. This is awkward. Part of me is dying to say something stupid like, *Fancy meeting you here*, but I force myself to look away and focus on the goods instead. The sooner I get out of here, the better.

"I'm pretty sure you're the youngest person to ever come in here looking for stationery. By about fifty years." He glances sideways, his lips lifted in a lopsided smirk.

"My mom's really into that kind of stuff."

Joey raises an eyebrow and starts flipping through the not-so-varied selection. He grabs a white and pink polka-dot set and waves it in the air between us. "This one?"

I reach past him and slip a set of pale purple cards from their hook. Purple is Mom's favorite color. At this point, I'd do just about anything to make her happy and change her mind about my punishment. "I'll take this one."

Taking in my air of decision, he shrugs and points me toward the checkout line. I follow him as he fiddles with the cash register and turns on the card machine.

"So. Do you have a pen pal?"

I choke out a laugh. "Um. No." What kind of question is that? Do pen pals still exist? But I guess my buying stationery is weird to him, and there's no good way to explain it without handing over my life story.

And I'm not about to do that.

"Okay." He stretches out the word like it has four syllables.

He rings up the stationery and I stare at the sleek black printing machines behind him. The air between us grows thick.

"I'll see you tomorrow when I drop off the pictures? They're almost done printing, but we have to look over them and discard any bad ones."

"Yeah, I'll be there," I tell him, a deflated note clinging to my voice.

It's the most boring summer of my life. Of course I'll be there. Turns out Mom and Dad knew what they were doing when they sent me here. As much as I love hanging out with my nephews, I'd much rather be in Washington with a secure future with my friends and familiarity. Blood rushes to my ears.

Of course, my parents would only pay attention when I'm doing something negative.

Nearly hidden in the cash register's shadow, a framed picture on the edge of the counter catches my eye. Pointing to it, I ask, "Is that your mom?"

Joey unclenches his jaw and his eyes soften. "Yeah. She puts pictures of herself around everywhere to remind Dad and me to 'behave'."

I smile. "She's really pretty."

Her black hair curls at the ends in perfect thick twists, and her lashes are so long they reach up to her eyebrows. But mostly what I notice about her is her lips. The same as Joey's, noticeable even when she's smiling, and he isn't.

Joey nods, watching me study her picture. "Yeah. She always says they make people better looking in Brazil." His chin lifts in pride.

Apparently. I laugh awkwardly, realizing that he might think I'm complimenting him.

I slip my hands toward the purse at my side, but I'm met with empty air. My heart sinks as I fumble through empty skirt pockets. I left my purse behind, and I didn't bring money with me. Ugh, this cannot be happening.

Peering over the counter, Joey frowns at me. "You okay?"

I shake my head. "Okay. Here's the thing- I don't have any money with me, but I can pay you back later today. I mean..." I force out a tiny laugh. "You do know where I live."

37

His forehead creases. "You want me to give you stuff for free?"

The way he says it, you'd think I'm holding him at gunpoint and demanding he hand over the contents of the cash register.

Leaning forward slightly, I meet his eyes. "Absolutely not. I'm just asking you to give me the stationery—it's what, five dollars—and I'll bring the money over to your house *today*."

Joey's mouth hangs open. I take a moment to replay my words to make sure I wasn't speaking gibberish. I sigh. "Didn't you say you live in the same neighborhood as my sister? I'll have her show me which house is yours."

His lips form a straight line. "Sorry. I can't do that."

Can't, or won't? "Well, maybe I'll make a call to your boss and tell him you wouldn't let me give you money. I'm a customer!"

His Adam's apple bobs as he swallows. "I think my dad will be *fine* with me refusing to help someone steal from his store."

With a shrug, I say, "I'm not stealing, and we'll see."

We stare each other down, waiting for the other to break. He looks away first; the tips of his ears burn red. "I can't give you the stationery if you don't pay."

My hands squeeze around my phone. "What if I send you the money right now? Like on my phone?"

He arches an eyebrow. "Fine."

After a virtually painless transaction, Joey slips the cards into a plastic bag embossed with the Prince Prints logo. He dangles it in front of me and I snatch it from his hands, letting the bag swing wildly.

He scowls. "See you around."

Biting back a sigh, I leave the store. I'm sure I will, Joey Prince.

CHAPTER Five

The first time I broke into an abandoned building came about organically, as these things do.

It was the day of the National Honor Society induction. Your classic high school ceremony where everyone's supposed to be dressed up in their nicest clothes. Only about one-third of the students wore slacks and dresses, then there's the group who wore black skinny jeans and collared shirts marred with wrinkles. And then there's this smaller group of students who claimed to have completely forgotten the dress code and showed up in the equivalent of their pajamas.

Dressed in my just-above-the-knee black dress with matching pumps and the string of pearls I got for my thirteenth birthday, I was firmly a member of the first group. I was *so* relieved I'd even gotten in. All my older siblings had been members, and Allison and Gavin were even vice president and secretary of their chapters. It was finally my turn to get my picture taken with the principal. Proof I was no longer the baby, but an equal.

Except there wouldn't be a picture.

When the ceremony began, and we all lined up in alphabetical order behind the stage in the gym, my heart fluttered with rare excitement. I was *finally* doing it. Living up to the family's expectations, joining my siblings' names on the wall listing our school's Honor Society members. Mom and Dad were going to watch me and whisper how proud they were, like they had for everyone else.

But the chairs all filled up, and Mom and Dad never claimed a set. After I trudged across the stage, tears welling up as I shook hands with Principal Ramirez and posed for a picture, I kept walking until I hit the packed parking lot. Griffin found me as I was screaming at my phone, which displayed the text message Mom sent letting me know Dad wasn't feeling well enough to come, so they'd have to miss the ceremony. Griffin wasn't being inducted; he came to watch me, dressed in ripped jeans and a baseball cap rimmed with dirt. "What are best friends for," he said. He dragged me to get ice cream, where we discovered the old diner a few buildings back from the ice cream shop was out of business.

The boarded-up windows were easy to bypass when I used the heel of my shiny black pump like a mini crowbar. We sat at a sawdust-covered booth inside the abandoned restaurant, my elbows jammed onto the tabletop, chin resting on my hands. Griffin slung his arm around me, and we sat in near silence. Then he lifted a hand to his baseball hat, tilted it up, and took my face in his hands to kiss me. After that we were together, same as always, but different.

Before we started dating, Griffin was soft, a little shy, and sweet. He still was after we got together, but I changed him without meaning to. I made him more like me, more rebellious.

I'm reminded of that faraway day when I spot a group of girls my age standing near the curb outside of Prince Prints. One of them is dressed in a white oversized football jersey with the number 24 in orange across the front. I'm not sure she's wearing anything underneath it. Maybe going without pants is a thing in Texas. On her head, she's wearing a baseball cap uncannily like Griffin's.

She spots me staring from where I'm walking my bike away and waves me over. "Are you here for the build-up?" The girl's platinum blonde eyebrows cock as she waves a blue piece of paper. As she moves, black cotton shorts peek from underneath the jersey. Her friends roll their eyes good-naturedly behind her.

I step back, still gripping my bike. "Um, I think so? I'm supposed to help build houses—or something?" This is the meeting spot sent in the introductory email. I kind of hoped no one would be here, and I could say I gave it a good effort.

She squints. "You're Paige, right?"

Slowly, I move my head up then down. "Yeah. That's me. How'd you know?"

She licks her lips and sighs. "You're the only new person on my list." She shrugs. "This is the first time there's been someone new in my, like, five summers of doing this."

I look past her to the destroyed buildings and understanding dawns on me. "I guess I thought we were building houses for impoverished families."

Someone snorts. "We do something different every summer, but this year we're focusing on the town. These are all small businesses who got hit really badly by the storm."

The pantsless girl nods. "Yeah, but I'm standing out here trying to make sure I catch everyone because it turns out we can't start today. They're doing the wiring and they need us out of the way. So come back tomorrow, okay?"

Can't wait. "Okay," I say to the group, pushing my bike past them and back down the hill. Mom and Dad's idea of penance can wait another day—it's not like I have anything better to do.

THE WHIR OF THE GARAGE DOOR OPENING AND CLOSING signals Allison's return from the grocery store with the kids. I meet her at the kitchen door to help unload. She's practically tripping over herself, shoving paper grocery bags into my arms the second the door opens.

"I have good news."

She beams at me and continues sneaking overstretched grins

in my direction as she settles Cam and Mattie at the kitchen table with animal crackers and juice boxes.

I exhale and lean on my elbows against the counter. "Okay, fine. What's the news?"

My sister makes a high-pitched squeal, followed closely by a copycat sound from baby Mattie, who's got at least three crackers hidden in each of his fisted hands. He's adorable. Her, not as much. Because whatever she's worked up about is bound to be less than exciting.

"Okay, okay. Stop looking at me like that," she demands.

I screw my mouth up into a nicer smirk. "What did you do, Ally? Does this have something to do with how all the kids at the build-up already knew about me? Are you forcing friends on me?" This is classic Ally. She's determined to mother no matter what.

Even as she's fixing me with a studying gaze, her eyes gleam with a familiar fervor. "I don't have anything to do with the build-up thing. I want that on record."

I roll my eyes. Guilty.

She holds up a finger. "But you're going to love this. I just scored you an extra day off every week. You can do whatever you want every Wednesday for the rest of the summer!"

Uneasiness slides through me. I run my tongue across my bottom lip. "You asked someone else to watch the kids?"

Her bright smile falters, fading into a thin line. "I thought you'd be relieved to have more time to yourself."

"Yeah, I am." I shrug. "I don't know what I'll do with the time off. It's kind of dead around here." I clench and unclench my fists. Dead as in my social life. Dead like my future plans if Mom gets her way and sends me away next year. And, as hard as I try, I can't seem to accept the offer as anything other than a reflection on my babysitting skills—or lack thereof.

"I'm sure you'll find something to do. Mr. Prince said Joseph —Joey—is trying to earn extra money, and he's tired of working for his dad every day. So you can leave the house and do your own thing for a few hours. All day if you want. It's good for both of you, really."

"What?" I clench my teeth. Maybe I heard her wrong. She can't be serious about this. "Joey Prince is going to watch Cam and Mattie?"

"Yeah. I told you, Cam couldn't stop talking about him." Ally tilts her head like she's testing out different angles hoping to understand me better.

From behind us, Cam's voice squeaks through the measured silence. "He's gonna teach me Mario, Piggy!"

Oh, yay. "I could teach you, Mario," I say.

Cam's nose scrunches. "You aren't good at Mario. But thanks."

Insults from a five-year-old aren't supposed to sting so much. Even if they are true.

Allison swishes her hair, gathering it in her hand and looping it over one shoulder. "Look, I know you think he's annoying, but you won't even be here when he's over. I'm just looking out for you, Paige. You've had a messy year, and you need time to reinvent yourself."

That stings. My throat bobs as I swallow in response. Reinventing myself is exactly my plan. How much has Mom told Ally about what could happen after this summer? About her promise to send me to boarding school if I don't change?

Has Mom mentioned that the severity of Dad's sickness is entirely my fault?

I nod. "Okay. I'm sure I can find something to do."

CHAPTER Six

I rock back and forth on my feet outside of Prince Prints once again, waiting for instructions with a group of kids around my age. The entire building project is supposed to be run by teens, for teens. Aside from the same redheaded construction worker I saw the other day—who I learn is named Valerie and has a house full of cats—there's only one other adult. And they both stand back and let the kids take the lead.

Whatever.

I'll milk this for all I can. Something new to tell Mom and Dad about. Further proof of how much I've changed. I'll spin my involvement in this project into an even bigger deal and cast the pantsless blonde as my new best friend, just to make the story sound good.

Dad will like the idea of me being part of a team. Mom won't believe a word, but it might be enough to sway her into letting me come home by September instead of sending me to Hopkins. I think Mom got the impression that I'd be building houses, too, but I'm sure she doesn't care what I'm doing, as long as it's some kind of work she knows I'll hate. Torture is the name of the game as far as Mom's concerned.

Blonde girl raises a hand and waves me over. I'm totally fine watching from here, but she's too far away to intercept my telepathic message. I jog toward her.

"I'm going to watch from back there so I'm not in anyone's

way." I point to where I was standing, where no one could clock me in the head with a hammer or accidentally chop my finger off with that scary saw they're all gathered around.

She opens her mouth to say something but stops and turns her head when someone else calls to her. "Yo, Callie. Are we starting or what?"

Callie. It would probably be good to stop mentally referring to her as the pantsless girl. Especially since her shorts are actually visible today. They're the same type of black cotton shorts as before, this time paired with a white form-fitting V-neck.

She drops her hands to her hips and screams back at the guy, "Hold on!" Rolling her eyes at the interruption, she focuses back on me. "We need you over here. I thought that's why you came."

I shake my head slowly because I'm starting to get the impression she doesn't understand me. "Uh. No. I only came to watch today. I've never built anything before. I'm not even dressed for it." Waving a hand down my body, I show off the bright yellow sundress I've paired with a pair of white Keds. My plan here is twofold. First, I'll show up late enough and just often enough that I'm more of a nuisance than anything. Second, I'll make so many excuses that I'll never have to lift a finger. No one wants a non-team player waving a hammer next to them. If I stay out of everyone else's way, in theory, they'll stay clear of me and the summer will hurry by while I relax in the shade of half-built storefronts.

Callie lifts a shoulder and lazily waves her hand toward nowhere in particular. "I've got shorts you can borrow in my bag. And those kind of count as tennis shoes."

I suck in a breath. She watches me, unmoving. I get the feeling Callie will not let anyone get away with not working. "Okay. Sure. I'll help, but don't say I didn't warn you." There goes my plan.

Her lips spread into a wide grin. "You'll be on my crew. You have nothing to worry about."

She's not exaggerating. By the time we're gathered in front of the first pile of lumber and tools, it's clear no one knows nearly as much about this as Callie. She divides us into two groups, and true to her word, I'm with her. Our goal for the day is to take inventory of the donated materials and sort it into two piles: useable and junk.

It sounds easy enough that I don't even blink until she points me toward one of the abandoned storefronts, where the tools and supplies are being stored. Surrounded by half-crumbled walls and exposed pipes, I do a double take. There's rotten wood and long metal stick *things* and window frames stacked up to the yellowed ceiling. Taking inventory is a nice word for what she wants us to do.

I swear three hours have passed by the time people on both sides of the street call for a water break. According to Valerie's watch, it's only been an hour. Sixty freaking minutes. Sweat beads on my neck and lower back and dust and wood shavings sting my nose. My hands have always been soft, but now I have more blisters than I can count, and I'm pretty sure my blisters have a few blisters. I follow Callie to a less destroyed storefront where she's left her stuff. She hands me an icy cold water bottle from a cooler. Then she passes some out to everyone else standing nearby. I gulp half of it down before a cramp stitches its way up my side. To say I'm out of shape would put it lightly, since I'm not sure I've ever been in shape.

Not like this, at least. Everyone else in my family loves sports. Most of my siblings were on the high school soccer team. By the time I was in middle school and still tripping over my own shoelaces, I came to terms with the fact that sports were not in my future. It wasn't hard to accept since few of their accomplishments were coming easily to me by then. And building things in the heat of the Texas summer feels a lot like playing sports.

Pressing the plastic bottle to my lips again, I take a tiny sip, steadying myself. A girl with short black hair stops in front of me, her matching water bottle in tow. She reminds me a little of

Lucy Liu from the *Charlie's Angel's* movie, especially with her matching black tank top and shorts.

She lifts her hand in a cute little half-wave, smiling shyly. "Hi, I'm Jen."

We both turn to glance over at Callie, who's wandered over to another group. She's yelling animatedly in either anger or excitement about a basketball game she watched on TV.

Jen's eyes meet mine, and we laugh.

"I'm Paige. I'm here for the summer, um, visiting my sister."

"Yeah, Callie told me. Her mom works with your brother-in-law, right?"

I frown. I knew Justin and Ally had something to do with this. "Yeah. I guess he thought I needed some friends."

Jen laughs again. It's a big laugh for someone so small and soft-spoken. My mouth turns up even though I'm not part of the joke.

"No one's as interested in all of this as Callie is. She probably forced more than half of us to be here."

I look around me and realize it makes a lot of sense. No one looks as purely athletic as Callie. Most of the girls are wearing regular clothes and slip-on shoes, and almost all the guys are lounging lazily on the bleachers. And she was running laps around every other person here, handing out tools, barking orders, and climbing up ladders like she's been doing it her entire life.

Jen shrugs. "We just do it for fun. And only in the summer since we're all too busy with school the rest of the year. Callie probably wishes it was year-round."

Back home, my definition of a fun summer activity is *very* different. No community service and no big groups. Usually it's just Griffin and me. If I weren't here, we'd probably be sitting at Lake Washington sunbathing right now. My stomach flip-flops, and I squish down the longing.

Right as I open my mouth to tell her about what my typical summer looks like in Washington, Jen pops up on her tiptoes and stares behind me. Callie pauses mid tirade and jogs past Jen and me.

"You finally showed up!"

"Yeah, I know. I'm way late, but I had to help my dad with something since I'm not working at the shop today."

My blood freezes. That voice. That know-it-all, nephew-stealing voice.

I whirl around to see Callie shoulder to shoulder with none other than Joey Prince. Jen skips toward him, throwing her arms around his chest and encapsulating him in as big a hug as she can manage.

This is so great.

I mean, there's nothing better than *almost* making friends only to find out they're fraternizing with the enemy.

Joey looks up from his circle of admirers and blinks at my dagger eyes. If he's smart, he'll pretend he doesn't see me so we can avoid the whole awkward thing again.

But he's not. He stiffens, pastes on his big fake smile, and waves me over.

Callie and Jen raise their eyebrows at me in tandem.

"You two know each other?" Callie points between Joey and me, her finger furiously wiggling like it's just as skeptical as she is.

What is it called when you keep running into someone, but neither of you has the guts to admit how much you don't care for each other?

The opposite of fate, maybe?

Joey clears his throat. "Her sister is a photographer," he offers.

The girls nod like that explanation makes perfect sense.

With a smile as wide and cheesy as his, I say, "And he's hanging out with my sister's kids."

Callie's head snaps toward Joey as she mouths the word 'kids' and adds a question mark to the end. Jen puts a palm to her mouth to stifle a loud giggle. "I think it's cute," she says.

He runs a hand through the back of his thick hair. "Hey, it's better than working for my dad. Are y'all still working, or what?"

At the mention of work, Callie leaps forward and starts yelling at the stragglers to get back into their groups. I inch backward to drink more water and buy myself time, but Jen catches my hand in hers and tugs. "Be in my group this time."

I nod absently as I watch Callie point Joey to the opposite side of the street and run after him. Following after Jen and Callie, I square Joey with a look from afar, so he understands this doesn't make us friends.

CHAPTER Seven

The next morning I wake up with a throat so dry it feels like a desert. I look out the window and the sun's already high overhead. There's also an unfamiliar car in the driveway. And I've got a good feeling about who it belongs to.

Make that a bad feeling.

But I can't spend the day covered in post-work sweat and with my hair mangled from dead weighting lumber. I crashed after getting home last night and decided to skip a shower. A decision that I now realize was all sorts of wrong and disgusting because I *reek*.

I deserve a shower, and Joey Prince can't stop me from taking one.

Ugh.

I *do* want a break, but does it really have to come at this price?

Seeing his smug face with my two favorite humans in the entire world is sure to send creepy crawly tingles across my body.

I can wash the sweat and dirt stains off my skin and sneak out of the house. I'll jump from my window if I have to. I trudge to the bathroom and groan loudly over the sound of running water. In the shower, I scrub at my skin until it's pink. Closing my eyes against the steaming water, the image of Joey's scowl replays. Despite my best efforts, I'm still seething when I finish, no matter how good Ally's guest bathroom shampoo smells.

After my deliriously long shower, I tiptoe downstairs. Cam's already positioned himself on the couch in front of the TV. Joey's next to him, looking oddly comfortable with baby Mattie nestled in his lap.

Mattie whirls like some demonic creature with supersonic hearing, his arms outstretched toward me.

Satisfaction pulls at my lips. Joey hasn't won *him* over yet. Mattie's cheeky smile definitely melts me, and I bend over the couch to scoop him up, nuzzling my forehead against the fuzzy white fluff on his head passing for hair.

Cam's eyes stay frozen on his video game, but Joey looks me up and down, a line drawn between his eyes.

"I thought you were busy today."

Oh. He's worried I'm staying.

I cluck my tongue. "Don't worry. I am."

I plant a kiss on Mattie's head and set him on the floor next to the couch. I rumple Cam's hair, then head through the kitchen without another word.

Stationery in hand, I let the door click softly behind me. Take that, Joey Prince. I wouldn't stick around and hang out with you if I got paid for it.

Okay, so I have no idea where I'm going. But I'm armed with my stationery and a plan, so that's going to have to be good enough. Honestly, anything's better than being stuck with Joey and his silent judgment. Plus, it should be illegal to swoop in like this and steal away my nephews' attention. It's kind of a major betrayal for Ally to hire Joey for a job I was already willing to do for free. She's bossy and sneaky like that. Older sisters are born that way according to every television show ever made. I didn't realize until now how accurate they were, though.

Biking down the street and out of Allison's gated neighborhood once again, I shake my head. I'm not going to think about Joey Prince for the rest of the day. This is my day off, after all. It should be a day to rest from everything, even obnoxious neighbor boys.

I pedal in the opposite direction of the town, down a road that looks more dirt than anything, and I stop once the landmarks turn into flanks of sturdy wide-leaved oak trees on either side. Up ahead a wooden sign on a post reads, *City Park.* An expanse of green grass dotted with blue and yellow wildflowers and even more tall oak trees make up most of the park. Wooden benches are scattered under patches of shade, and off in the corner sits a playground where kids are running in circles under a red plastic slide.

After I park my bike against a nearby tree trunk, I fold myself onto a rough wooden bench and spread out my stationery and the black ballpoint pen I "borrowed" from Allison's desk. I also unfold the letter from my parents and prop it against the back of the bench. For motivation.

The letters to Mom and Dad are easy enough. I know exactly what they want to hear from me. I end my letter to Mom with a desperate plea against boarding school. The letter to Griffin stays blank.

Leaning my head back against the bench, I squeeze my eyes shut. Then I pull my phone from my bag and press call.

Griffin answers on the second ring.

"I'm sorry I let you take the blame. And I'm sorry you're stuck picking up trash. That should be me."

He makes a few unintelligible noises, and then nothing. I shocked him into silence.

I sigh into the phone. "I'm just, you know, trying to fix things."

"It's okay, Paige. I was never mad about that."

Somehow, I always manage to forget how deep his voice is until the next time I hear it.

"Oh."

"How are your nephews?"

"They're adorable and weird and kind of crazy sometimes."

"That's good."

I guess it's my turn to ask him something. "How's your dad?"

His voice goes softer, muffled, like he's dropped his head onto his pillow.

"He's the same. Has a new idea that's gonna make us rich."

Griffin's dad has been coming up with money schemes for as long as I've known his family. And according to Griffin, for as long as he can remember. They all fail. That's why Griffin's mom works two jobs.

"Maybe it really will this time."

His laugh is husky. "I miss you. I know you don't want to talk to me. I tried not to call, but..."

I swallow. A little kid wanders past me, turning her head slowly, looking around carefully. A few feet in front of her, another little girl with black braids crouches behind a tree, hand pressed against her mouth as she watches her friend approach. "You don't have to apologize." I tug at a piece of my hair. I shouldn't have told him not to call. I shouldn't have been that harsh.

"Do you remember the Honor Society induction?"

"Yeah. Kind of hard to forget."

Heat creeps its way up the back of my neck. The first time we kissed. And the beginning of all my mess-ups. I think it means something different to Griffin, something memorable in a nice way. For me, it's mixed up with all of this.

It's kind of hard to separate Griffin from the string of events that got me sent to Texas for the summer.

I'm not sure I should even try.

"What about it?" he prods.

"I was thinking about how I could have just gone home afterward. Or you could have. We could have done something different, and we wouldn't have gotten in trouble. You wouldn't have community service. And I wouldn't be trying to build things I have no idea how to build."

"Yeah, but then we wouldn't have kissed." Of course, that's all he's thinking about. Not the community service, not that I might be stuck at boarding school. My life is in ruins and all Griffin cares about is us kissing. That's all I used to care about too, but that was before I destroyed my own family. Before my parents couldn't stand to look at me.

"I have to go. Thanks for picking up."

He sighs. "I'll always pick up."

WHEN I GET BACK TO THE HOUSE, NO SOUNDS COME FROM THE backyard, and the inside is eerily quiet. I tiptoe through the front hall into the living room, clutching my bag close to my side in case I need to clobber an intruder.

Clunk.

Something thuds from behind me, and before I can stop myself, a screech curls its way out of my lips.

"Shhh."

Joey emerges from the kitchen, water bottle clutched in one hand. He points a finger to the darkened living room where Cam lies on the couch, his open lips quivering in perfect time with his shoulders, and a floral blanket from Allison's collection of useless house decorations draped over him.

"Mattie's sleeping upstairs," he adds.

Pressing a palm to my galloping heart, I frown. "You seriously scared me."

He pulls his lips together. "Sorry."

I slip into a chair at the kitchen table, tucking my legs under me. My heart still thuds in overtime as I slump onto the tabletop. "We need to talk."

While I'm on an apology kick, I might as well keep going. Not that I have anything to be sorry about with Joey. But this awkward tension between us has got to end. Apparently, he's not going anywhere, and I'll be here the entire summer. I'm not sure

I can handle two and a half more months of tiptoeing around him.

He sits in the chair next to mine, turned so we're facing. His hair shines in the ultra-bright afternoon light streaming from the windows.

"Let's call a truce, okay?" I glance over at Cam. His little body sprawled out from exhaustion, a sleep-induced smile across his open mouth.

"A truce?"

I roll my eyes and stare at the bright white ceiling. "You're Mr. Rule Follower and I'm... not. We don't get along. But Cam likes you, and that's going to have to be good enough for me."

A frown creases his face. "You don't like me because I follow rules?"

It's like he's trying to prove my point or something. I wave a hand in front of his face, and his deep brown eyes blink.

"Focus, okay? Let's play nice for Cam. I'm tired of the arguing."

He pulls himself up straighter, flexing his shoulders. "We do run into each other a lot."

No kidding.

"Sure. A truce for Cam." Reaching toward me, he extends his open hand. I hesitate before I slip my palm against his. Then we shake.

CHAPTER EiGHT

E arly Thursday morning, I park my bike against a
building covered in orange caution tape. I give a
resigned sigh at the sight of everyone else already
busying themselves with tools and buildings scraps. They're all so
intense about it. If Griffin were here, we'd sit back against one of
the remaining awnings and laugh at them. Maybe we'd get something from that intoxicating smelling bakery down the street
while we sat on our butts.

If Griffin were here. If things were normal between us.

"You came!" Jen runs up to me, bringing me back to the
present. She tips her head, smiling brightly. She looks genuinely
happy to see me. Like a friend.

I pause mid-stride. "Is that good?"

Her surprisingly big laugh bounces around us. "Yeah. I was
afraid you got scared off. It's nice having someone else to hang
out with while Callie and Joey take all of this way too seriously."

Being wanted is a pleasant change. "I'm on my period today,
so I plan on being extra un-serious. We can be mediocre builders
together."

She hooks her arms with mine and gives me a sympathetic
frown. "I'd say tell Callie that you're sick, but don't bother. She
doesn't care."

Across the field, everyone else is already divided into teams.
Callie balances a pink measuring tape on the end of her pointer

finger and stares down at Joey, who's standing opposite her. When she spots Jen and me, she bounces on her toes and claps. "Here they are. Paige, you can be in my group."

I walk toward her, but Joey's voice stops me. "I already called dibs on Paige. You get Jen."

From behind me, Jen grumbles something about being fought over. Frowning to myself, I sidestep toward Joey and the rest of his group. Maybe he wasn't paying much attention last time, but I'm very new to this. A short boy with a blond buzz cut leans toward me. "Joey loses to Callie every week."

I cock an eyebrow. "How exactly do you lose at *this?*"

He laughs. "Ask them. All I know is they turn everything into a competition. How much their groups get done, how many hours they put in, whatever. They're crazy."

"Then he shouldn't have picked me." He *really* shouldn't have picked me.

The boy grins. "I have a feeling that's not why he wants you on his team."

Uh, what? I glare at buzz cut boy. Turning away from him, I face Callie and wait for her to say something. Anything but talk about Joey and his motivation for choosing me. Maybe he wants to get revenge by making sure I humiliate myself. Or maybe this is his way of living up to the truce we made. He thinks by picking me for his group we'll be working toward a common goal or something.

Callie holds up her hands, the measuring tape still dangling from her fingers. Her voice booms over the street, silencing everyone. "Let's get to work!"

People scatter, but I slowly follow Joey and the rest of my group. Why hurry? Especially with my cramps on full blast.

"I'm not sure I'm going to be much help today," I say, watching as Joey instructs half of our group to lift steel beams out of the way.

Jen winks at me as she hurries past. "Sorry. Can't talk now that we're rivals."

Joey yells something to the buzz cut kid that I can't quite make out. He disappears into one of the buildings and comes out with an armful of tools. Joey turns to me, arms folded across his chest. "Paige, can you help me with staining these boards?" He nods to a gigantic stack of wooden posts, a virtual vat of wood stain, and a pile of paintbrushes still in their plastic packaging.

I nod. "I've never done it before, but it doesn't look too hard." I've gathered enough to know by now that I don't have a choice. The faster I work, the faster I'll be done. In theory, at least.

Joey grins. I've never seen him smile so easily before, and it occurs to me that he looks like a completely different, non-annoying neighbor boy when he does. I cross my legs and sit on the sun-kissed cement. Joey crouches next to me and we unpack the brushes, staining the wood in complete silence. Every once in a while, Joey disappears to bark orders at someone else or to spy on Callie's group to see how much progress they've made.

Rinse and repeat until the end of our work day when Callie cheers so loudly that she's won. It leaves the rest of us dizzy. I still don't understand the score system, but Joey scowls and concedes that she won—somehow.

Groaning, I trudge toward my bike. I'm not sure my legs can even pedal home right now, but what other choice do I have? I flick the kickstand with my foot and flex my hands against the handlebars.

"Hey. Do you need a ride?" Joey watches me atop a stack of wood, where instead of drinking water, he's pouring a bottle of it over the back of his head. His hair glistens, but he shakes off the droplets like a dog, spraying water everywhere. Callie and Jen don't seem bothered by the spray. They laugh and shove his arms from where they sit on either side of him.

I shake my head. "No, I'm good. I can't leave my bike here."

Callie stands. "It'll fit in Joey's car. He shoves lots of crap in his trunk way bigger than that."

For whatever reason, my new friends actually like Joey. And

there is that truce I called with him last night. And it's not like I'm dying to exercise my achy legs any further.

I throw my hands up. "Okay. Sure. A ride would be nice."

Callie and Jen wave goodbye while I follow Joey to his car, a silver 4-Runner parked neatly in the back of the parking lot, away from all the other cars.

He takes my bike from me and hoists it into his trunk. Callie's right. It fits easily.

The inside of his car is immaculate. No trash by my feet, no empty fast food cups, no sweaty boy clothes thrown across the back seats. The exact opposite of Griffin's perpetual disaster of a tiny red Mitsubishi. The scent of fabricated woodlands hits my nose. One of those green tree-shaped car fresheners dangles from his mirror.

Joey catches me staring at his pristine interior. "What?"

I raise an eyebrow. "It's so clean in here, but I guess that shouldn't surprise me."

He frowns. "Right. You think I'm really boring."

"Not boring. Just..." Tapping my fingers against the middle console, I search for the right word. "Predictable, I guess."

He stares straight ahead as he drives out of the parking lot.

"So you knew I was going to offer you a ride home?"

Irritation itches at me. I should have known he'd take everything I say way too seriously.

"Yep," I answer.

"And you knew I was going to choose you to be on my team?" One eyebrow slides upward. That's right. He picked me for his group, which seriously doesn't make sense.

"Okay, no," I admit. "What was up with that?"

He breaks out into a huge smile. "Maybe I'm trying not to be too predictable."

We reach our neighborhood and he pulls in front of Allison's driveway. He even gets out and unloads my bike.

"Thanks for the ride."

I steer my bike toward the garage door, waving over my shoulder.

MY LEGS ARE JELLY WHEN I CREAK OUT OF BED IN THE MIDDLE of the night.

Have to get to the bathroom.

My knees feel like they have pins stuck in them, and each rushed step is an enormous effort. My stomach gurgles as I near the bathroom door.

I collapse. My cheek hits the icy cold tile and I wrap my arms around myself, letting out a near-silent whimper as I curl into the fetal position next to the white porcelain toilet.

My stomach hurts so badly I'm convinced there's a knife slicing through it. I blink and look down, but there's nothing. Just my own pale hand wrapped around my abdomen.

Pain and nausea grip me for minutes. Hours. What feels like all night. When it finally dulls, I creep back to bed, pulling the covers up to my chin until I pass out into a deep sleep.

CHAPTER Nine

C hange.

It's halfway through June and I'm supposed to *change*. My list from the first night here still has the word followed by half a dozen question marks. I'm living in Texas, working as a nanny for little kids, and in my free time, I haul wood and nails and tools I previously never even wanted to know the names of. How much more change is even possible?

Mattie is finally asleep for the afternoon, and Cam sits at the table with ten different cans of open Play-Doh in front of him. I drop into a chair and squeeze a yellow ball of Play-Doh in my fist. A day inside is the only thing I can manage after last night. And the only way I can hide how craptastic I still feel is to move as little as possible. Enter: Play-Doh. My phone sits on the table, and I press call and lean back in the chair.

"Hi Mom."

"Paige! Hang on, let me go get your dad."

There's a shuffling sound, and I picture her scooting down the hall in her pink slippers to their bedroom. Dad's probably reading in bed, one arm folded behind his head as he props the book up with the other hand, his brow creased in concentration.

Another shuffling noise. "Okay. Are you still there?"

I squeeze the Play-Doh. "I'm still here."

"Is that my little girl? We miss having you around here." My dad's voice is softer than I remember. Almost winded, like he's been jogging instead of reading.

Still, the amount of effort it takes to not respond with something cutting is staggering. What's the point of pretending to miss me when they sent me away in the first place? When they want me to attend boarding school after I leave Texas?

"I miss you guys too." As much as I'd like to deny it, it's true. Allison and Justin are great. But the familiarity of Mom nagging me and Dad trying to explain the plot of his latest favorite mystery novel are the things I never thought I'd miss so much.

Dad speaks up again. "We got the letters you sent. That was really nice."

I wait for Mom to say something, but she doesn't. Maybe she's not even in the room.

"I'm trying, Dad. I want to go back to school in September. I want to come home."

Mom's voice sweeps over mine. "We can talk about that later. I've almost finished the registration for Hopkins."

I push a hand to my chest where the wind nearly cuts off, and my entire body sinks heavily. "What? No, I mean, I want to go back to *my* school. Not boarding school." My voice cracks on the words 'boarding school.' I'm sure it's fine for some people, but all I can picture are dungeon classrooms and bowls of cold soup in the cafeteria and lonely, endless days and nights of studying. It's in Connecticut, far away from Texas and Washington. Far away from anything—anyone—I care about.

What would I do if something happened to Dad while I was that far away?

Dad starts to say something, but Mom talks over him. "We'll talk about it later. Tell us what you've been doing in your spare time. Allison said you've made some friends?"

I pause. "Boarding school, Mom? I can't do that. I won't. Trust me that I will not do anything bad anymore, okay?"

"Paige, don't be dramatic. It's not all punishment. It's a top-rated school, you know." She smacks her lips. "They have tons of extracurriculars, an optional off-campus lunch hour, and teachers from all around the world. It's an amazing opportunity."

Breathing through my nose, I squeeze my eyes shut. Mom will not listen to me. She never has. "Have you guys seen Griffin?" Maybe he can talk some sense into them. Not that he's their favorite person, but I at least trust him to argue my case. I know *he* doesn't want me away from home any longer than necessary.

Silence swallows the line.

"I've talked to him a few times. I just wondered if he's come by the house at all."

Mom answers. "We've seen him once or twice, but you shouldn't worry too much. I'm sure he's busy with his other friends."

Griffin in my house, with my parents, without me, would be weird. I don't know why I expected him to be there when I'm not. Maybe because I don't know a world without him hanging out after school, eating all the food in the pantry, expertly timing stolen kisses on the living room couch when no one's looking.

A pang hits my chest that has nothing to do with missing my parents and everything to do with the other things I've left behind.

I have to prove to my parents I'm different. That I deserve to come home. That I won't stress Dad to death.

I exhale into the phone. "Mom, please. What do I need to do? I'm trying to change here. I haven't done anything bad since I've been here, I swear. Ask Ally, ask Justin. Ask Mattie and Cam. I'm being perfect. As close to it as I can."

There's the desperation I've been holding back. It cracks through my voice until it's raw and my face is tight and my eyes sting.

"We have the rest of the summer, Paige. Love you, sweetheart. I have to go check on Dad's lunch."

She hands the phone off to Dad, and he lowers his voice.

"Honey, we'll talk about it. I promise. Mom's got a lot to worry about right now, okay? You know how stressed she gets."

And there's the signal that they couldn't care less. Because when isn't Mom stressed, and when isn't Dad too tired to intervene?

A tear streams down one cheek, catching in my peripheral as it gathers and drops onto my T-shirt. "Love you, Dad."

"I love you so much, Piggy. Stay out of trouble."

The ensuing silence once they hang up echoes in my ear longer than it usually does. Why do I feel that it doesn't matter what I do? I could win the Nobel Peace Prize this summer, and it wouldn't change Mom's mind. She wants to send me away from home and Dad, and there's a huge chance she'll never budge.

CHAPTER Ten

"I refuse to put any of that on my ice cream." Jen pokes her fluorescent pink spoon at the mounds of gummy worms and sour candies in the topping line-up.

Callie sticks out her tongue and balances more sour gummies on her scoop of vanilla than should be able to fit in one cup.

I stick with chocolate and peanut butter, but I pluck a green gummy worm and position it on top of my ice cream in place of a cherry.

We sit down and Callie makes a big show of clearing her throat and exchanging glances with Jen. "Ahem. So, you and Joey..."

I catch on and lick my spoon slowly while they lean in. My eyes scan both of their faces, which are eager for details, eyes wide. "There's no me and Joey. You're his friends, aren't you supposed to know that already?"

Callie tilts her head toward Jen, a satisfied smirk on her lips. "Told you."

Jen shakes her head. "Wow."

"What?" Honestly, I'm surprised he hasn't told them about how hard I am to get along with. The idea of Joey and me as anything more intimate than neighbors, tentative allies, mutual friends to my nephews—is crazy. A word stronger than crazy. But maybe it's a sign that my new persona is working. If Callie and

Jen see me as the kind of girl who'd go gaga over someone like Joey, I must be doing something right.

"So are you saying you don't like Joey?" Jen swirls her ice cream with her spoon, her eyes on the tabletop. A flush of pink covers her cheeks.

"Jen used to have a big crush on him," Callie chimes in as red splashes Jen's cheeks.

"Wait, what? *That's* what you're asking? No. I don't like him like that at all. I've barely stopped hating him."

Jen looks up and smiles. She stops spinning her spoon.

Something green and icky crawls its way across my chest, threatening to turn my dessert sour in my stomach.

Jen and Joey?

I can't see it. She's so sweet and silly, and he's so frustrating and organized.

Picturing Joey in a relationship with *anyone* is almost impossible. He'd probably be the kind of boyfriend to text you goodnight before bed every single day. He'd probably show up at his girlfriend's door with a limp bouquet of roses, just because.

Callie spoons ice cream into one side of her mouth and talks out of the other. "Okay, but answer honestly—do you think he likes you like that?"

"No way." I shake my head at Callie. I'm hyper-aware of Jen next to me, quietly studying the tabletop. Even if part of me thought Joey was misguided enough to catch feelings, I'd lie through my teeth. I'm not about to hurt Jen's feelings after she's been so nice to me.

"You look kind of pale today. Are you *lovesick?*" Callie asks me, nudging Jen with her elbow and guffawing into her spoon.

I make a mental note that I look pale and need more bronzer if I'm going to avoid questions about being actually sick. I'm not sick. I won't be sick. The other night was a fluke. Kind of like this conversation.

Raising an eyebrow, I point my spoon at Callie. "Why so many questions about Joey?"

She smirks and holds up three fingers, ticking them off one by one. "One, he picked you for his group even though, no offense, you have no idea what you're doing. Two, he offered you a ride home even though you already had your bike. Three, he was staring at you the entire day, which is part of the reason your team lost."

Voice soft, Jen chimes in, "Yeah. I saw him staring at you too."

I shake my head again. "You guys are ridiculous."

Was Joey really staring at me? I did my best to ignore him until he drove me home. Even then, we didn't talk much. Maybe he was looking at me because he was trying to figure out how to get me kicked out of the group? That makes more sense than the alternative.

We all spoon bites into our mouths in silence. A vibration startles me out of contemplation.

My phone buzzes in my pocket for a solid minute before I accept the call. Gesturing to my friends that I'll be right back, I step outside. The sunshine warms my face where the yogurt left it cold.

"Griffin," I sigh into the phone, "I'm kind of busy. What is it?"

"Sorry. I can't sleep."

I suck in a breath through my nose. "It's not nighttime here, so there's no way it's bedtime in Washington."

"Oh, yeah. Must be why I can't sleep."

His voice is groggy and throaty like he really is lying in bed. Squeezing my eyes shut tight, I try to erase the image of his hair standing on end, his body sprawled in bed, eyes dark with exhaustion. I miss him *so* much, but I still can't talk to him. It's too much.

I choke back a laugh instead of giving him the satisfaction of letting him think he's funny.

"You used to like my jokes." His voice climbs an octave.

"I'm out with friends. Can't we talk later?" I *can't* reconcile my friendship with Griffin backed up to the bizarre conversation with Jen and Callie. The two worlds refuse to combine in my head, and they shouldn't. The only way I survive is by keeping my lives separate, which means keeping Griffin at arm's length.

"Fine... Hey, wait—"

I hold my breath. "What?"

"Promise me something?"

"I don't know if I can."

"Promise you'll pick up when I call."

I owe him that much. I owe *myself* that much. Swallowing saliva down my suddenly dry throat, I nod, even though he can't see it. "I will."

When I get back to our table, what's left in my cup is soupy and melted. Jen and Callie's cups are empty, and they're both scrolling through their phones. I rescue the lone gummy worm from the bottom of my cup, chewy and sugary.

"Hey, sorry for making you guys wait."

Jen squares me with a questioning look. "Who was it?"

"A friend from back home." I tuck my phone into a pocket in my purse, like I can hide Griffin away from their questions.

Callie purses her lips. "Are you cheating on Joey with someone?"

She and Jen giggle while I roll my eyes, heat creeping along my ears.

"Mari-o! Mari-o! Mari-o!"

Cam's incessant chanting pounds in my ears as he waves a pair of matching game controllers in my face. His big brown eyes are even wider than usual, and his lips are pulled downward in a pout.

From my lap, Mattie stares up at me. He doesn't really talk, but if I could read minds, I have a feeling he'd be thinking along the same lines as his brother. He's also got a controller in one hand, hanging upside down and with the batteries missing. Sneaking grins at Cam, he doesn't seem to notice anything different. He's happy to be like his big brother.

I groan into a nearby couch pillow. "I thought you said I wasn't good enough at Mario to play with you," I remind him.

His face slides into an angelic smile. "I'll teach you. I'm really good at this game."

Ding dong.

The doorbell chimes right in time, saving me from giving in. "Be right back." I slip Mattie from my lap and hand him a ball from the toy basket near the couch.

Swinging open the front door with one hand and brushing through my hair with the other, I look up into Joey's face.

"What are you doing here?"

Even for me, it's kind of rude. But it's not Wednesday, and he already delivered Allison's prints for the week. Can't I have one day free of Joey Prince?

Considering he's standing on the porch, apparently not.

"I brought something for Cam and Mattie. I promised Cam the other day, and then I forgot."

A likely story.

He swings his hand forward, revealing a giant clear plastic bag full of little race cars. Looking past me, he cranes his neck inside the hallway. "Are they awake? It's not naptime, right?"

I sigh. Bringing toys is kind of non-annoying of him. And I'm pretty sure the only polite option is to invite him inside.

"They're awake." I point him to the couch and lead the way to Cam, whose eyes light up as he races toward us.

"You got the cars?" Joey hands over the bag, and Cam doesn't wait more than half a second before plopping down on the spot and emptying the entire bag on the floor. Cars roll in every direction, sliding under the couch, down the hall, and into the kitchen.

Mattie screeches as he lunges for a pair of yellow cars

heading for under the table. He crawls lightning-fast, tongue out in concentration.

"Are these all yours?" I scan the cars littered at my feet, at least fifty or more.

Running a hand through the front of his wayward hair, he nods. "Yeah. My dad used to buy me one for every 'A' I got in elementary school."

I glance down at the cars again. "You must have gotten a lot of 'A's.'"

He lifts a shoulder. "Now all I get is a lecture about how I need to study business and become a 'self-made man' like he is." Joey's voice is lined with bitterness, and his mouth twists into a sour smile.

But, hey, at least his parents pay attention to what he's doing. I had to go completely AWOL for my parents to take notice. And then they sent me away because they couldn't be bothered to deal with me.

I'd tell him that, but it's Joey. He doesn't care.

Neither of us says anything as we stare at the boys playing with the cars. Cam lines his up horizontally, prepping for a race. Mattie has somehow managed to stuff three in each of his hands. He chases after another greedily and loses grip on two of his originals. His bottom lip trembles and his eyes zero in on me as he throws his head back and starts wailing.

I scoop him into my arms and hug him tight. Joey reaches over my shoulder with a handful of replacement cars. On the rug next to the couch, I set Mattie down and we pile the cars in his lap like he's King of the Cars. No more crying.

Both Joey and I settle back onto the couch and sigh at the exact same time. We eye each other, challenging the other to say something. It's weird, working together with him. We've been on the same build-up team, but that's just painting and lugging materials in silence.

This is us on the same side for once. He may be my opposite in a lot of ways, but I can't hate someone who obviously cares about my nephews like I do. I was telling the truth at ice cream with Callie and Jen—I don't hate Joey Prince at all. He's growing on me, which should irritate me more than anything. Instead, it warms me, a small buzz building where an iced-over part used to sit.

Joey stretches his legs and looks over at them like they're intensely interesting and new. "Jen, Callie, and me are going to this party tonight. It's supposed to be just a few people at our friend Ben's house, if you want to come."

He twists the folds of a couch cushion between his fingers, watching as the fabric bounces back each time.

Hmm. On one hand, I was starting to think parties hadn't caught on in oh-so-fancy Old Oak, so it's good to know they exist here. But I can't help remembering how Jen and Callie teased me at the ice cream shop. Should I be concerned this is more than an obligatory I'm already at your house, so I might as well bring it up invitation?

I chew on the inside of my cheek.

A ratio of three girls to one boy doesn't constitute a date. Plus, if it's a party, there will probably be so many other people I may not even run into Joey, much less feel like I have to talk to him.

"Can you promise nothing crazy will happen?" Ally and Justin might be cooler than my parents, but they've made it clear I have limited chances. I will not risk losing their trust over one party.

He tilts his head like he's considering it. "I can't guarantee that it won't get crazy, but I *can* promise that it won't be the illegal kind of crazy. Ben's grandpa is a retired police chief, so Ben's really careful."

A police officer approved party? Ally will eat that up. Flashing a smile, I say, "I love parties."

His mouth curves upward, warm and full. "Cool. Well, I better go. I just wanted to drop off the cars." As he walks to the front door, he waves goodbye to Cam, who ignores him and continues *vrooming* his cars along the patterned border on the rug.

"Yeah, thanks for that. You saved me a few hours of entertaining them on my own." I put a hand on the open door as he steps outside.

Turning back, he pinches his lips together, blowing a breath out slowly. "So, I guess I'll pick you up at eight?"

"Aaaaghhhh!"

A scream pierces the room. Out of the corner of my eye, I see Cam's hunched over, using a wailing Mattie's flattened back as a human racetrack. It's impossible to concentrate on anything Joey says. I can't even hear my own thoughts over the death howl letting loose from Mattie's tiny mouth.

I nod. "Uh huh."

Joey's face relaxes as I try and fail to refocus my attention on him amidst Cam's cries that have added to Mattie's. Both little boys roll around on the floor, their faces growing red. "Cool," Joey says.

I close the door, run to rescue Mattie, and freeze, heart pounding in my ears.

Wait, what?

Am I crazy, or did I agree to a date with Joey Prince?

CHAPTER Eleven

Brain buzzing, I text both Callie and Jen to ask if they're riding with Joey, too.

Jen says no. Callie says no and then adds ten question marks and a kissy-face emoji. A second later, she texts that she changed her mind.

Callie: We're all riding together! Tell Joey to be there on time!

Crap.

For the rest of the afternoon, Mattie naps and Cam zones out in front of a Disney movie we've watched three times this week. The hours tick by until Allison gets home from her last photo session and I can get ready.

"Who's throwing the party? Is it someone I know?"

I lift an eyebrow. "You sound like Mom's clone."

She sets a hand on her hip. "Well, I am a mom, so."

"I don't know if you know him. Ben somebody. Joey said it'll be a small party, but all my friends are going."

"Callie too?"

Nodding, I cross my arms in front of my chest. "Callie, plus Jen from the build-up. And Joey is the most boring teenager in the world, so you don't have to worry, okay? Plus, the guy's grandpa is a police officer, so everything will be very G-rated."

She smiles, but her forehead still wrinkles in concern. Feeling kind of ridiculous, I pat her arm a few times. "Thanks for worrying about me, but I promise to be careful." Her concern sparks something foreign and sisterly in me, and it's strange, being worried over instead of grilled like an at-risk prisoner.

Allison squeezes my hand. "That's what big sisters are for. Just promise me you'll be safe."

JOEY KNOCKS ON THE DOOR AT 7:59. I SWING IT OPEN AND invite him inside. When he sees Callie and Jen waving from the couch, his mouth twists.

"It's easier if we all go together," I say. "That way we get to hang out more, too."

He shrugs but doesn't look at me. "Okay."

When he turns to say something to Jen, Callie wiggles her eyebrows. I ignore her. I figured Joey wouldn't mind the girls riding with us since we're all going to the same place. But trying to figure him out is impossible. When it comes to emotions, he's a robot: totally devoid of any.

Until he isn't.

Out in the driveway, I shove Jen in front of me toward the passenger seat. "I like sitting in the back," I lie. I can't subject myself to any more awkward situations with Joey, not right now. Only he knows his motivations for asking to ride together, and I want to keep it that way.

Jen skips to the door and climbs into the spot. Joey says nothing. In the back, Callie shows me pictures on her phone from a party last year. Apparently, Ben is notorious for throwing bonfire parties every summer.

"You know Ben, right?"

The name sounds familiar, but I've met so many new people since the beginning of the summer. Their faces and names all blend together into one big Texas-shaped blob.

I shrug. "Probably."

Jen turns from her seat in the front. "You'll know him when you see him. He's always at the build up."

Unlike the too-big shiny new houses in Joey and Allison's neighborhood, these houses are spaced so far apart you'd need to take a car to knock on your neighbor's door. The farther out we drive, the more land each property sits on. Some of the buildings look as old and crumbling as the ancient sprawling oak trees billowing down over us. But when we pull into the crowded dirt driveway in front of Ben's house, it's obvious his parents have updated a lot.

Instead of a dilapidated farmhouse from the beginning of time, the house we walk up to looks like it materialized straight out of the end result of an HGTV show. The outside's a light grey, and everything is trimmed in white. Tidy white wooden shutters frame the windows, and the double front doors are painted a deep navy blue.

Before Joey even knocks, the door jolts open. The blond buzz cut guy from the build-up looks at each of us and grins. "Come in, y'all."

As we follow him, my phone buzzes from inside my purse, and I reject the call without even looking. I set up one of those cheesy ringtones for my parents in case there was ever an emergency, so I know it's not them. Anyone else can wait for me to call them back tomorrow..

Buzz cut guy—Ben—leads us through his house and into the kitchen where every surface is covered in food and coolers. He waves a hand at the spread. "Here's all the snacks and stuff, but the real party's outside."

He points to another door past the kitchen at the end of the main hall. It's slightly ajar and the echo of loud music pounds through. A group of girls seated at the long wooden table near the wall call Ben over, and he waves at us before swaggering toward them.

Jen snatches a bag of chips from the counter. She tosses another bag to Joey, who catches it with a smirk.

Callie rolls her eyes. "I don't know how y'all can eat those." She slips a cookie off a wide platter and bites into it with a groan. "Ugh. So good." She shoves the rest in her mouth, wipes the back of her hand across her lips, and sucks her teeth. "Okay, I'm going out."

I lean forward to get a better look at the chips Joey and Jen are now sniffing and pulling out one by one to inspect closer.

"Have you ever had hot Cheetos?" Joey taps the bright yellow plastic packaging. "These are an off-brand version, but they're three times as spicy."

Jen coughs into her hand. "At least."

Joey nods solemnly. "Possibly more."

He extends the open bag, revealing bright orange puffy chips covered in a red-orange powder. Just the smell alone stings my nose. I shake my head.

"No thanks. I kind of want to keep my taste buds. You guys have fun burning yours off, though." I'll leave them to bond and sacrifice myself to the outside party crowd—alone. Jen looks happy to hang out with Joey, and if he's getting any weird ideas about where our relationship stands, maybe time with Jen will set him right.

They grin at each other and continue searching through their open chip bags for the perfect challenge.

Down the hall, I follow the beat until I reach the back door. Once outside, the music becomes recognizable, but only kind of.

This is country music, and I'm not familiar with any of the songs. I'm not one of those people that have a vendetta against country music; I've just never listened to it. Now it's blasting in my ears, courtesy of a set of sleek black speakers tucked in the tree directly above my head. A singer croons about some guy leaving her and never coming back, even though what they had was perfect.

I sort of did that to Griffin, and I hate myself for it. For all the times I complain about how stupid he is, there's one hundred more where I miss him in a part-of-myself-is-missing kind of way, even if I've chosen to move on from him, from us.

Maybe there's a reason I never listen to country.

Not a lot of dancing is happening, even with the music so loud my ears ring. Instead, most of the darkened silhouettes surround the biggest bonfire I've ever seen. It roars yellow and red and whips into the air where it sits near a grove of trees at the edge of the clearing.

Once I get to the fire, I stop outside the circle of strangers. Next to me is a long plastic table lined with marshmallows and roasting sticks. I take my time picking out the fluffiest marshmallow I can find before I squeeze through and find a spot. Besides the people standing around the fire talking, others sit on giant logs that serve as benches. I crouch down into an empty spot and let my stick hover above a smoky corner of the fire pit —the perfect roasting conditions.

My eyes focus on the melting marshmallow, but across the fire a familiar outline knocks me off balance. As I'm squinting across the fire, I let my hand drop for a second too long, and my marshmallow, along with the end of my stick, chars black.

Dang it!

Joey walks around the fire and sits next to me on the log. I hand my burnt stick off to him, glaring. "You ruined my marshmallow." He's supposed to be talking to Jen! Eating spicy chips and bonding! Not following me outside. Leave it to Joey to choose this moment, this night, to break character and get all aggressive on me.

While I stalk off to get new supplies, he calls after me, "What? I didn't do anything."

I ignore him while my new marshmallow toasts, then carefully remove only the crispy golden-brown outer shell and pop it into my mouth. I flick the gooey center into the fire.

Joey's mouth opens. "What was that?"

I shrug. "That's the only part I like." Griffin was the one to convince me not to waste my time with the rest of the marshmallow once I admitted the outside is all I like. I should be with him tonight.

"I can't believe you got mad over a burnt marshmallow when

you only eat one-tenth of the whole thing. You made me actually feel bad for a minute."

I look at him sideways. "You should feel bad. You were staring at me like a creep, and I burned my marshmallow."

His mouth turns down. "I wasn't staring at you. I was looking at the fire, and you happened to be there."

My fingers stick together as I curl them into a fist.

Laughing drily, he puts his hands behind him and leans back. "Is that why you're in Texas for the summer? You yelled at everyone in Washington too much, so they sent you here?"

I suck in a breath. "No. I—" Suddenly, the curling smoke from the fire is too close, too much." My throat closes up. "I'm trying to change, okay? You annoy me so much you make it really hard."

He blinks. "Change?"

"Yeah. I'm obviously a huge screw up. My parents got sick of me, so they sent me to stay with Ally and Justin." Why am I admitting this? I keep my tone light and sarcastic, but my words sound as sour as they taste.

Something warm tickles against the back of my dress. Joey's breath blows across my neck as he scoots closer, and his hand pats my back awkwardly. Whoa—what?

Joey's voice is soft, gentle. "Hey—I'm a jerk. I was embarrassed you caught me looking at you. I didn't mean it."

My face heats more than the fire should warrant. This conversation took a turn I wasn't expecting. It's not like I was trying to make Joey feel bad for me. The opposite, really. The truth spilled from my lips before I could stop it.

"Um, it's fine. My parents are going to send me to this fancy all-girls boarding school if they don't think I've changed enough by the end of the summer. The thing is, I'm not sure what else I need to do. I messed up, and I'm trying, but they don't seem to care. Mostly my mom. She thinks I'm the reason my dad's been tired and sick lately. Which I guess I kind of am..."

I swallow as all those fears rush back at me, threatening to tear me apart on the spot if I don't push them back down. Dad getting sicker. My stomach pains. I can't think about it or it will consume me. Once I start talking, more truth spews from me. Joey listens carefully, a line drawn between his brows.

My back grows suddenly colder as he shifts, taking his arm with him. "Boarding school? I didn't know those even existed anymore. Seems kind of extreme, to be honest."

"Well, my dad's sick a lot, and I think my mom is done raising kids. I'm the last one left at home, and I'm not sure she thinks I'm worth the effort."

Why am I telling him all this? Why can't I stop? And why am I not as embarrassed as I should be? Joey and I aren't close, not like this. We don't spill secret fears while sitting around the fire. Just a second ago, I was annoyed at him for following me out here.

His voice cracks. "You are. Worth the effort, I mean."

Turning, I squint up into his eyes lit by the dancing firelight, and they're warm brown with flecks of yellow fire reflected in the irises. I tilt my head. "Thanks."

We sit like that for a few more seconds until my stomach flips into my chest, and I break the spell. As subtly as possible, I scoot a few inches in the opposite direction and gaze around. The fire's starting to die, and all the marshmallows are gone. Less than half of the original crowd still sits around the fire. Judging from the laughs and shrieks echoing from a few feet away, most of the people have gone back inside. We shouldn't sit out here alone—people might get the wrong idea.

I should probably go look for Jen and Callie. I stand and squint into the distance. "Didn't Callie come outside a while ago? Have you seen her?"

Joey stands, too, and stuffs his hands in the front pockets of his grey shorts. "Don't worry about her." His eyes flit to the sky, then the ground.

Huh? Did I miss something? I chew on my bottom lip.

Everyone seemed happy enough on the drive over, but I could swear Joey looks annoyed at me for bringing up Callie.

"Are you guys fighting or something?"

"No. We're good. She has a habit of disappearing at parties. It's kind of her thing."

"What's whose thing?"

Ben sneaks up from behind Joey, grinning widely into his face before stepping close enough to nudge my ribs with his elbow. I'm tempted to elbow him back in the face; my arm itches to swing forward, but instead I cross my arms over my chest and scowl. I don't like being touched without permission, so what's with tonight? It shouldn't be a free for all.

Joey shrugs, so I speak up. "Callie. Joey says she always disappears at parties."

Ben's smile stretches, his teeth glinting in the glow from the fire. "Ohhh yeah. That is definitely her thing."

The way he says it makes my skin crawl.

Joey slugs him in the chest. "Dude. Stop making everything sound perverted."

Rubbing the spot Joey hit, Ben shakes his head. "Relax. I'm sure she's fine. I'll go ask around." He jogs away from us, back toward the house.

"What's Callie's thing?" If my friend has a habit everyone else is worried about, I should be out looking for her too. If I were a better friend, I'd probably already know.

Joey shrugs, a smile flitting across his lips. "It's seriously not a big deal. It's just awkward."

Who could have guessed Joey Prince would be the type to hold a secret over someone's head? Or maybe he's being secretive because he doesn't know if Callie would want me to know about her *thing*. I might not be secured enough in the friend group to know everything. Still, Joey doesn't have to be smug about it.

I grit my teeth. "Are you enjoying this?"

His mouth goes straight, but his eyes laugh and laugh and laugh. "A little," he admits.

One measly party and he goes rogue on me. Where's the serious boy with the chip on his shoulder when I need him? I growl and smack his chest, just like he did to Ben. Except he pretends like it doesn't hurt. He smiles so big it barely fits on his face.

"Fine. Callie has this guy from the other high school that she only hangs out with at parties. He's a creep, and we all hate him, but she won't get over him."

"That's it? A make out buddy you don't approve of?" There's the Joey I know, showing up right on time to get all judgmental and weird. Hands on my hips, I shake my head.

A muscle in his jaw twitches. "He's a douche bag. You'll see."

As if on cue, Callie's voice carries over the back yard. Her hair's so light it shows up in the dark, and whoever she's with is tall with matching nearly fluorescent hair.

I wave my arms above my head and yell her name. "Callie! Over here."

They change directions and walk toward us, Callie's voice still floating over the music. Once they reach us, the tall blond guy she's clinging to smiles, but it's more of a sneer.

"'Sup, y'all?"

He bro nods at each of us, his gaze lingering on me longer than anyone else.

Callie notices and reaches out to squeeze my shoulder. "This is Paige. She's here for the summer."

He lifts one half of his mouth into a lazy smile and bro nods at me again. "I'm Kevin. You should come hang out with me next time Callie's busy," he says, his voice deeper than it was only a second earlier.

My eyebrows shoot up, along with everyone else's. "I don't think so." Callie won't look at me. Kevin seems to read the room because after a second of all of us glaring at him, he shrugs. "I'm just messing with y'all."

Something pokes my side, and I shift my eyes to see Joey stabbing his finger at me pointedly. Okay, okay. I get it. This

Kevin guy is exactly what Joey said he'd be. I widen my eyes at him to *stop it already*, and he seems to get the picture because he lets his hand fall and swing by his side.

Callie clears her throat, her eyes wide. "We're gonna go listen to some music in Kevin's truck. He's gonna take me home later, so y'all go ahead, okay?"

She trots off, loser Kevin trailing behind like he's determined to keep up a cool, disinterested pace.

When they're out of earshot, I raise my eyebrows. "It seriously pains me to say this, but you're right about him. What a creep."

He rolls his eyes. "Great. You finally agree with me, and I don't even get to feel good about it."

I can't say why, but a sense of calming relief comes over me that Joey can tell the difference between a guy like Kevin and a guy with good intentions. That he actually cares about who Callie spends time with.

We track down Jen, who's inside sitting at the farm table debating the merits of romantic comedies and their inevitable comeback on the big screen. She pauses when she sees us.

"Jen, are you ready to go? I think it's past Joey's bedtime."

"Callie wants me to wait for her." Her bottom lip dips into a pout.

I flash a sympathetic smile. "Are you sure?"

Jen nods. "Yeah. She'll owe me for this, but yeah, I'm sure. We'll get a ride with Kevin."

Joey and I walk to his car, climb inside, and situate ourselves in total silence. I guess I ended up riding alone with him after all. So much for my plan tonight.

And then, whoosh!

Right as I buckle my seat belt, something whizzes past my head and lands at my feet. I bend down to retrieve the empty chip bag from the party. Holding it by the ends of my fingers, I wave it in front of Joey's face. "What's this? You're throwing trash at me now?"

His face is gleeful, bordering on giddy. "I can't make you happy, can I? First you complain that my car's too clean, now you complain about a little trash. Make up your mind, Paige."

My eyes narrow to slits as I try and fail to glare back at him. I drop the chip bag onto his lap, nose wrinkled. "Have you ever considered that I like to complain when it comes to you?"

He starts the car. "Never. But it makes sense."

I study him as he drives down the dirt road we came from. His perfectly imperfect mop of hair, his smile that's somehow made more appearances tonight than in all the weeks I've known him combined. Why do I like to complain about him? Why does he bother me so much—why do I care? My face warms.

I think I kind of, sort of, maybe *don't* hate Joey Prince.

Crap.

CHAPTER Twelve

"We have to be quiet while Mattie sleeps, okay Cam?"

Cam nods. He shifts his eyes to Joey, then me. "Okay. But I'm huuuungry."

Joey's watching the kids right now, not me. But I barely walked in the door from swimming at Jen's house, and my stomach rumbles as soon as he mentions being hungry.

Joey looks up from his video game, eyebrow raised. "What are you hungry for?"

Cam scratches one side of his chin. "Hmm... maybe chocolate chip cookies?"

Shaking my head, I cross to the pantry. We're all out of cookies. I might be guilty of eating the last of them during a stressful late-night phone call with Griffin earlier this week. "Maybe pick something else, Cammy."

Joey stands, rubbing his hands along his pockets. "I bet we have everything to make them, though. Let's see."

He stops behind me, peering over my shoulder into the pantry. As he eyes each shelf, he makes little humming noises under his breath. His arm bumps mine as he reaches to check behind a giant bag of flour. Then he claps his hands together.

"We already have all the ingredients. Ready to help me, Cam?"

"*You're* going to make cookies?"

I turn to give him a look. Reaching past me for the flour and brown sugar, Joey presses his lips together. "Well, not without my sous chef."

Cam bounds forward, lining up next to Joey with a grin cracking his face. "Yay! Cookies!"

I cross my arms against my chest. This should be good. Somehow, I just knew that Joey was the kind of guy to bake cookies and be great with kids. He probably adopts stray puppies and bottle feeds abandoned baby birds. I already know he builds houses every summer just for fun. What a weirdo.

"I'm going to take a shower. Can I trust you two not to burn the house down?"

Joey shrugs and Cam giggles.

By the time I come back downstairs, Cam's face is splattered with flour and his mouth lined with chocolate. Joey is hunched over and points to the oven, explaining the fluorescent green numbers lighting up the screen.

"See the number ten? When it says zero, the timer will make a sound, and our cookies will be ready."

I peer into the yellow-lit oven. A dozen mounds with chocolate dotting the tops sit in rows. They actually look good. My stomach gurgles angrily at the warm brown sugar smell.

Drumming my fingers on the black kitchen counter, I click my tongue. "You bake?"

Joey looks at me, chin pointed. "Yeah. I'm a great baker. You'll see." I get the sense that this is not his first time making impromptu cookies.

I wish I could accept his unspoken challenge, but I'm a truly awful baker. I couldn't even get my Easy Bake Oven to work right as a kid.

"What else can you make?" Mom's rare batch of homemade muffins or elusive bread loaves tick through my head. She's never offered to teach me how to make either of them.

Joey lifts an eyebrow, studying me. "Anything. All you have to do is follow a recipe, it's easy."

Frowning, I bend to peek at the cookies again. Not as easy as you'd think.

Cam tugs on my hand, his chocolate lined lips pinched together. "Don't worry, Piggy, we'll share with you."

I kiss his head, and my chest grows warm. Good to know that I can't be dethroned as his favorite with a batch of warm cookies. "Thanks, Cam. You're the best. And those cookies sure smell delicious."

"So, are you ever going to explain the 'Piggy' thing?" Joey tilts his head, looking between Cam and me.

I shoot Cam a warning look, like *don't you dare*. If only five-year-olds were in on that sort of thing.

He squints his eyes and mashes a finger to the ball of his nose. And then he oinks like a pig. Of course he thinks it's hilarious.

Joey erupts into a stream of laughter that ricochets against my ears.

If embarrassment could kill a person, I'd absolutely melt into a puddle of shame right here and evaporate. Instead, I cover my burning face with my hands and shake my head.

Oh man.

From behind my fingers I say, "My name starts with a 'P,' and I was always hungry. It was a bad combination."

What I don't say is that it's tough being the youngest sibling, especially with three older brothers who eat like they're on death row. I learned early to grab food as soon as it appeared and swallow it before it got snatched from my hands. But of course, my family thought it was hilarious, and so the piggy nickname was born.

And apparently it will never die.

I clear my throat and drop my hands. Whatever. Who cares what Joey Prince thinks, anyway? He's still shaking with silent laughter when I look up, and next to him, Cam scoots backward on the floor while sneaking glances at his new hero.

These better be amazing cookies.

Joey fake-coughs into his shoulder. "You'll murder me if I ever use that nickname, right?"

Nodding once for confirmation, I lift my lips into a smirk. "You better believe I will."

He laughs softly under his breath, then tucks his hands into his pockets. "Okay. At least I get a warning."

Cam ignores both of us and wanders into the living room to look for a very specific Happy Meal toy that hasn't been found in weeks. Joey leans back against the counter opposite the oven.

Neither of us says anything else until the timer sounds, beeping loudly until I leap forward and turn it off. Above me, Mattie's cries start. Joey sets the baking sheet on top of the stove and jogs up the stairs to get Mattie from his crib.

I slip two fresh cookies onto a paper plate from the pantry and sneak out to the front porch. My restraint lasts approximately one point five minutes before I burn the ends of my fingers and the tip of my tongue inhaling them.

Dang it.

Best cookies I've ever had.

CHAPTER Thirteen

"**F**ireworks?"

Justin's eyes widen, making him look even more like a giddy little kid than normal. He rubs his hands together as he cackles maniacally.

Allison strolls into the kitchen, Mattie on her hip. "What's going on?" She looks to me for the answer because, clearly, Justin is on a separate plane right now.

I roll my eyes. "Callie and Jen invited me to watch fireworks with them tonight. I was telling *your husband* about it, but this was as far as I got before he went all weird on me.

She nods knowingly. "Oh. Got it." Stepping forward, she snaps her fingers sharply in front of his face. "Justin, snap out of it."

He shakes his head, slowly at first, then faster like a wet dog drying itself, his hair flopping side to side. Mattie giggles, clutching at his chubby belly. Ally sucks in her cheeks and rolls her eyes, looking at me like "See what I put up with?"

Justin laughs and reaches to take Mattie. "If you go out with your friends, you'll miss the best fireworks show in Texas. I'm not sure you wanna do that."

Ally levels a look at me. "He's talking about *his* fireworks show. Trust me, yours will be more fun. Ignore him."

Grinning, I poke Justin in the bicep. "Save me some of the poppers. I like those."

He dips his head to sigh—a long, drawn-out, dramatic thing. I'm glad, not for the first time, that Ally ended up with Justin. He's probably the one person in this family right now, aside from my baby nephews, who doesn't judge every breath I take. I need to thank him for that. For now, I flash him a smile and shake my head about his fireworks thing.

Ally shoos me away with one hand, wrapping an arm around Justin's waist. I hurry upstairs to change my clothes. Callie texted earlier to warn me about mosquitoes around the lake we're going to. Reluctantly, I take off my blue-and-white striped dress and pull on my favorite pair of jeans. I scan the shirts in my closet until I land on a plain red V-neck. I pair the outfit with silver strappy sandals and skip down the stairs.

Outside, Cam and Justin wave sparklers against the orange sky. The sun sets so late that Cam will fall asleep before the real fireworks start, but he loves sparklers—who doesn't?—and he gets to stay up later than normal tonight to play with them. It was the same when I was little. The Fourth was probably the one day a year I got to stay up late with my siblings and run free in the front yard. I almost felt like an equal.

I wave down the driveway, watching as Allison hovers over Cam, paranoid he'll set fire to his hair or something. Callie texted this morning to say we'd all meet at Joey's house and drive over to the lake together. Normally, I'd be hesitant to waltz over and wait with him without knowing for sure that someone else would be there. But after the party and the ride home, plus working together at the build-up, and our truce, I'm not worried. We clearly can get along when necessary. And maybe even having fun while we're doing it. Though I'm not prepared to let Joey in on that shift just yet.

Although the houses in the neighborhood are huge, they're still pretty close together, so it doesn't take long to walk over to Joey's. I ring the doorbell and step back on the porch. Several seconds later, a man's voice booms from inside the house.

"Not going anywhere..."

"Too many parties.... when is he going to grow up...."

"Start thinking about a future...."

Click.

The door pulls open, and I stumble backward in surprise. Joey glares at me.

"Oh, hey. I was, uh..." I bite my lip. "I wasn't trying to listen, I promise. I was just waiting." I turn, seconds too late, and try to pretend like I heard nothing.

Joey follows me and his lips form a thin line. "It's fine. Let's not talk about it."

I flash a tight smile. Pretending I heard nothing is great. I can do that, no problem.

Jen's baby blue convertible chugs past Joey's house, stops, and zooms backward before stopping to the side of his driveway. Callie leans over the rolled-down top. "Happy Fourth of July, y'all!" Jen giggles and waves both arms overhead like we're in some sort of teenage beach movie.

I wave back and grin.

Joey stuffs his hands in his pockets and stalks toward the car. I follow him, wishing I could think of something to say to smooth things over. But is it really my job? It's not my fault his dad was yelling loud enough for me to hear. It's not Joey's either, but the point is I'm not to blame here. And he's the one who asked me not to talk about it. The least I can do is humor him and keep my mouth shut.

The backseat of Jen's car is cramped. If I were purposefully sitting on Joey's lap, I'm not sure we'd be much closer than we are already. I cling to the side of the car, wishing there was a door handle instead of smooth metal siding. Joey leans his head against the window on the opposite side, his eyes closed. Clearly, he's still butthurt.

If I hadn't heard his dad crapping on him a few minutes ago, I'd think he's purposefully being a killjoy. But he has a good reason. Still, we're headed to the lake to see a fireworks show Jen promises will be amazing. Plus, no parents are around.

I nudge his foot with mine.

He opens one eye, lifting his head an inch or so. I raise my eyebrows and smile. Shifting his body, he sits up in his seat. He smiles back at me briefly, nodding as if he understands what I'm trying to convey.

His shoulders move with a heavy breath and his eyes meet mine again briefly before he nods at the front of the car. Leaning forward, so his head hovers in between Callie and Jen, he says, "I heard Kevin's coming tonight. You gonna run off with him again?"

Callie sucks on her teeth. "It's none of y'all's business what I do."

From the driver's seat, Jen shakes her head.

I lean back. Callie is right; this is clearly none of my business. This is between old friends. I don't know Kevin, besides seeing him briefly at the party. He seemed like a jerk, but I have nothing real to add to the conversation. And Callie's right, her opinion's the only one that matters in this situation.

Still, Joey's eyes shift toward me. No way am I backing him up. I shake my head "no."

He widens his eyes. He must think this is payment for what I overheard. Technically, I owe him nothing. But it was a sucky thing for his dad to say, either way.

"Callie—" I suck in a breath. "What's with this Kevin guy?"

She flips her hair, combing it with her fingers. "He's older, a senior, and that's why everyone hates him."

Jen makes a choking sound and Joey's nostrils flare.

Callie holds up a hand, like she expected their reaction and doesn't want to hear it. "He's always been super nice to me. Neither of us is looking for a relationship right now. That's why we only hang out at parties and stuff. I don't know why everyone has to make a big deal out of it." Her voice turns low and whiney.

Jen reaches across the seat to squeeze her hand. "We worry about you."

Pulling her hand away, Callie huffs. "I could beat him up on my own. I don't need anyone to worry about me."

I understand that. Having tons of people obsessing over what you're doing and why you're doing it is humiliating. I've always felt that way as the youngest in my family. Like I'm growing up in a fish tank with a crowd gathered around to see me run straight into the glass every night. It's not ideal.

"I mean, if he makes you happy..." I shrug, letting my words trail off.

Joey glares at me, and I ignore him. Or try to, while he not-so-gently kicks my foot with his shoe across the back of the car.

Callie sighs. "Yeah. He does most of the time."

No one else says anything until we swing around a woodsy bend and reach a darkened parking lot. Jen turns the car off and she and Callie get out. Joey and I are stuck in the back until they pull their seats flat for us to crawl out. While we wait, Joey points at Kevin's approaching figure. Callie leaps toward him and mauls his face with hers. My nose wrinkles automatically.

"*That,*" Joey says, "is what you encouraged."

I climb from the back of the car, watching as Callie and Kevin disappear toward the soft orange glow of a fire. Turning to Jen, I point in the same direction. "I guess we go this way?"

She winces. "Sorry. I'm meeting someone too." Her head turns right as another car pulls into the parking lot and a tall guy with a head full of curly black hair jumps out of the back. She waves enthusiastically before spinning back to me. "Sorry," she says again. "I figured you'd have Callie and Joey to hang out with. I didn't know Kevin would be here..."

I shake my head and wave a hand. "Don't worry about it. I'll be fine. You have fun."

She doesn't wait and runs off giggling toward her *friend.* I've been abandoned. Or, I guess, *we've* been abandoned.

Behind me, Joey grunts, as if coming to the same realization.

So much for not being worried about being alone with him.

He started out the night in a bad mood; it wouldn't surprise me if he stays that way. Especially now that it's just the two of us.

"So, this way?" I point again toward the smell of fire and the curling stacks of smoke. He nods. "Yeah. It gets kind of crazy, though, so watch out."

Crazy isn't the word for what we step into.

Past the parking lot, through the grove, the lakefront is filled with kids our age. Tents speckle the sand, along with fires of all different sizes. The black water glistens from their glow and the air ripples with music and shouting and premature fireworks.

Even if I wanted to find Callie and Jen, it'd be impossible in this mess.

Boom. Boom. Boom.

Instinctively, I step closer to Joey as a trio of fireworks blasts through the air from the middle of the water. Joey's arm circles my waist as he attempts to steady me.

Hands out for balance, I inhale. "Thanks." My breath doesn't quite return in full force. Because of the near tumble, not at all because of Joey's arm and their freaky warmth.

Straining my eyes, I might be able to make out a boat way out there. But everything's so dark and hazy with the smoke all around us.

Joey steps back a few inches. "Come on."

We weave through bodies stretched out across the sand, girls in bikinis on beach towels, and a group of guys playing the most intense game of beach volleyball I've ever seen. Under a weeping willow, up on the grass, a big group is gathered, and someone yells, "Go! Go! Go!" and pumps their fist into the air. The group sticks together too tightly for me to see what's happening, but I don't think it's necessarily a secret.

By the time Joey stops walking, my ears buzz against my skull, and blisters form on the backs of my feet where my sandals rub. Hands on my hips, I lean forward and yell loud enough for him to hear, "Where are we going?"

He gestures vaguely ahead. We leave behind the majority of

the people, and the space between fires gets farther and farther. Maybe he's taking me away from everyone else so he can push me into the lake without any witnesses, pretending to tolerate me long enough to not be the main suspect in my eventual drowning. Or maybe he's as wary of the crowds as I am and wants to find an emptier spot. At this point, I wouldn't be too surprised either way.

As if reading my mind, he suddenly stops and turns his head toward me. "I'm not leaving the beach to murder you or try to kiss you or anything."

Interesting that he lumps those two very different scenarios together. Really interesting.

One of my eyebrows shoots upward, questioning.

"I happen to know of a better spot to watch the fireworks. And since we both got ditched, I'm letting you in on my secret."

Despite myself, I grin. Something about knowing one of Joey's secrets makes my cheeks spread with an unbidden smile.

Joey leads us around an overflowing trashcan with fat flies circling it. He points ahead to a bench covered in sand near the edge of the blocked-off sand dunes. I follow.

"So that stuff my dad was saying? You know, earlier at my house?"

"Yeah." Here we go. I guess he's going to talk about it after all.

Joey ruffles his hair. "He's not, like, mean or anything. He's crazy about me making something out of myself. He wants me to be super successful and own a business like his. Exactly like his."

I nod. "He wants you to take over his shop?" The day Joey helped me find the stationery stays burned in my brain. His voice hits the same frustrated tone now as he explains his dad's expectations.

"My mom's kind of like that," I say. "She doesn't expect me to be successful, though. It's kind of like she thinks the opposite. That's the whole reason I'm here in Texas, because she's scared

I'll end up a complete loser or something. I guess that's why she wants me to go to boarding school."

Joey laughs softly. We sit on the bench, and I tuck my feet under myself.

"That sucks. My parents would never send me anywhere. They'd be too afraid I wouldn't come back. They wouldn't even let me go off on my own when we visited Brazil last summer."

I shake my head. "You'd come back. Believe me."

He stretches his arms behind him. "Don't you hate it here?"

Combing the ends of my hair with my fingers, I stop to think. Do I hate it here?

I hate that I was forced to come. But Ally and her family, and Callie and Jen, even Joey—they make it better than what I had in Washington. It's that Mom left me no choice that needles at my nerves every time I'm reminded of how my summer *should* have gone.

I scoop up a round pebble near my feet and rub at the smooth spots with my thumb. "I don't hate it here. I hate feeling like I'm my family's unwanted afterthought."

Joey's head tilts to the side like he's absorbing my words, saving them for later. "What's it like having so many siblings?"

Rearing my arm back, I toss the pebble as hard as I can into the water. It lands with an echoing *plonk* as it sinks to the bottom of the lake.

"Sometimes it's really fun. Like holidays when everyone's home together, we don't need anyone else to come over because we already have a full team for anything we can think of. Board games get really crazy because we're all so competitive, and my twin brothers always cheat." Of course, most of the time, I was left out of the fun. Too little, too whiney, too late. A bunch of excuses that, more often than not, made me burst into tears and stomp away.

Joey laughs, warm and happy sounding. I watch him a second too long before tearing my gaze away to speak again. "What about being an only child? Do you love it?"

Even though I'm not looking at him, I can tell his words contain a smirk. "Will you hate me if I say yes?"

Boomboomboom. Boom.

The explosions start with a burst of white and red light directly over the water, interrupting our conversation. They pause long enough for me to consider his question.

"No." Being the last one stuck at home with my parents has sometimes felt like being an only child. It'd be a lot simpler if it didn't come with the weight of everyone else's accomplishments hanging over me at all times.

We lean against the bench and tilt our heads to the sky as light explodes above us.

CHAPTER
Fourteen

"Sure you don't want to come to the zoo?" Justin waves a flyer featuring a giraffe chewing on a pile of leaves.

I moan into my cereal bowl. "It's Saturday. All I'm doing today is watching TV and eating my weight in Cinnamon Toast Crunch."

Allison makes a big show of covering Cam's ears with her hands. "Shhh. Stop being a bad influence on my kids. You're going to make them rebellious like their aunt."

Justin lightly taps her head with the flyer. "Stop calling your sister names. You're going to give our kids more ammunition for later."

They roll their eyes at each other and Justin winks. I get the feeling if the kids and I weren't here, they'd be sticking their tongues down each other's throats.. I'm not sure I'd even mind— as long as I were safely out of view.

They scatter out the door, and I pour another bowl of cereal, dragging myself to the couch to eat it while Ally's gone and I can get away with it without her making me sit at the table. It was past midnight when Joey dropped me off last night, but even after I was upstairs in my pink polka dot pajamas, my eyes wouldn't shut. Every time I tried to lay my head on my pillow, the blazing fireworks reflected in Joey's eyes haunted me. That, and my stomachache resurfaced right on schedule. I'm officially sick of feeling sick. But I can't mention it to anyone because they'll do what they do best: worry. I can do that just fine on my own. A stomachache doesn't mean anything, I tell myself as I swirl my cereal. I'm still eating, aren't I?

Going to the party last week, I thought Callie, Jen, and I would hang out and ditch Joey as soon as we got there. It ended up being the opposite. And stranger still, being stuck with Joey wasn't awful. And last night at the fireworks... It was nice. More than nice. Kind of great.

Apparently, he knows how to have fun occasionally.

But now my eyelids weigh twice as much as normal, and they won't stop sliding over my eyes whenever I stop moving. Not even the lure of adorable, brown-spotted giraffes can shake me awake long enough to get anything done. I'm determined to have the laziest of Saturdays.

From its spot on the table next to my cereal bowl, my phone chimes with the sound for a new email, my mom's name attached to it.

Gritting my teeth, I open the email and scroll through. My heart sinks right down to my stomach.

It's a forwarded email confirming tuition has been paid for the upcoming school year. It's official: my parents are sending me to boarding school. Just like some poor orphan girl, except I'm *not* an orphan, and this is so messed up.

They promised to give me this summer. I've been busting my butt to prove to them I'm more than my screw-ups. All of that's wasted now.

Tears blurring my vision, I fumble with my phone and press call on Mom's number. It rings and rings and rings. Nothing.

I try Dad's number even though he habitually can't find his cell phone to save his life. No answer there either.

Phone still pressed to my ear, I call Griffin. He's the only person who will understand. He's the only person who will make any of this better.

Except it rings for barely a second before switching to voicemail. He always answers my calls, no matter what. Even if he's in the middle of an art project, he'll drop it to talk to me.

I'm so painfully alone, my bones ache with the thought of it. Boarding school. Never going back home. Permanently disappointing my parents. Hurting Dad. It's too much.

Pressing the call button one last time, I call Griffin back. It sends me right to voicemail again, so I leave a choked, frantic message.

Griffin. I don't know what to do. Call me. I'm scared.

The back of my neck is sweaty and hot, so I lean it back against the cool couch fabric, letting my eyes slide closed.

My phone rings loudly.

Scrambling, I shove it to my face. "My parents enrolled me in boarding school. Without even telling me."

A loud sound like a rush of air is followed by, "Holy crap. That's what this is about?"

I suck in a ragged breath. "Yes."

"Paige. I thought you were being chased down an alley or something. I thought you were being murdered!" Griffin's voice is sharp.

I squeeze my eyes shut. "Why would I call you if I were being murdered? You don't think I'm smart enough to call 9-1-1?"

His voice is rough. "I think you're too smart sometimes."

"What's that supposed to mean? Are you mad at me or something?"

Here I am looking to Griffin for comfort, and he's decided to lose it over something dumb. My life is falling to pieces, and Griffin wants to pick a stupid fight.

I'm met with silence.

Seriously?

Blood pounds in my head as I try to keep my composure. It's so unfair of him to ignore me right now. It doesn't matter that we haven't been on the best of terms lately. This is real. This is important.

"Ugh," I groan, sucking back more tears. "Fine, tell me what I did so I can apologize."

He doesn't say anything, but his breath blows steadily through the phone, so I know he hasn't hung up.

"Griffin."

Tears tug at the corners of my eyes, threatening to make an appearance. It's all too much. I can't lose what hope I had for the summer and Griffin in just one day.

I sniff.

"Are you crying?" His voice cracks, sounding half-shocked, half-horrified.

And honestly, he should be. If he'd handled this better, I could be at least a little cheered up by now.

"Just tell me why you're mad," I say, willing away the rest of my tears. It's true—I can't make anyone happy. I'll live the rest of my life disappointing everyone I meet. Something is wrong with me.

"Remember the promise you made me a few weeks ago?"

I have no idea what he's talking about. How am I supposed to keep promises when we're across the country from each other, forced to resort to phone calls whenever either of us has a free moment?

Phone calls.

It hits me like a snap of lightning: I promised to always answer his phone calls, and he's been calling like crazy lately.

"Griff, I—" I gulp.

Am I sorry? It doesn't seem fair of him to expect me to drop everything to talk to him. I'm here, and he's there. It's why I ended our relationship in the first place. Well, one reason.

I clear my throat. "I don't want to fight. I need your help. I know you're mad, but can we forget about that for a second?"

The pause that follows is as quiet as death, but it screams Griffin's name. He's scowling into the phone, hating me. "I know you do," he finally breathes. "And I can't do it. You don't even want to know why I've been calling you?"

Sighing, I lean my head against the couch again. "Because you miss me?" I need to hear him say it. Please say it. Someone needs to reassure me because my parents won't talk to me and I'm so, so alone. If no one misses me, if everyone wants me gone, then it's true. I'm too far gone for them to care about.

Griffin makes a sharp strangling sound. "I'm over this. Good luck with your drama."

Even seconds after he's hung on me, I keep my phone cradled to the side of my head.

It feels like my chest is hollowing out, slowly cracking. I don't know what just happened.

All I know is how alone I am. No one cares that I don't want to go to boarding school next year. No one cares that I'm trying to change, to become who they all want me to be. No one cares that I might be sick like Dad.

There's no one left to call. All my other friends back home ditched me when I started spending my free time sneaking out and breaking in rather than attending study groups and weekend parties.

I grab my Keds from by the front door, slip them on, and lock the door behind me with the spare key Ally gave me. Then I simply walk. According to my sister, there are four different parks, each at a different corner of the neighborhood. I turn in the direction I guess one might be located, down the end of the street next to Allison's, which leads to another street and a cul-de-sac that sparks a sense of deja vu.

The rumble of a lawnmower engine sounds from around the corner, and when I turn down the road from the cul-de-sac, sure enough, someone pushes a mower across already-short bright green blades of grass. Not even Ally and Justin, with the lawn care company they hired for the summer, have such a nice yard.

And who else could be behind the mower but Joey Prince?

I'm still in my pajamas. They're cute pajamas—pink with tiny polka dots on the shorts and a matching cotton tank top—but my neck still warms as Joey squints at me from behind the lawnmower. I should have thrown on a bra at least. He raises a hand in a hesitant half-wave. Like he's not sure he should acknowledge knowing me because I'm the crazy girl walking around by herself in her pajamas at noon with puffy pink eyelids.

I wiggle my fingers back at him, instantly regretting turning down his street. He turns off the lawnmower and wipes his palms on his black basketball shorts. In the sun, his forehead shines with sweat droplets as he walks to the edge of his yard in confusion. "Going for a walk?"

My mouth opens to say something snarky, but I close it. I'm the one in front of his yard on a Saturday. I'm the one in pajamas. And I'm the one with no one left to talk to.

I lift my shoulders. "I'm going to the park." He follows my gaze to the end of the street where thankfully there's a green-and-white sign advertising an exclusive community park. "Have fun with your yard work," I say, striding toward the park.

Behind me, he sighs. "I can take a shower real quick and meet you down there if you want."

My heart swells. I want, more than anything, to not be alone right now. Lifting a shoulder, I glance back. "Sure. You can come."

His lips twitch.

I keep walking until I hit the park entrance. A short black gate blocks my way. I lift the latch and walk through it until I find a green metal picnic table positioned under the shade of a grove of trees. I'm the only person here. I thought there'd at least be someone walking their dog or pushing their kids on the swings. But no. More silence.

The squeak of the metal gate signals Joey's arrival and with it, some of the weight leaps from my chest. Even if he's only here to lecture me, I'll take the company. When he sits down across from me, his hair is wet, his face free from sweat, and he smells like vanilla body wash.

Inhale. Exhale. My lips settle into a satisfied smile, in spite of the fact Joey's watching me, clearly concerned.

"Do I stink or something?" He rotates his head to the side and sniffs the air around his arms.

I shake my head. "You don't stink. I'm glad you're here." He still smells a little like fresh-cut grass, and I have to turn my head to keep myself from inhaling and completely creeping him out.

"You are?"

I wrinkle my nose. I'm not going to say it twice; it's embarrassing enough to admit it the first time.

"Why didn't you ride your bike over here? By the way, you know you should wear a helmet when you're riding that thing. Especially on the roads."

A helmet never occurred to me, which is probably one of the key differences between Joey and me. I seriously doubt a bike ride around the neighborhood is going to kill me. Joey seems to think just about everything is dangerous. I stick my tongue out at him.

"I left in kind of a hurry. I had to get out of the house." I gesture down at the pajamas I'm sporting in lieu of actual clothing.

He chuckles under his breath. "Oh yeah. I was wondering about that. You okay? You look kind of..."

I let him trail off, conceding the moment. I look concerning, clearly. I stretch my palms in front of me, laying them on the table. Technically, I'm fine. But my parents ignoring my pleas to give me another chance before registration, coupled with Griffin's inexplicable anger, has left my heart and mind raw.

"Kind of," I say.

Joey runs a hand through his still-damp hair, combing the ends with his fingers, even though it's as smooth and straight as always. He tilts his head, studying me. "What's up?"

"My mom paid the tuition for boarding school without even telling me first." I bury my face in my hands as soon as the words leave my mouth because saying them makes it real. Saying them makes it *hurt* again.

"So that's it? You have to go now, no matter what?"

"I guess so. I'm not gonna give up, but it sucks she would do that." I exhale before adding, "Plus, I got into a fight with someone from home and he hung up on me and now won't answer my calls." I suck my teeth, regretting the words as they leave my mouth. The mood changes as soon as I say them.

"Your boyfriend?" Joey's eyes bore into the top of the table. He taps his fingers against the side of his leg and doesn't look at me.

I swallow. "It's complicated, but he's not my boyfriend anymore."

What Griffin and I have is indefinable. Even if I could define it, talking about relationships is where I draw the line with Joey.

He doesn't seem to get the hint, because he drags his eyes to mine and adds, "Callie told me about some guy you liked back in Washington." His gaze is steady and unblinking.

A frown swallows my face, followed by a pang of betrayal. I guess I should have known Callie would tell Joey things. I just didn't think those things included my personal life. But Griffin feels less personal now, especially considering our very recent conversation.

"We broke up, but we're still friends."

Joey nods, looking down at his hands like he's thinking this over. "So what did y'all fight about?"

I narrow my eyes. What's with all the personal questions? Did a couple of decent nights together really change things this much, or is this the Joey that Callie and Jen see all the time? I'm starting to think I don't know him as well as I thought, and the realization is unnerving. Like I'm not just sitting in the park alone and half dressed with Joey, certified nice guy and babysitter. He's also Joey, a guy who really cares and is trying to see if I'm alright.

Sniffing, I raise a shoulder. "I don't even know. I called to tell him about the email from the boarding school, and he was already in a bad mood."

"Sounds like he still likes you." Joey says it so simply.

I raise an eyebrow. "Because he's mad at me?" The thing is, I know Griffin still has feelings for me. It's not like we could end things nicely. It was abrupt and painful and forced. I had no intention of breaking up with him before my parents told me I had to leave for the entire summer. Before it became clear that we were two different people who'd be spending the summer in two different places. And now we're stuck in this limbo where our feelings are the same, but we're separated by too many miles to do anything about it. And I don't even know if we'll live in the same place again anytime soon.

Joey sucks in one of his cheeks. "Guys don't get mad at girls they don't like. That's a fact."

I roll my eyes. "I didn't know you were such a relationship expert."

He steeples his hands, grinning slyly. "Well, I am. Tell me more about the friend who's mad at you, and I can analyze him for you."

Grimacing, I shake my head. "I think you're getting a little ahead of yourself. Nobody asked you to analyze anything."

"Hey—you're the one who showed up outside my house. I didn't ask you to spend the day with me."

My chin drops. "I was just walking by. And I didn't recognize your house because the neighborhood looks different at night. Don't flatter yourself, okay? It's not like I was hanging around the street corner waiting to catch a glimpse of you covered in grass and sweat."

We scowl at each other until Joey breaks into a sly grin. "Don't worry. I'm not *actually* mad at you. So disregard what I said earlier."

My cheeks flush as I scowl deeper. For a second there, Joey was dangerously close to flirting with me. And I was even closer to reciprocating. I'm supposed to be the one controlling things here, not him. The last thing I need is Joey messing with my head, not when I think we might finally be friends.

AFTER I'M IN BED FOR THE NIGHT, MY EYES HEAVY AND HAZY, Griffin calls me back.

I mumble a greeting into my phone.

"Are you sleeping?"

"I was trying to..."

He's so quiet I start to wonder if he's fallen asleep. Finally he whispers, "I'm sorry."

My shoulders loosen. "I'm sorry, too. I don't want you to hate me."

"I could never hate you. And it's nothing. It was stupid."

I lay my head back down on my pillow, hugging the phone to my cheek. "Being far away from you is harder than I thought it would be. I really miss you."

He clicks his tongue. "I knew it'd be hard."

"Yeah, yeah. Don't be a know-it-all."

His words smile into the phone. "Tell me what you miss about me."

I sigh. "I miss everything. I miss your hugs and I miss our jokes." My voice grows softer. "I miss seeing you every day."

His voice sounds sadder than it should when he responds. "We'll see each other soon. Get some sleep, okay?"

"Don't 'ang up 'til I'm asleep." My words slur with exhaustion.

My eyelids slide closed as Griffin's voice lulls in my ear. "Good night, Paige."

When I wake up the next morning, something's wrong. It's not the weather. The sun's already shining, bright yellow in a cloudless summer sky.

It's also not Griffin, since he kept his word and stayed on the phone until my snoring probably got too obnoxious. We resolved whatever was bad between us. For now, at least.

I see a text from Mom asking me to call once I'm awake. Nothing too out of the ordinary besides the fact it was sent at three in the morning Washington time, and I've never known my parents to stay up anywhere near that late.

I stand up and immediately start pacing. As my phone rings, I trace the grooves between my fingers, trying to practice mindfulness in a tense moment.

"Hello?" Mom's voice is terse, businesslike and formal, even though she can clearly see it's me calling.

"Mom. Is everything okay?"

Voice wavering, she answers in a watery tone, "Things have been better. We've been at the hospital with your dad since yesterday morning. We thought we might get to go home, but he hasn't healed like he was supposed to and they're about to take him into surgery."

Blood drains from my face, weakening me. Her words echo slowly, and my tongue feels heavy and numb in my mouth. "Surgery? Why didn't you tell me about any of this?"

She sighs like my question is just another inconvenience. "I was about to call Allison to ask her to bring you to the airport. Dad wants you here for the next week. He's going to need cheering up."

As if on cue, there's a *tap, tap, tap* on my bedroom door. Ally's head peeks along the side. "Can I come in?"

Judging by how tentative she's acting, she already knows what's going on. The sight of her sucks the rest of the strength from my jelly legs and they nearly buckle beneath me.

Mom tells me she'll send an email with my flight information and hangs up, leaving me and Ally staring at each other from opposite sides of the room. I walk toward her and crush her in a hug.

"Ally, will you come with me?"

She nods. "Justin and I already talked about it. He can stay home with the kids for a few days. Our family needs us right now."

"Is Dad going to be okay?" I whisper the question, posing it to the universe, to God, to anyone who is capable of answering me.

With her free hand, she smooths my hair back. "I think so."

WHEN WE BOARD THE PLANE A FEW HOURS LATER, OUR FACES are washed, and our hair is brushed into matching low ponytails. Sometimes the fact that we're sisters isn't surprising, even with the twelve-year age difference. Then Ally pulls out a nonfiction mammoth of a book to read and pops anxiety pills she has specifically for flying. I feel myself starting to drool as my eyes droop. And all's right in the world of sisters again.

Once our plane lands in Seattle and we've retrieved our luggage, we huddle together near the exit door, waiting. After a minute, a tall man with Ally's smile and my green eyes wave at us from the doorway. We rush over to him and exchange quick hugs.

"Gavin, you finally shaved that gross beard off your face." Ally taps a finger on our brother's smooth skin.

He grins, holding his hands up in defeat. "You and Sarah bullied me into it." Sarah and Gavin got married last winter, and she reminds me so much of Ally it's scary.. There's something about weird family attraction in there, but I'd rather not think too hard to try to dissect it.

He grabs our suitcases, one in each hand, and motions us forward to the parking garage. I slip into the back of his rental car and lean my head against the chilly window. I listen as they talk about marriage, kids, college memories. All the things I'm years away from experiencing. Sometimes it's easy to forget when we're not all together how much of an outsider I am, even in my own family.

Still, being back home is nice. An ache forms in my chest at the thought of missing out on this for longer than a few months. Boarding school in Connecticut would be a prison. A lonely, boring, maddening prison.

My heart leaps into my throat as the car slows and Gavin parks in front of a red brick two-story house with white front doors. Home.

Leaving my siblings to slowly find their way inside, I trip over myself to rush in. Hesitation overcomes me at the front door. Do I still have the right to open the door and march inside? Should I knock? From where he stands at the open trunk of the car, Gavin calls, "It's open."

I turn the knob, suck in a breath, and tiptoe inside. "Mom?"

Silence. I drop my suitcase and tuck it against the wall as I look around.

And then a skidding sound, followed by a high-pitched barking.

"Pepper!" I drop to my knees to greet the tiny tan

Chihuahua. He rubs his wet black nose against my arms as I scoop him up and hold him against my dress.

Ally appears behind me in the front hall, dropping her black leather suitcase with a *thud* on the hardwood floor. She pets Pepper's head with a trembling hand and meets my eyes.

"Ready to go visit Dad?"

CHAPTER
SiXTeeN

Everyone agrees I should be the first to see Dad, which is about the only perk of being the baby of the family. I hold my breath the entire way. His room is quiet and dark, except for the beeping and flashing screens from the equipment surrounding him. I sneak across the gray-tiled floor to his bed so slowly and carefully it's like I'm six years old, playing pretend spies.

His eyes are closed when I peer down at him, but his lips curve into a half-smile. They twitch.

"Dad! Stop trying to scare me," I demand, letting out a long, withering breath of half relief, half annoyance. He's forever playing pranks on me, and they're never funny. This time I'm torn between freaking out because a hospital is *not* a great place to play dead and fake laughing because I feel sorry for him. I settle for shaking my head and not murdering him for giving me a split-second heart attack.

"I've missed having you around." He reaches for my hand and gives it a squeeze. His hand is almost twice the size of mine, but right now it feels breakable, like if I squeeze too hard his bones might crumble underneath the pressure.

"I miss you too, Daddy." Something tight constricts against my throat, making it impossible to deliver any words without sounding totally ridiculous. But I won't let myself cry right now. The doctors say he's going to be fine. His life isn't on the line or anything, I'm just scared. I really am the baby of the family, too young and too immature for any of it. I can't let them see my fear.

Fear for him and me. My stomach hasn't hurt for a few days, but it's still a secret. If I tell anyone about the stomach pain, will I end up like Dad? If I *don't* tell them, will I still end up like Dad?

He misinterprets my hesitation and clucks his tongue, patting his belly. "We're okay, Paige. Everything's the same, except I weigh a little less now. So it's actually good news."

I chuckle for his benefit. Jokes are what Dad always falls back on, but it's hard to laugh right now.

Eyeing his dressing gown, he blinks up at me. "You don't wanna see, do you?"

I shrug. I am kind of curious. I've heard about colostomy bags before. It's always been something that was a possibility for Dad with his Crohn's disease. But he was doing so well, barely sick at all, for almost ten years. Then out of the blue last year it flared up. And now this. "So they took out your entire colon?"

"Fifteen feet of it. So, like I said, I'm a lot lighter now. I can probably eat as many of your mom's snickerdoodles as I want this Christmas."

Dad lifts the side of his gown so only his stomach and chest are visible on one side. Rib bones show through his skin where they didn't before. A small clear pouch connected to a clear tube lies flat against his stomach, taped to his skin with thick clear medical tape.

I force saliva down my throat. "It's smaller than I thought it would be," I offer. I wish I could think of something similarly witty to say. I wish I didn't take an involuntary step backward, shrinking from the sight.

He nods, understanding. "Yeah. It will take some getting used to, but I'm thankful for it. I think I'll feel a lot better with this little thing than I have the past year."

Meeting his eyes, I match his smile. Everything's going to be okay. The smile hurts my face until I drop it outside of his door.

When I get back to the waiting room, my other two brothers have arrived. Ted and Peter smirk at me. Matching mouths, matching glasses, matching blue-green eyes, and matching shaggy college haircuts. I roll my eyes at them out of pure habit.

"Well, if it isn't baby sister Paige here to visit her twin brothers." Ted wraps an arm around my waist.

I push him off. "Yep, that's right. I flew all the way here to see you two jerks."

Peter frowns at Ted, who wiggles his eyebrows. Too quick for me to react, they each grab an arm and a leg and scoop me up. I kick at them furiously until they unceremoniously plop me into the nearest waiting room chair. The middle-aged blond lady next to me glares over her Starbucks cup.

Peter pastes on a sweet smile. "We're twins, you know." He points a finger between him and Ted like the lady might need an extra visual to be fully impressed. She presses her lips together and turns her head in the opposite direction.

Ted, Peter, and I walk to the other side of the waiting room, hands pressed to our mouths to stifle our laughter. Sometimes they can actually be funny, and I've never needed something to laugh at more than in this moment. It's easier to laugh at the twins than at Dad's sad attempts at hospital humor. Their matching grins ground me, buoying me from seeing Dad so small.

Even though I'm left out of a lot of things, this is perfect. Being with my family is necessary, no matter how crazy they drive me ninety-nine percent of the time.

Ally's there too, sitting demurely in a metal chair. She rolls her eyes at us. "How did Dad look?"

I bite my lip. The image of his colostomy bag still hovers at the front of my mind, alien and scary. No one wants to hear the truth, though. What she's really asking is for some reassurance, even if she'll never admit it.

"He was good. He seemed a little tired, but he was talking about cookies. Oh, and he tried to trick me into thinking he was unconscious or something, so he's feeling good enough to be annoying."

We all smile faintly at each other. I guess it's slightly irreverent to make fun of Dad when he's in the hospital.

Ted slaps a hand on my back, way too hard. "It's not the time for Dad jokes. Now who's the jerk?"

I rub the spot of impact and give him a serious frown. He and Peter guffaw at each other. Ally pretends not to hear them and types on her phone. In the corner, Mom and Gavin huddle together, their voices barely a whisper. When I step toward them, Mom leaps out of her seat and pulls her arms around me.

"You saw Dad?"

I swallow. "Yeah. He looked okay."

Mom runs her hands over my hair. Her fingers are cold and shaky. "I missed you, baby."

I breathe into her shirt. "Missed you too, Mom. I just wish I wasn't home because of *this.*" She squeezes my arm in response.

It's not until all of us—minus Dad—go out for pizza that I notice Mom and Gavin are still separated from the rest of the conversations. They're still whispering, Mom's lips pinched, and Gavin's eyebrows drawn close together. I nudge Ted with my foot under the table. He turns his head to look at me, half a slice of pepperoni pizza hanging from his mouth.

Ugh, brothers.

I tilt my head toward the end of the table at the conspirators. "What's going on with them?"

He stares me down as he chews the rest of his pizza, swallows, then wipes his mouth with the back of his bare hand.

I repress a shudder and bob my head toward them again like, "Well?"

"What about it? Mom's a worrywart, and Gavin's always too serious. They're probably still talking about Dad."

"Dad's okay though, right?" I'm not usually insecure, but seeing Dad in the hospital bed so frail and *old*-looking leaves me shaken. That and the prompt return of my stomachache. My pizza tastes like glue, and nausea twists when I look at the pile of slices in front of me.

Ted sucks loudly from his straw. "You can't die from what Dad has, you know that, right?"

I shoot him a *look*. I stand up to go to the bathroom. Ally follows me. "I need to go too." She bumps me with her hip as we walk. "You know Ted's just being a brat."

I say, "He used to be funnier."

We push open the restroom door and stand in the empty white openness. I don't really have to pee, and it seems like she lied, too. Ally moves toward the sinks while I lean back against the tiled wall. Puckering her lips in front of the mirror, she pauses to apply a fresh coat of nude lipstick. "That's college guys for you. They all think they're hilarious. They're not."

We stay in the bathroom for another minute and Ally shows me the latest pictures Justin sent of Cam and Mattie. She scrolls through a series of silly shots of the boys on the neighborhood playground. I laugh at Cam's blurry figure crashing down the slide. Ally touches my arm. "Don't let our brothers get under your skin, okay?"

I nod and feel a bit better. Sometimes Ally's big sister tricks actually work.

But as we're walking back to the table, my gaze travels from my empty seat to the table where the contents of my purse are now spread between my brothers.

"What the heck?" I stomp toward them and snatch my purse away. I hold out my hands for my wallet, my cherry ChapStick, and the fancy pen Dad got me for my birthday last year. Peter, at least, has the decency to avoid my glare. Ted widens his eyes, pretending to be innocent. But he's smirking underneath the pretense, and I've got an unsettling feeling that he knows something I don't. I pick up another piece of cheese pizza and nibble the end, inhaling garlicky red sauce like I have an appetite, stealing looks at my brothers as I do. They're doing that twin telepathy thing where they communicate without speaking.

The next time I look up, Peter's fiddling with something under the table while Ted sips soda with one hand. His free hand slides under the table. They're totally passing something back and forth. The next time it happens, I duck my head under the tablecloth. Tad's got whatever it is now, and his fingers move rapidly as he... texts.

I whip my head up so quickly it slams against the edge of the table. Blood pounds in my ears and along my throbbing skull. "You guys stole my phone! Give it back!" I dive toward Ted, who passes the phone like a football above my head to Peter. Peter waves it high in the air, out of my reach.

"What are you guys doing? Downloading joke apps? Taking embarrassing pictures when I'm not looking?" The possibilities are endless, each more horrific than the next.

Peter slides it across the table, and I catch it in a swift move that would probably make me feel really cool if not for the circumstances. It's open to my text messages, where my latest message is from Joey, asking if I want to talk on the phone later.

I scroll back to see more texts that I didn't write.

Trembling with rage, I look up at their waiting faces. My chest heaves. "What. Did. You. Do?"

Ted steeples his fingers, resting his elbows on the table. "Tell us about this Joey guy."

Ally, who's been pretending to be absorbed in her glass of water until now, peeks over the top of the glass at me, eyebrow raised.

I grind my teeth together. The entire time Peter and Ted smirk at each other. Finally, I force my eyes to focus on the messages they sent. The first one's innocent enough. Just a message saying, *hey*.

Then Joey wrote, *What are you doing today? Want to meet at the park?*

The make-out park? Not-me says.

I will kill my brothers.

Joey hasn't responded, but three little dots blink at the

bottom of my screen. He's typing something. Probably something awful. I squeeze my eyes shut, then blink them open and furiously type a message before he sends his.

Stupid brothers. I'll explain later.

My face burns as I slip my phone into my purse and glower at the entire table.

Ally leans forward, her best mom voice in play. "That was *not* okay. You two better grow up. And apologize to Paige." She doesn't even know the worst of it.

They glance at each other. Ted shakes his head, still smiling at his prank. "Paige knows it was a joke, right Paige?" This is a thing he does. If he can use his powers as the older, slightly cooler brother to convince me to forgive him without issuing an apology, he will. Every. Time.

I take a shuddering breath and turn my back to him. It's not that easy, not this time.

Peter mumbles to my turned head. "Sorry, sis." It's halfhearted, but I twist my neck and nod at him—and only him.

Laying it on thick for Ted's sake, I say, "Thanks, Peter. That means a lot."

Ted's lip curls.

Ally lifts a breadstick to her lips and takes a delicate bite, her cheeks curved in a hidden smile. She has more experience than I do dealing with annoying brothers, but she always lets me figure things out on my own before stepping in. I appreciate her taking her role as big sister/honorary second mom seriously.

My phone vibrates from inside my purse. I slip it into my hands under the table and away from obnoxiously curious siblings.

It can be the make-out park if you want...

My heart double-beats in my chest. What?! Joey Prince does not flirt. Joey Prince doesn't even joke. So what's going on?

My fingers fumble as I scramble to come up with a response. Should I flirt back? I don't even know if he's actually flirting. He could have accidentally sent that text and he's staring at his phone right this second, trying to figure out how to awkwardly let me know. Or, he could have *his* awful relatives over, and they've also stolen his phone.

I drop my hand from my phone. Those made-up scenarios make infinitely more sense than anything else does. Because predictable, safe Joey wouldn't respond to texts like those other than to shoot me down. The only reasonable thing to do is ignore whatever just happened until it straightens out.

But I've never been a very reasonable person.

Hands shaking slightly, I bite my lip and type so quickly even I barely know what I'm writing.

Next week?

I toss my phone into my open purse and shove it away to the edge of the seat next to me. My phone buzzes approximately five seconds later. Instead of diving for it, I slide my hands under my butt and sit tall in my chair.

"Mom, Gavin, what are you guys talking about down there?" Partly because I'm curious, but mostly to distract myself from the bold and nonsensical thing I just did.

They both lift their heads, blinking guiltily at the rest of us.

Peter waves his hand in a big arch over his head. "Hello, the rest of your family's down here, Mom. Come talk to us."

Her mouth lifts in a lopsided and tired smile, and she scoots over a chair. Gavin follows, folding his arms in front of his chest and leaning back in his chair.

"What are you guys talking about that's so secretive?" Ted raises an eyebrow and leans in close, pretending to whisper.

Gavin sets his mouth. "It's not a joke, so quit it."

Ted frowns at Gavin, but he shuts up.

"Is everything okay?" Ally's voice is calm, her back straight in her chair, her glossy hair framing her face.

Mom nods quickly. "Yes, of course. I'd tell you all first thing if something else happened with Dad."

That's not exactly true. He was in the hospital a whole day before things got serious enough for her to call me. I still haven't had time to tell her how much that sucked. I probably won't ever get the chance, present circumstance considered.

Everyone fake smiles back at her, and we finish the rest of the pizza and head home in studied silence. I can't stop calling up the image of a grey Dad, cracking not funny jokes about his condition. I hate hospitals.

After all this, I need a nap. I haven't slept in my room, in my own bed, in way too long. My pillow at Ally's house is too new to form perfectly to my head, and the sheets are silky and expensive, but they don't smell like home. My room here is a mixture of the perfume I've owned since my thirteenth birthday and the special laundry detergent Mom uses to wash my clothes so it won't bother my sensitive skin.

One whiff of that and I'll take the world's longest nap and be in heaven.

Mom pulls into the driveway and we file out. Gavin parks in the driveway next to Mom, and the twins follow him up the walkway.

Peter and Ted say something to each other about a race and then dash for the front door around the hedges surrounding the porch. They shout something unintelligible, and then my name clearly echoes from their mouths, followed by laughter.

This can't be good.

I speed-walk past everyone and peer cautiously around the corner to the front porch and my brothers.

My stomach flutters up into my chest.

Griffin.

CHAPTER
Seventeen

"How'd you know I was home?"

The house is so stuffed with my siblings I manage to smuggle Griffin into my bedroom without anyone raising an eyebrow. We keep things PG, obviously, and leave the door cracked open.

He tilts his head, his smile lazily unfolding. "Your mom told me you were flying up for the week." Sucking in his cheeks, he pauses. "Sorry about your dad, by the way. Is he doing okay?"

My hands form into loose fists at my sides. "He's going to be fine." My eyes glaze over the bookshelf across the wall, filled with some of my favorite books and a few unread nonfiction books Mom insisted on.

I drink in the sight of him, my sometimes-boyfriend, some-times-closest friend who I haven't seen in weeks. His tall frame leans across the end of my bed, his back against my bedroom wall and his feet dangling off the side of my bed frame. He's exactly the same—short blond hair and pale blue eyes, a smile perpetually playing across his lips. But *something* is different.

I stare and stare and stare until my eyes water. Griffin sits still, letting me study him.

Squeezing my eyes shut, I sit next to him and drop my head onto his shoulder. He shifts and wraps an arm around my shoulders, pulling me close to him. His chin rests on top of my head.

Somewhere down the hall, Pepper's nails skid across the

wood as he chases his own tail. My siblings' voices carry through the house, rising and falling with the sounds of teasing and debating—sounds so familiar they could lull me to sleep if I weren't so aware of Griffin's skin on mine. I'm not used to it anymore.

Being here with him is my happy place. Being with Griffin like this, in my home, in my room. It's so comfortable.

I've really, really missed it. All of it. I sigh into his neck. "Will you take me back to the house? For tradition's sake?"

His mouth tickles my hair. "Right now?"

I nod, inhaling his scent—a mix of deodorant and too much cologne.

He shifts to look at me and his lips slide sideways, spreading wide and slow.

"Sure. Why not?"

�🕊

"How many buildings have you broken into in Texas?"

I don't look at him as I sidestep over a flattened tree stump. "Zero."

He pauses as his hand circles my wrist. Specks of dried paint freckle his fingers. Eyes wide, he says, "What?" He's either surprised, or he's making fun of me. Either way, I'm not in the mood for it.

I shake my arm loose, pushing past him. "I don't have time for messing while I'm there." Frustration seeps into my voice. It's hard to explain the last few weeks to Griffin. He hasn't been there to see the build-up, the way my new friends have fun without alerting the police, the trusting, wide-eyed look Cam and Mattie give me across the table each morning.

He says nothing, but the crunch of his footsteps on branches and loose rocks lets me know he's still following me.

After a few minutes he calls ahead, his voice casual and deep. "What do you do in Texas, then?"

Gazing backward over my shoulder, I frown. "We talk all the time. You know what I've been doing; the build-up and watching Cam and Mattie. That's all."

The sound of his sigh washes over me. Suddenly I'm as frustrated as he is. What's with all the questions? Why does it matter what I do when I'm not here?

I shake my head until the world spins around me. "What do you want me to say, Griffin? That I'm miserable? I kind of am. Does that make you feel better?"

He doesn't answer.

At my elbow, he closes in, holding up a palm for me to stop. "I'm just trying to talk. It makes me feel awful that you're stuck there. I did everything I could so you wouldn't get in trouble."

A hint of betrayal seeps into his voice, and my throat constricts.

Feeling small, I say, "I know. That's not what I meant."

Griffin took the blame for all of it. When the police dragged us home, in the back of a siren-paraded police car, he told everyone who would listen that he'd surprised me and taken me to the abandoned house.

That he'd been the one to pick up a paver from the overgrown front yard, that he'd smashed it through a front window.

That I was completely innocent.

The police believed him. I'm barely five feet tall, so clearly, I wouldn't willingly break into an old house that had belonged to a widow who died a few months earlier.

Mom and Dad listened and nodded.

They thanked the police officers, drove Griffin home when his parents wouldn't answer their phones, and explained the police's offer of community service instead of something worse.

Then they sat me down on the living room couch and told me about going to Texas for the summer. They never explicitly said they didn't believe Griffin's story, but they also never acted like I was innocent. Truth is, they know Griffin well enough to see what had been going on all along.

Me corrupting *him*.

His hand swings by his side, and I reach for it, giving it a squeeze. "Thank you for taking the blame. I swear I never would have asked you to. But it was sweet of you."

He runs a hand along his short fuzzy haircut. "I love you, Paige. I mean, you know I still love you, right?"

Blue, steady eyes wander down at me. Like he sees me more than he sees anything else. Like I'm *enough*, just how I am. Even if I don't change. Maybe especially if I don't change.

Licking my lips, I squeeze his hand again. His skin is so warm, his fingers calloused from weekends spent mowing lawns and pulling weeds.

Watching me is something that never seems to get old for him. When we switched into the not-just-friends phase of our relationship, it bothered me. What did he want? Why wouldn't he stop looking?

Now, I gaze up at him in equal silence. We don't need words. We're happy together. Even if—

Even if we're not together romantically now.

A hand sweeps in front of my face, reaching for hair that's fallen out of place. So, so gently, he tucks a strand of wayward hair behind my ear. Softly, he runs his hand along the side of my face. I don't move. Maybe I don't even breathe.

Griffin's head ducks toward mine. The movement's so familiar, my toes reach up on their own. I'm not even in charge of my own body when it comes to him. To this. But...

"Stop." I put a hand against his chest as I stumble away from his lips. My forehead presses into him so he won't see my face.

If he saw me, he'd know how conflicted I am.

His arms circle me protectively. Head ducked over mine, he whispers, "What's wrong?"

I sigh, breathing into his shirt. It's impossible to be close to him and not inhale his scent. It smells like Washington. Like home, like trees, like kissing until your lips are so chapped they sting.

"Nothing. We're not together like that anymore. We can't just make out like everything's the same."

He draws a breath against my hair. It's warm and ragged. It's agony.

I tilt my head to look at him, and he leans back so we can gaze at each other and still touch. It's wrong. I know it's wrong to want him to hold me and tell me things will be okay, and at the same time push him away like this.

"Okay," he says. He looks past me, at the ground behind us, but I catch a glimpse of his eyes, and they're wet. Griffin doesn't cry.

Something sour twists in my gut. The look of hurt splashed across his face is too much. "I'm sorry. I'm so, so sorry."

My shoulders press tight against my neck. If I were a little kid, I'd lie down here on the dirt, in the middle of nowhere. I'd curl into a ball and cry until my voice was hoarse and my face was tight with dried tears.

But I'm changing. So I don't.

"The house can wait until you get back in the fall." He gestures a hand lazily at the house in the distance. Like it wasn't our plan all along. Like it doesn't matter if we go.

I set my jaw and nod. "Yeah, I should probably get back. My family will start looking for me, and that never goes well."

He raises his eyebrows.

Maybe we both know better. We're too mature for stuff like this when there are more important things on the line.

That's what I tell myself as Griffin drives me home in stiff silence. And that's what I tell myself when he unlocks the car door and waves goodbye, sending me home without a hug for the first time ever.

I let myself check my texts before I go to sleep. Nothing from Griffin, but one message from Joey—short and simple.

Deal. Next week

CHAPTER
Eighteen

Wednesday morning, Dad is coming home from the hospital. Ally wakes me up the second there's the tiniest crack of light spilling through the blackout curtains I installed freshman year. She raps on my door and lets herself in without waiting for an answer. She peels the covers off my body, starting by my feet.

Purely by accident, I kick her in the stomach as I'm rolling from the bed.

"You're worse than Cam." I stumble around the room, trying to regain consciousness.

She smiles. "I'll take that as a compliment."

We get to work cleaning the kitchen, emptying the trash and all the takeout boxes from the fridge we've amassed over the last few days of everyone being home. She vacuums and I make the bed in Mom and Dad's bedroom. Meanwhile, all three of my brothers put their empty heads together to figure out the new fancy water bottle they bought for Dad.

We line up—oldest to youngest, even though no one tells us to—on the front porch as soon as Mom texts that they're five minutes away. When the car pulls up, Dad is in the passenger seat, and Mom pulls in slower than I'm sure is legal.

We make a big show of cheering as they walk up the driveway and around to the front porch. Dad raises one fist in the air like a champion. We collectively pretend it's an exciting event and not... I don't know... terrifying having him home, away from the careful hospital nurses. Mom rolls her eyes at us and hooks an arm tightly around his waist as he hobbles forward.

"Take it easy on him, you guys."

She doesn't have to remind us. All she's been talking about for the last several hours on our group family chat is how gentle we'll need to be. No shouting, no partying, no staying up late. And to the twins—absolutely no pranks.

Everyone gets it. Even Ted curled his lip up and looked downright disgusted at the thought of doing something to Dad after he's home from the hospital. Even something minor, like switching his lemonade for water dyed yellow with food coloring. Which I'm pretty sure Dad can handle. He's not the baby Mom makes him out to be. But I don't want to see him back in the hospital, either.

The rest of this day has to go really smoothly because it's the last day everyone's here together. Ally has a flight after dinnertime to get back to her family. Justin only has so many days off work available per year, and they've already booked a vacation with his family later this year. Ted and Peter have to drive back after dinner, too. They don't have summer classes, but they both work as resident advisors for on-campus housing, and they're technically not supposed to be gone at all. Not that they're big on rules, but still. They're not totally useless, it turns out.

I thought of everyone, Gavin would stick around as long as me, if not longer, given how serious he's been. But he's mentioned his wife so many times in the last twenty-four hours, I think Mom and Dad would kick him out if he didn't also need to get back to the Walgreens he manages.

We all lead Dad up the stairs to his bedroom. All seven of us squish along the hallway, then the stairs, and then the doorframe of my parents' bedroom. It'd be hilarious if it weren't a nerve-wracking moment.

I've set up five different board and card games Mom asked me to get down from the hall closet. They're ready to go on his bedside table. But Dad smiles real big for everyone and then announces he's going to take a nap.

We all slowly scatter after that. My brothers say they need to pack, but video game sounds ring from their closed doors as I pass by.

Ally comes up behind me so quietly I don't know she's there until her hand drops on my shoulder.

"I saw you sneak off with Griffin yesterday."

It's neither a question nor an accusation, but the tips of my ears still burn. Ally's so perfect, and I'm *me*.

It's okay when she's far away in Texas with her idyllic family, and I'm here making a mess of things. But there's something very raw and icky about her seeing me.

And I didn't even do anything wrong this time, technically.

I rub my eyes, weary all of a sudden. "Nothing happened, Ally." I don't know why I take on such a serious, self-important tone.

Allison doesn't seem to understand either. She drops her hand, squinting. "I didn't think anything did. What's going on?"

I step into my room and collapse onto my bed, lying on my back to stare at the mismatched paint and the crusty glow-in-the-dark stars.

Ally's stars that became my stars.

Ally's room that turned into my room.

She lags after me, each step tentative. I wonder if she's looking around the bedroom with wide eyes, hand brushing through her perfect hair because she can't imagine herself here. To be fair, it's a far cry from her current house.

"Nothing's *going on*. I keep telling everyone I'm going to change. I want to be more like you and less like me." I bark out a laugh as if everything I'm saying is just a snarky joke. Silly Paige, she refuses to take anything seriously.

Ally's gaze is fixed on the glued-on stars. Her words come slowly, like she's pulling them from somewhere else. "But... why,

Paige? You're perfect the way you are. You're everything I'm not."

I let out a slow, noisy breath, my brows knitted tightly. Everything she's not. It sounds like an accusation coming from her.

She tears her eyes away from the ceiling. "That's a good thing. You're brave and fearless, and excited about life."

I snort. Sounds like she's reading from a magazine article advertising exotic locations. Besides, I'm not any of those things. Not in the ways that count. Not brave enough to take what I want. Not fearless enough to change Mom's mind. And, yeah, I'm excitable. But what does that get me?

Nothing good.

She joins me on my bed, tucking her knees up to her chest and hugging them.

"I've never gotten in trouble. But I also took things so seriously, I never had much fun. I still struggle with that, with letting go and enjoying things."

I wrinkle my nose.

She sighs, slipping a hand over mine. "I wish I was more like *you.*"

Pressing against her hand, I say nothing. I'm at a loss, and part of me has never felt closer to my perfect big sister.

In unison, we tip our heads to the stars, both of us lost in thought.

WHITE LIGHTS ILLUMINATE THE LINOLEUM UNDERFOOT AS WE huddle together outside the airport doors. My siblings line up, minus me, by pure habit, in order of oldest to youngest again. It's a funny leftover from our childhood holiday pictures. I stand next to Mom, letting her lean on me like a prop to hold herself up. Unlike the Seattle airport in normal hours, the early morning lines are short to nonexistent, and there are hardly any other people dropping off.

Even with Dad asleep at home, we're still a big group. With the airport virtually empty, we stick out more than ever. Ally and my brothers take turns hugging Mom and patting her back and telling her, again, everything will be fine. I'm glued to Mom's side, so I get hugs right after her.

Ted and Peter squeeze me at the same time from either side, lifting me off my feet and stealing my breath away. I swat at them until they let go, waving my arms like a baby bird trying to fly. "Put me down," I manage to shriek.

They drop me unceremoniously, and Peter rubs his hand back and forth over the top of my hair. "You still mad at us, baby sister?"

Still mad? That implies I was mad in the first place and not completely livid. Mad would be if one of them used up all the hot water before my turn to shower. Mad is what I am after I stub my toe on the corner of the downstairs bathroom door for the fifty-millionth time.

My brothers stole my phone and texted flirty messages to Joey. I'm way past mad.

And besides that, fire blazes in my ears at being called a baby. I'm always called a baby, and being a measly two years younger than the twins doesn't give them the right to torture me.

Crossing my arms over my chest, I *humph* and tilt my head away from them. I smooth the frizzy hairs pulled up by Peter's noogie. "Yeah. I'm still mad."

Ted slings an arm around my shoulder. "Don't be. We were trying to help you out."

Peter shrugs. "I already said I was sorry."

I inhale, biting the inside of my cheek. Mom watches the three of us out of the corner of her eye. Gavin talks at her and she nods, but I know she's spying. I pull my arms around my brothers. Voice light, I say, "You're right. I'm over it. It's not a big deal."

Ted, momentarily stunned, grins and slaps my back. Peter

mumbles another apology and walks off to say goodbye to Mom again.

I can pretend to not be furious at my brothers for a little while if it means I get the chance to show Mom how mature I am now. The old me would have held that grudge forever. The current me still plans on it. But Mom doesn't have to know that.

CHAPTER
Nineteen

Ally's not here to wake me up, but I still find myself crawling from bed way too early to make Dad breakfast. I've fallen into a kind of routine during my time with her family in Texas and it turns out it's hard to shake even now that I'm home.

"Is he allowed to eat this?" I hold up a package of bacon as Mom pads into the kitchen, twisting her hair up into a bun.

She blinks at the package, then shakes her head emphatically. "Only liquids for a few more days. Hide that, though. If he can see it, he'll try to eat it."

We both laugh, remembering times Dad snuck into the kitchen after a party and cleared out the remaining food.

I stick the bacon back in the fridge, sliding it behind a package of hotdogs that might have been there since before I left for Texas. He'll never find it here. I pick up a bunch of bananas hanging from the fruit basket on the counter, turning them in my hands. "So, a smoothie?"

Mom nods, eyes vacant as she thinks about something else. Worries about something else. "He'd love a smoothie, hun."

Digging under a stack of mixing bowls and a horde of old plastic cups, I retrieve the blender from the top cupboard and set it on the counter. Mom hands me a plastic container of blueberries. I reach behind the milk cartons and find peach yogurt. We work together, moving seamlessly and silently as a team.

Dad's never been big on smoothies. When Ally went through a green smoothie phase, he made a point of telling her every time he saw her chugging one how nauseous it made him. Bacon is better, obviously, but this smoothie smells like a tropical vacation. It's gotta be better than hospital food, at least.

Tiptoeing upstairs, Mom and I sneak into their room and present the icy cold smoothie. Dad lifts himself up on one elbow and takes the glass, sticking his tongue out at it when he thinks Mom isn't watching.

He winks at me, takes a big drink, and delivers a thumbs up. "It's actually pretty good."

I exhale.

Mom looks at me sideways. It's the first time she's spent any time with me since I've gotten here. Between the hospital visit and my siblings taking up her time, she's been too busy.

She's always too busy.

"What are your plans today, Paige?"

I lift a shoulder. I don't have plans other than help look after Dad. It didn't occur to me I could be doing anything else while I'm here.

My parents look at each other, silently communicating. Dad gulps another swig of his smoothie, then sets it on his bedside table, smacking his lips.

"All your mom and I are doing today is resting, unfortunately." He pretends to glare at her, like she's the reason he can't go out and have an adventure.

She smiles tightly at him. It's not that she doesn't appreciate his jokes, it's that she's still too worried about him to laugh along.

To me, she flashes a genuine smile, even if it's thin. "Go take a break. Why don't you call Griffin? He's missed you, you know."

Griffin and I had our time yesterday. Besides, whatever we are to each other now is too complicated to navigate. We proved that yesterday when we tried to pick up like normal and got stuck in total awkwardness.

I tug at the end of my ponytail, watching my parents. What are they getting at, trying to push me toward Griffin? Mom always has an ulterior motive, even if I can't figure out what it might be just yet. "I thought you guys hated him after everything that happened?"

Mom narrows her eyes, issuing a silent challenge. "Why would I hate Griffin? He's always been so sweet."

Dad's eyes flit over mine and Mom's. He doesn't like to get involved in our arguments, and I can hardly blame him. Mom is scary, and I *am* her daughter. If I didn't know better, I'd swear they are both hiding smiles. "I haven't always been his biggest fan, but you've been hanging around Griffin for a long time, even before you two started dating. He's always been honest with us," Mom says with a shrug.

"Honest with you?" I know, logically, that I should let this conversation go, but I can't help but push.

My mind must be drawing a blank because I'm not sure what there's been to tell the truth about before breaking into old houses caused so much trouble. Griffin's always been my friend, and he's been to my house and out to dinner with my family plenty of times. But how has he been this perfect model of honesty? And what about?

I sink to the end of the bed, next to Dad's feet. He leans forward and runs a palm along my back, rubbing softly like he used to when I was younger and sick in bed. "Maybe ask him," he offers.

I lean into Dad's touch. Mom watches us, then pats my leg. "Let's let Dad rest, alright?"

I give him a quick kiss on the cheek, and we shut the door behind us. I shake my head, at a loss for Mom's motivations.

"Hanging out with Griffin is too complicated now. I mean, I broke up with him. We can't pretend that didn't happen."

Mom turns back, spinning on her heel, her eyes wide. "Is this about that other boy?"

My mouth opens. "What?"

She shakes her head, almost like she's arguing with herself instead of talking to me. "The boy Ally knows in Texas. She said you don't get along with him. We didn't send you there to date, you know that, right?"

The urge to call Ally immediately and chew her out for ratting on me to Mom is overtaken by curiosity. I don't want Mom to know about Joey. I can't even pinpoint why it bothers me, but it does. Joey feels like a secret, like part of the new thing I have in Texas that I don't want to share yet. That I don't want Mom to control. "Yeah. I know. What does he have to do with Griffin though?"

Angling her head toward the closed door behind us, Mom puts a finger to her lips. "He needs to sleep. If we're going to talk, let's do it in the kitchen over breakfast."

We sit across from each other at the kitchen table. I grab a bagel and chew and chew and chew until I can't stand it anymore. Pushing my plate away from me, I lean my elbows on the table and sigh.

"Tell me what you're talking about, Mom. Tell me what you and Dad meant about Griffin telling you the truth. And tell me what Ally said about Joey."

She picks up her muffin, nibbles the top, then sets it down. "I don't remember you being this demanding a few months ago. I thought being around Ally would make you more respectful, not less."

It's painful trying to mold my face into a nice expression without letting my eyes roll to the ceiling. I'll forever be compared to Ally and always, always be a disappointment to my mom. It shouldn't surprise me at this point. Going on sixteen years and some things never change. No matter how much blood, sweat, and tears I put into trying to please my parents.

"Allison said the other boy was helping out with her kids and that you didn't like him very much." She shrugs, eyes piercing mine. "But I'm your mom. I can read between the lines, even if your sister doesn't think I can."

Okay. Who knows what she means by that, but points for Mom, I guess. All I can say for sure is that maybe I used to, but I definitely don't *hate* Joey anymore.

I shift in my seat, tapping my bare toes on the cold wood floor. "And what Griffin told you? What's that about?"

She tilts her head to study me. Maybe she's looking for a better version, one she's more compatible with. Maybe she realizes that version doesn't exist.

"It's not a real secret, Paige," she says witheringly. "But way before you were dating and you were just friends, he came to the house looking for you one day. Dad and I were the only two home. You were off with one of your brothers, I think, running errands, and we were working out front in the garden. Dad made some sarcastic comment about how nice it was that you two could be friends, and he looked back at us and shook his head. 'I'm in love with her,' he said. And then he swore us to secrecy."

I don't realize I've been slowly inching forward until she stops talking and my forehead nearly brushes the tabletop.

"Wow." I straighten, shaking my head. If that's true and Griffin's liked me all this time, it's big.

And it makes the way I brushed him off the other day even worse. But the truth is, I don't know how I feel anymore. I don't have the luxury of trying to decide if I'm in love with my best friend or not because I have other things on my mind. And if he really loves me, he'll respect that.

I huff and Mom pinches her lips together. She can't know what I'm thinking, but my narrowed eyes probably tell her enough. If she thought this news about Griffin would change things, she's very wrong.

The damage is already done; we're already broken up. And I refuse to be pressured into anything else.

For now, at least, we're friends. Period. Even if my parents have apparently liked him all along.

I stand, brushing nonexistent muffin crumbs from my skirt.

"I think I'll go visit some friends. If Dad's going to sleep for a while."

Without missing a beat, she stands, too, nodding fervently. "Just come back after lunchtime so you can play Phase 10 with your dad. I think he'd like that."

I slip on brown leather sandals that wrap around my ankles like a ritzy gladiator. Then I swing a small cross-body purse over my shoulder and head out. I'd be willing to leave the house barefoot if it meant escaping this conversation with Mom.

The thing about our neighborhood is it's completely walkable. From our front porch, I can walk to all my old friends' houses, the corner grocery store, the neighborhood park, and a small farmer's market down the street. And none of those trips will have me breaking a sweat. Still, I kind of miss my pink beach bike back in Texas. Never in my wildest dreams would I have pegged myself as the kind of girl who bikes anywhere, let alone enjoys it.

But living with Allison and Justin is so different from life here.

Down the street, around the corner, and up a hilly cobblestone road, tons of restaurants and shops are tucked close to the surrounding neighborhoods. In under ten minutes, I stand outside Dad's favorite sandwich shop.

Swinging open the door, I'm greeted by the smells of sweet pork, onions, and baking bread. I inhale, soaking in the warm comfort of the familiar food. The girl behind the counter must be new because I don't recognize her. She greets me with a lazy scowl before disappearing into the back.

I don't even glance at the menu since I practically have it memorized, but I don't mind waiting either, so I settle into one of the two tables set up in the tiny shop. If I had to live inside a smell and I could only pick one for my entire life, it'd be fresh bread, hands down.

Mom used to bake a lot when I was little. Now that it's just me and her and Dad, she rarely does. But there was this one birthday—my thirteenth—when Mom surprised me by baking a six-layer cake frosted in pink vanilla buttercream and decorated with intricate white and pink fondant roses.

I'm not sure I even said thank you. Maybe that's why she doesn't bake for me anymore.

The front door of the shop chimes and I look up reflexively. Griffin smiles at me from the doorway, shrugging sheepishly, his ears pink.

"I didn't know you'd be here." He says it quickly, like he's got to get it out before I start assuming things.

I nod. "I know."

We live in the same neighborhood. I'm not so egotistical to believe he's stalking me. We've been here for lunch together too many times to count. It's only a coincidence.

A really unfortunate coincidence.

He sinks into the chair across from me, leaning back far enough for me to admire the muscles on his arms when they're flexed back like this. How awkward it is to be torn between the impulsive desire to touch him and the logical truth of how wrong it would be to lead him on.

Tilting his head, he opens his mouth like he wants to ask what I'm thinking. Instead he asks, "Are you staying or ordering out?"

Virtually no one eats inside the shop since the area's so small. I haven't decided yet, but I click my tongue and decide on the spot. "I'm eating here and taking sandwiches back for my parents."

Griffin taps his fingers on the table. "Mind if I eat here with you?"

My smile spreads, slow and reluctant. "You're my best friend. You know that, right?"

I mean it as a compliment, but we both interpret it like it is: a reminder. Griffin shakes his head, his baseball cap bobbing with the movement. "Believe me, I know."

Ouch. I grimace, my heart pounding along a sad beat.

The girl finally reappears from the back, and Griffin and I stand in line to order our sandwiches. I go first while Griffin lags behind.

"I'll have two turkey subs to go and one pork slider for here, please."

Behind me, Griffin fumbles with his worn leather wallet, threads pulling along the sides and middle. He counts to himself, loud enough for me to guess he's using the last of his cash to stay and eat with me. Maybe the last of his money, period.

I pause, biting my lip. "Actually, can you make that two pork sliders for here? And two chips and lemonades, too. Thanks."

Griffin makes a frustrated sound as we sit back down at the table. "You didn't have to do that. I have the money."

I roll my eyes. "I owed you lunch. From that one time."

He arches an eyebrow. "What one time? Pretty sure I've never gotten you lunch. I mean, I probably should have, but you know I'm broke."

Shrugging, I grab my lemonade and slurp through the straw. I set down the cup with a *plop*. "It was a long time ago."

He sighs. "I can tell when you're lying, you know."

Wrinkling my nose, I stare at him. "If you're going to say I have a tell, you're wrong. I have a very good poker face."

He squints, inspecting my face until I find myself squirming under his gaze. "You have a perfect poker face."

The way he says the word "perfect" makes me think he's talking about something else. He's studied me enough, he should know. If anyone knows me as well as I know me, it's Griffin. It's comfortable and uncomfortable at the same time to be so *seen* by someone else.

He reaches for the straw in his lemonade cup and swirls it around. "But your voice cracks when you're lying." He smiles. "It's cute."

My face goes warm, and I look at the table for longer than is socially acceptable.

"You can't flirt with me anymore, Griff."

Under the table, I catch a glimpse of his hands tightening into fists.

His voice is gruff. "Why? Because you don't like me like that anymore?"

"Yes," I say. My voice cracks.

The girl behind the counter appears, balancing our sandwiches and bags of chips nestled in plastic baskets.

Ahh. The food smells so good I want to melt into it and disappear from this conversation.

Griffin grabs his and starts stuffing bites in his mouth like he's one of those guys in a hotdog eating competition. I wouldn't be surprised if he started dunking his bread in his lemonade to make it easier to finish his food all in one go.

"Ahem." I clear my throat and give him a withering look.

"Are you eating fast because you're mad at me and you're desperate to escape?"

Gulping down the enormous bite of pork in his mouth, he nods. "Yeah. Pretty much."

I huff. "You're not allowed to be mad at me. If you care about me at all, you'll understand where I'm coming from."

He sets down his sandwich in its basket, smiling a smile that doesn't reach his eyes and slices across his face in a cold, sad way. "But that's the thing. I have no idea where you're coming from because you refuse to talk to me. You're upset about your dad, which I get. But I could be there for you, I could help you. And this whole time you've been in Texas, you've been avoiding me. I call and you ignore it most of the time. And when you do answer, you're annoyed with me. I'm not stupid, I can hear it. I know you."

I open my mouth to tell him exactly how stupid he sounds right now, but he keeps going.

"And right when I'm about to call it quits and leave you alone because I don't want you to start telling everyone how pathetic I am and how I can't take a hint, you randomly send me late night pictures of you in bed or you call me just to say hi or I see a picture of you and I remember...." He runs his hands over his red face. "Everything."

My sandwich turns to sawdust in my mouth. Griffin's just poured his heart out and I'm staring at him with a half-open mouth full of pork gone cold. My heart's beating slowly in my chest like it's stunned and trying to keep up.

"Griffin." I shake my head—at myself, at him, at all of it.

"I don't want to hurt you. And I don't want to lead you on. That's the last thing I would ever want."

I gaze around the small cozy sandwich shop like the right words will materialize and hurl themselves into my mouth.

They don't come. The truth is, I don't know what I want.

"I'm sorry." I'm small and fragile and scared.

Griffin scoots his chair back and stands. One hand on the door, he looks back at me. "Thanks for lunch."

Then the door chimes and I'm left alone.

CHAPTER *Twenty*

Dad is terrible at Phase 10, like he's terrible at every other card game in existence. But the thing is, he loves them more than anyone else I know. It's ironic and hilarious, the way he can muster up excitement for a game he'll, without a doubt, lose.

I always deal the cards and Dad always sits patiently, his hands folded in his lap, his eyes trained on the stack of cards. We've been playing together since I was five and barely reading enough to get by in games like this. Instead of Candy Land or Hungry Hungry Hippos, it was Uno and Phase 10 and Monopoly. Basically, whatever my older siblings had moved on to by that point.

His sandwich wrapper sits on his bedside table—we'll have to hide it from Mom so she doesn't throw a fit about his special diet—and we're both sitting on his bed with the cards spread out between us. Mom's off to the store with the promise of calling to check in and see if we need anything every ten minutes. I can't be positive, but I'm pretty sure Dad switched his phone to silent and slid it under the bed as soon as she left.

"How do you feel?" I steal a glance at him. He's pale and thin, but not as ghost-like as he was in the hospital.

"On top of the world," he says, grinning and flashing non-existent arm muscles.

I roll my eyes and poke a stringy bicep. "Seriously, Dad. Does your stomach hurt?"

My own stomach clenches, as if a reminder is all it takes for the pain to start up again. What I really want to ask Dad sits on the tip of my tongue, both too afraid to tumble out and too late. I should have asked him about his symptoms a long time ago. It didn't matter what the specifics were until it did. Now it just feels insensitive to talk about my own problems.

"It doesn't hurt right now," he assures me, squinting slightly as if reading my mind. "Are you feeling okay?"

Because it's what he expects me to do, I roll my eyes again. "Dad. I'm good."

He laughs. "Talk to me about this boarding school situation." He shuffles his hand of cards back and forth before looking up at me.

I glance around like Mom might pop up at any second to explain *again* how badly I've messed up. "You know everything, including that I'll do anything not to go," I grumble, looking down at my hand.

He bobs his head once. "I want to hear how you feel. Tell me your side."

Voice low, like I'm on the verge of being caught in a lie, I say, "My side?"

Looking me square in the eyes, jaw tight, he nods again. "Start with the truth."

BY THE TIME MOM WALTZES UP THE STAIRS, STILL ON A shopping high, Dad and I are both slapping down cards like nothing happened. I realize one second too late that I'm smiling wider than I have this entire trip home.

"What's going on?" Mom drops to the edge of the bed, watching the game—and my face—closely.

Dad sets down his cards and gestures to me. "We had a good

talk. Paige, tell your mom what you told me." He nods reassuringly and I stiffen.

Sweeping my hair behind my head with my hands, I twist and twist and twist. Dad coughs.

"When the police brought me and Griffin home, I let him tell everyone it was his idea, but that was a lie." Every word I speak sinks right down to the bottom of my throat.

Mom's face is blank. A perfect stage for the storm that's about to hit, I'm sure.

I let out a shaky breath and drop my hands from my hair. "It was all my idea. He didn't even know where we were going until I brought him there. Then I broke the window. And I tried to run from the police."

Tears slide down my face. I didn't give Dad all the details, and now a horrible thought hits me. What if this shock puts him back in the hospital? What if I've changed for the worse, and everything that happens with his health is my fault? My stomach clenches and I fold into myself, my head hitting my knees, my dress soaked with salty wet tears. Sniffling, I inhale into my legs, trying to compose myself.

Mom's voice calls from above me. "Paige. We've been waiting for you to tell us the whole truth. Why do you think we sent you to your sister's?"

I shake my head, lifting it just enough to glance at her through my loose hair. "I thought you were still mad at me for being a part of it. I thought you were trying to get me away from Griffin. That's why I broke up with him." I pause, my voice softening to a whisper. "I thought you blamed me for Dad being sick."

My parents glance at each other, eyebrows raised in their own private language.

A hand strokes my hair. I lift my head to see Dad's arm reaching over me. "We weren't thrilled at the idea of you and Griffin to begin with. But we can't blame him, not when we *know* you. We wish both of you would have told us the truth. That's why you're in trouble." He meets my eyes. "And my being sick has nothing to do with you. Got it?"

I inhale. Dad's eyes are wide with concern, which makes me feel about one inch tall. I should be reassuring him, not the other way around. But I still feel better when his hand strokes my back in soft, sweeping pats. My breathing slows enough for me to offer a weak, semi-convincing smile. "Okay. So now that I've told you, can I come home?"

Mom presses her lips together. She doesn't even give Dad the chance to answer. Isn't he supposed to be involved in this decision too? "You promised to help your sister for the summer. We'd like you to see that out. And then, like we said before, we'll assess where we are at the end of August."

Whipping my head between the two of them, I let out another sob. "What? I thought you said you weren't upset!" Mom won't forgive me no matter what. I *knew* she sent me away for more than the break-in.

Mom narrows her eyes. "The fact remains that we can't trust you. You lied to us about something really serious. And then you broke into someone else's property on more than one occasion. We can't ignore those things, Paige."

"So boarding school?" My eyes burn. The world tumbles around me and not for the first time.

Mom's nostrils flare. "I said we'll decide once summer is over. Don't be melodramatic. We told you the terms when you left for Texas. You've had weeks with this information."

Dad shoots her a nervous frown. He doesn't want this to turn into a fight. We had such a good talk, and it felt like Dad was really listening to me, like he cared. I have to swallow my argumentative side for his sake. He can't handle a huge blowup right now, and I can't handle the implications of what the stress could do to him.

And Mom—even though she's treating me like I'm a baby throwing a tantrum—is right. They've been telling me boarding school is a big possibility since the beginning of June. I guess there's still a part of me that hoped they were bluffing.

That part of me shrivels, and I sit up straight with the realization.

Wiping my eyes with the back of my hand, I steel my shoulders. "Okay. It's a fair punishment, I guess. Just tell me what I need to do to show you I can be trusted. I'll work on it for the rest of summer. And I'm really committed to the build-up, but I'll do anything else you need. Ally can help me, even." Hope clings to my words because they could what convinces Mom. Maybe she's waiting for me to prove myself to her.

Dad reaches over to squeeze my hand. "That's a great plan."

Flexing my fingers, I squeeze back. At least Dad doesn't seem like he wants me gone for good. Mom heaves a breath, a palm to the side of her face.

"We can't tell you what to do. It's not ticking off boxes, honey, it's gaining a sense of maturity. It's becoming the kind of person who's inherently trustworthy. That's what we need from you, but you're the only one who has control over it."

So basically, she refuses to tell me.

We stare at each other like a distorted mirror image. I always wished I looked more like Dad, like Ally, like Gavin. The twins are at least a solid combination of both our parents with Dad's eyes and chin and Mom's mouth and hair. But I'm a clone of Mom. Seeing pictures when she was my age and in high school is like gazing at a version of me that existed in the eighties. On the outside, at least.

"I can do it. I swear to you." I don't even blink as our stare-down continues.

A smile curves her lips. "I look forward to it." My stomach sinks with a heavy dread.

CHAPTER
Twenty One

With two days left until I fly back to Texas, I take the opportunity to raid my closet for more clothes. I'm getting sick of wearing the same dresses and single pair of Keds, so I replace all the clothes I originally brought with new outfits.

Once I'm done organizing and pre-packing, I sit on the edge of my bed, surveying my bedroom. I've slept crappy since I got here, despite thinking my bed here is superior to all others. I hate to admit it, but I miss the silky sheets and fancy plush mattress on the guest bed at Allison's.

I miss Cam and Mattie, too. I've only been able to video-chat with them once since I've been here, which feels like practically nothing since I've gotten used to seeing them all day, every day.

My hands go to my phone and I scroll through my recent texts, fingers hovering over Ally's number.

Under her name is Joey's. We haven't talked since our semi-flirting from the other day. Before I can stop myself, I click on his name and tap the call button.

The phone rings.

Why exactly am I calling Joey Prince?

I could say I'm bored or I'm lonely or maybe because my mom is on my tail and Griffin and I aren't speaking. But there's more to it than that.

Call me crazy, but I might actually *like* talking to him.

Texas has messed me up in the worst way. The longer I stay in Washington, the more apparent it becomes.

While the ring tone echoes in my ear, I twirl the end of my hair around a finger, anxiety gnawing at me. If he answers, what am I going to say? *Oh, hey, it's me, Paige. I know I'm always acting like I hate you, but I've recently realized that you're cool, so what's up?*

Leaving a voicemail might be worse, though.

"Um. Hello?" Joey's voice is formal, like he's expecting his history teacher to be on the other end instead of me.

"Hey. This is Paige." Oh wow. I didn't know it was possible to make this more awkward, but there you go. I did it.

"Heh. Yeah, I know. I texted you the other day, remember?" I imagine he's smiling like he did the night of the party at Ben's house. A real smile.

"Yeah. Just checking."

I hear a rustling sound, like he's settling in somewhere comfortable. "So, a weird thing happened yesterday."

I bite my lip because I've got a feeling about where this is going. "Oh yeah?"

"Mm-hm. I stopped by your sister's house to see if you wanted to...umm...hang out...like we texted about the other day, and she told me you weren't home. That you weren't going to be home until Sunday."

What.

The.

Crap.

Is Joey Prince admitting that he stopped by Ally's house to take me to the park and make-out? How do I even respond to this?

I open and close my mouth. My hand slips around the back of my phone, clammy and warm. "Um." I inhale and shake my head, trying to focus. "Uh, yeah. I guess I forgot to mention I'm in Washington this week." My voice falters.

"I was joking about seeing if you wanted to go to the park. You know that, right? You're not going to hang up on me over that, are you?" He laughs a little, like he's joking, but we both know he's not.

I snort into the phone and regret it immediately. "I definitely knew you were joking. Get over yourself."

"Just checking." He clears his throat. "So how's your dad?"

Something tight curls its way around my chest, squeezing away my coherency.

"Fine," I breathe. This isn't the conversation I wanted to have. Honestly, I can't say what I wanted to talk to Joey about. We don't exactly have a history of comfortable conversation. But the times we have talked—really talked—I feel like he actually heard me. Maybe that's why I called.

"Okay. That's good." Joey's voice dips low.

Now's the time to say something. Anything. Before the silence gets too thick and awkwardness settles in. I blurt the first thing that comes to mind. "It turns out my parents are not joking around about boarding school, so that sucks."

I hear him take in a breath. Maybe relief that I've broken the silence first. "Did you think they were? Joking, I mean?"

"I guess I hoped they were."

"You must have done something pretty bad."

"I broke into my dead neighbor's house and let my ex-boyfriend take the blame when the police found us." I dig my bare toes in the carpet as I wait for his reaction. Somehow, I care more about what Joey thinks than my parents. They expect me to mess up, but Joey might still have some faith in me.

"Ooooh. Yeah. That's bad."

I spit out a laugh, relieved that he doesn't seem too bothered. I've missed his candor. "Yeah. I bet it's awful compared to anything you've ever done."

Joey doesn't say anything for a moment. What's this about? Did I accidentally hit on a terrible secret? Then he says, "Yeah. True."

I bite my lip. Guess Joey Prince is as good and pure as I

thought. No hidden dark secrets to share. Maybe this is why I called him. I need a little good and pureness in my life.

A voice I can't make out cuts over the background and a rustling sound blurs the conversation. Joey doesn't say anything for half a minute and then returns, his voice flatter. "Hey—um, I have to go. My dad needs my help at the store."

He has to go? Already?

"Oh. Okay." What's this feeling running through me? Disappointment? At the end of a not-so-awkward conversation with Joey? I shouldn't have flirted with him, even after I got my phone back from Ted and Peter. But I did and I don't regret it.

Joey sighs, the sound carrying between us. "Thanks for calling me."

Even though I'm alone in my room and half a country away, I smile. "See you next week, Joey Prince."

CHAPTER
Twenty Two

"**D**ad, come look at what we got for you."

Mom and I unload armfuls of grocery bags. The green fabric bags lined up on the kitchen counter are stuffed full of food from our "quick stop" at the store. I only went along because Mom swore she wanted to get ice cream and check out a new vintage clothing shop in Ballard.

Clearly, she had other errands planned as well.

Shopping with Mom is always an extravaganza. It's not like on TV sitcoms where the parent pushes a cart down the aisles of the store, their hand gripped to a list of items they need to purchase.

I mean—I wish.

This is how it usually goes. Step one: Mom convinces someone to tag along with her, usually by lying to or bribing them. Step two: She just "happens" to remember something we're out of, and we just "happen" to be right next to the grocery store. And don't worry, it will only take a minute. Step three: It's over. You're doomed. You're at the grocery store and you won't leave until there's one of every single item in your cart.

We're talking hours here.

From the couch in the living room, Dad cranes his neck. "Hmm?"

I grab the special yogurts Dad loves and wiggle them in the air. He grins and pulls himself to a standing position.

"Thanks, sweetie." He bends over and kisses my cheek, even though Mom's the one who bought them. I'll gladly take some credit, since I did barely survive that shopping marathon.

Methodically, I line up the contents of our bags and put them in their places in the pantry or fridge. Next to me, Mom selects the food she bought for dinner tonight—my last dinner at home before I leave tomorrow morning—and starts chopping and washing and separating.

Ding.

Dad nods toward the door. "Someone coming over?"

Mom shakes her head. They both turn to me.

I haven't invited anyone, but I have a good feeling I know who's here, anyway.

I bite my lip as my parents exchange a knowing glance. They must guess who it is too. I steel my shoulders. "I'll get it."

When the door opens, Griffin smiles widely at me, pulling something from behind his back. The gold foil catches my eye, and I stand on tiptoe to reach for it.

He waves it over my head. "If you accept this Twix, that means we're not fighting anymore."

I eye the candy bar, pretending to weigh my options. There's no real choice, though. Griffin is my oldest friend—period. We've fought before, during, and after our relationship, and I'm guessing we still have a few more fights to come. "Fine," I say as I grab the Twix. I unwrap the top and take a bite. Griffin rolls his eyes. "Can I come inside now?"

With my toe, I nudge the door open another half-inch. He steps inside, his arm extended toward the chocolate.

"Hey! No take-backs." I frown over the wrapper as I tear off another bite with my teeth.

Dad peers around the corner from the kitchen. "Do I hear Griffin?"

Griffin jogs toward him so Dad doesn't have to walk down the hall. "It's me. Paige wasn't going to let me in, but I bribed her." He juts his head back at me, and I scowl for both their benefits.

"I'm right here, you know." People talking over me like I'm invisible is one of my pet peeves, and Griffin knows all about it. He used to be the one I'd go to when my siblings treated me like a pest or tried to convince me I was half-dog and needed to fetch things for them and carry them in my mouth.

Mom appears from the kitchen, wiping her palms along the hem of her apron. "Hi Griffin. Staying for dinner?"

I slip the Twix behind my back. Mom has a strict no-candy-before-dinner rule. Technically all her rules are strict, but this is one she rarely goes soft on. Some sort of 1960s line about spoiling dinner and giving yourself a stomachache. I'm not in the mood for another battle.

Griffin nods eagerly. "Yeah, I'd love to. Whatever it is smells amazing."

Suck up. Mom steps back into the kitchen and Dad follows. Griffin sinks down onto the couch, patting the cushion next to him. Sighing, I collapse onto the couch, my legs tucked under me.

"Thanks for the Twix." I break off a piece and hand it to him.

He chews slowly, mulling something over.

Caramel and chocolate swirl together in my mouth. I roll my head to the side until it hits his shoulder. He scoots closer.

"I wish we'd never fought."

Draping an arm around me, he says, "Me too."

"Do we have to talk about it?" The fabric of his t-shirt is thin and soft. I close my eyes and bury my face in it.

His chest rumbles against my ear. "We probably should."

Reluctantly, I sit up. "I'm sorry you think I'm leading you on. I'm not trying to, I just—"

Just what? If I don't know what I want from Griffin, how am I supposed to tell him? He deserves the truth, either way. After our argument, I want things to feel normal between us.

His hand lifts to my hair, tugging at a piece in front. "What is it?" His voice is low.

I drop my head onto him again. "I don't know what I want. All I know is I want you in my life, and I'm scared of losing you. Of losing this."

His arm tightens around me. "You won't lose me. Not ever. Do you want to go back to being best friends and that's it?"

As soon as he says it, my heart screams *no*. I never wanted to break up with him in the first place, and every part of me aches that I'm causing him pain. But there's a chance I'm not coming back to Washington in the fall. There's an even bigger chance saying yes will hurt him even more in the long run.

"I can't promise anything. I don't even know where I'll be in September."

He runs his hands over his face. "But if you're here?"

I swallow. "If I'm here, it still won't be the same. We're friends, Griffin. That's all I can promise right now." Choking back a sob, I cover my mouth with my hand. I should tell him the full truth. That I'm not sure we're good for each other. That I'm *pretty sure* I'm the problem and he can find someone better. A better friend, a better girlfriend. Someone who cares enough about him to be there all the time. But I don't open my mouth again. My family is right about me: I'm a coward.

Wordlessly, Griffin laces his fingers in mine and squeezes. We stay that way until Mom calls out that dinner is ready, then we pretend everything's okay.

A TAP TAP TAP ON THE DOOR SIGNALS DAD'S ARRIVAL IN MY bedroom. He walks carefully to my bed, where my suitcase is open, and my clothes lie folded in an impossible mountain around it. He lowers himself down to sit, knees wobbling.

"Gonna miss you around here."

From my spot hovering over my already overstuffed suitcase, I smile. "I'm going to miss you too, Dad."

That's what this is all about, right? I've got to prove I'm mature enough to stay out of trouble and stop causing Dad stress. I can't live at home and constantly stress him out to the point of needing hospitalization. I'd like to think I'm not that self-centered. I do miss Dad, and despite the push and pull of our relationship, I miss Mom too. A weird new part of me misses Ally and Justin and my nephews, though. And even my new routine in Texas—the build-up and Callie and Jen. And—okay. Maybe one percent of me misses Joey.

"I'll work on your mom, okay? I want you home. This is where you belong." Dad tilts his head. "Just play nice for a few more weeks and she'll drop the whole boarding school idea. Your mom worries too much. But I'm fine now. My doctor said my chance of disease coming back is low." He smiles, his voice even. Dad knows how to calm me, even in the rockiest of times. Where Mom stirs things up, Dad smooths them over.

I exhale. I'd trade my irresponsible sense of adventure for the promise that Dad could stay healthy forever. I'd make that swap anytime.

I set down the shirt I'm pretending to fold and sit next to him on the bed. It creaks under our weight. This old bed has probably seen a lot of parent pep-talks.

"I'm going to really try. I want to come home so bad." My hands shake as I reach around Dad's torso and side hug the crap out of him. Still, I'm careful not to squeeze him too hard.

Please, please let Dad get better for good. For both of our sakes.

CHAPTER
Twenty Three

At the Houston airport, I scan the crowd near the luggage belt. Allison didn't say if she would come inside or if her plan is to drive through the pickup area. Her silky hair isn't in the crowd of people, so I heave my luggage off the belt and head toward the exit. The noise in the airport escalates with people yelling back and forth across the building.

"Hey."

"HEY."

"Hey, Paige!"

I whirl. About one hundred feet back, Joey stands, car keys in one hand and a clear plastic bag in the other. His mouth pulls in a half-grimace, half-smile as he shifts his feet and waits for me.

I stand rooted to the spot. Why, why, *why* is he here?

He waves again, and I make my way toward him. Because I can't just ignore him, right?

"Where's Allison?" The first words out of my mouth are rude. Joey seems to bring that out of me. I shake my head. "I mean, hey, what are you doing here? I'm just surprised to see you. I thought my sister was picking me up." I twist my fingers around and around my suitcase handle.

Joey runs his hands through his hair once, then twice. "Yeah, she was planning on it. I was over playing with Cam, and I... offered." The car keys spin around his fingers and the bag swings at his side as he adjusts his feet.

"Oh."

I grip the rubber handle of my suitcase tighter. "I bet she was glad you offered, to be honest. She's scared of flying, you know. Even being at the airport freaks her out."

His eyebrows shoot up. "Wow. I didn't know that, but it makes sense. She did look relieved."

"Yep." Texting Joey, and even calling him, while I was back home was easier because of the distance between us. It didn't feel quite real from one thousand miles away. Now, standing in the airport with just us—it feels very, very real.

He walks ahead to the exit I'd been heading toward and I follow. "Yeah, I kind of thought she was dreading you coming back."

Is he serious?

Turning his head, he grins at me. *There it is.* So elusive, but so worth it when he smiles like that. Too bad it would be rude to tell him he needs to smile more.

"Psh. Yeah, right. She already told me she misses me like crazy because I'm good at keeping the boys entertained." Ally has been texting me daily and sending little updates. I can't tell if it's because she *does* miss me, or she knows I miss her family. Either way, I'm ready to get back and hug those little monsters.

"Those kids are crazy, but I like them a lot." Joey's smile flashes again at the mention of my nephews.

Something warm washes up in my stomach. "They're a little obsessed with you. Cam especially. After that day at the arcade, you were all he could talk about. It almost got me in trouble with Allison because she thought 'Joey' was some guy I'd hooked up with when I was supposed to be watching Mattie and Cam."

Joey stops. "What?" He turns all the way around, his mouth an open circle.

I nod, my ears warm and uncomfortable. That was maybe, possibly, TMI. I have the tendency to word vomit when I'm nervous, hence, the no filter admission. I swallow and try to play it off. "Yeah, crazy, huh?"

His brows furrow all the way into each other. "Yeah. Very crazy," he agrees.

We walk until we reach the parking garage. "So, which level are you on?"

I gaze around the bottom level like Joey's immaculate 4-Runner might be hiding in plain sight.

He groans, rubbing a hand along his neck. "Not this one."

Once we *finally* find Joey's car, I load my suitcase into the trunk and buckle up in the front seat. Last time I was up here was after the party at Ben's house. When I started the night planning on avoiding Joey at all costs and ended the night bonding with him over just about everything.

The inside is exactly the same as it was before. Way too clean to belong to anyone our age. The carpeted interior even has vacuum lines across it. I inhale to confirm—yep, no stinky boy smell lingering in the upholstery.

"Thanks for picking me up. You could have waited in the pickup line. I wouldn't have minded." I suddenly feel shy about him driving nearly an hour away, paying to park, and waiting for me to deboard and get my luggage. How long was he standing there before I finally noticed him?

"It's not a problem. How was your trip? Is your dad feeling better? Oh—these are for you." His voice breaks a little as he hands over the plastic bag, and I open it to find a row of brownies on a paper plate. The tops are swirled with peanut butter.

I poke one and it's still soft and warm. "Wow. Thank you." He shrugs, like it's no big deal, but my chest tightens as I gaze wide-eyed at the brownies. No one has ever made me welcome home brownies before. I can't imagine anyone other than Joey doing something like this. It's... really, really nice.

I guess Allison filled him in on the reason for the impromptu trip back home. At the mention of Dad, my heart pings. I pinch off a tiny piece of brownie and slip it into my mouth. It melts instantly, and I'm in chocolate and peanut butter heaven. I'd eat more, but no way can I let Joey see me potentially make a mess in his car. I will not get blamed for a stray brownie crumb anytime soon.

"He's a lot better." I swallow. "He's going to be fine."

"So, did you take care of him the whole time? Did you do anything fun in between all that?"

He asks the second question like he already knows the answer to the first. Joey plugs our neighborhood address into his phone's GPS. He sets it into a suction cup holder on the windshield, so the directions are at eye-level.

I blow out a steady breath. "Pretty much, yeah. We played card games, and my mom dragged me to the grocery store, which was a nightmare."

"You didn't see any of your friends?"

My eyes slide sideways toward him. Either he's acting suspicious or I am. We can't both be gearing toward the same thing. I'm trying my best to steer the conversation away from Griffin and anything related to *that* disaster, but it seems like....

"Okay. What did Ally tell you?" I should have known my sneaky sister would go behind my back and spill.

He lets out a low chuckle, his eyes still glued to the road. "It was actually Justin." Ugh, even worse.

Bringing my hands to my face, I groan into them. Is nothing a secret in my family?

"I mean, just a little bit. About a boyfriend back home. They said you'd probably see him while you were there." Maybe I'm crazy, but his voice sounds like it's getting higher and faster for absolutely no reason.

I shake my head. "Ex-boyfriend. That's the important part." And I don't know why it's an important distinction, but it suddenly is.

"Justin said on-again, off-again. Which means he's your boyfriend some of the time."

I roll my eyes and set my brownie plate carefully on the floor before letting out a dramatic groan. "We are not on-again, off-again. We broke up once, and we haven't gotten back together."

Joey doesn't respond to that, but his shoulders go from tight and raised down to a normal level. Dare I say, relaxed. It's weird. Why would Griffin and I together stress him out? Unless...

"If you're not together, why does your brother-in-law think you are?" Do I detect a challenge? Jealousy? What is this? Joey says whatever's on his mind, but we've never talked about relationships before. Maybe my time in Washington has him curious about my life there. Or maybe he's just making small talk, but it feels like more than that. There's been a shift in the way we act around each other, and it makes my head spin.

"Because he's misinformed. And a big idiot," I say. Justin and Ally are *so* going to hear about this. I'm going to ban them from gossiping about me, starting as soon as I get to their house.

Joey laughs loudly. "Fair enough."

I pull air into my cheeks, then let it leak out slowly. "Griffin and I are best friends, that's why it's complicated. Everyone expects us to get back together because we actually do love each other. I'm not sure it's like that anymore."

Joey sucks at his teeth. He doesn't look at me. "Did you tell him that?"

Why does everyone expect me to break Griffin's heart as easily as snapping a twig? I'm not ruthless, and I can't turn my feelings on and off. For the moment, they're stuck in between. So, ugh, no. I didn't exactly tell him. "I tried."

"I've been led on before, for like two years, and it sucks. I wish she would have just made up her mind. Even if it wasn't what I wanted to hear."

I dip my head and study my hands. He makes it sound like I'm purposefully hurting Griffin. But it isn't like that. "I don't want to talk about this anymore."

"Oh. Okay." His voice is muffled because I'm staring straight out the passenger side window with my back turned to him. Who knew he was so nosy? Leaving Washington, I felt fine about how Griffin and I left things. It's not like we gave it a name, but we felt like friends again, which is the most important thing to me. Now Joey is asking too many questions and turning my intentions sideways.

"But did you see him? Griffin?"

I turn so quickly my neck cracks and snap, "I said I don't want to talk about it. Why do you even care?"

He stares, stares, stares at the road. I narrow my eyes on him. He doesn't get to pester me and then ignore my questions.

I huff. "Seriously. Why. Do. You. Care?"

"I don't."

"It sure sounds like you do. But, yeah, I saw him a few times. Like I said, he's my best friend." I blow a breath through my nose and lean back in my seat. Maybe if I lean back far enough, I can pretend Joey's not even here for the rest of the drive.

"Hey—you're the one getting all defensive. I'm just trying to make conversation here." He has this Texas drawl that only comes out when he's agitated. Instead of "here," he says it like "her." It'd be kind of endearing if he weren't forcing me to the point of insanity.

Drumming my fingers on the middle console, I groan. It's so like him to call me out for my mood swings. Like I said—he hears me, maybe better than most people. "Ugh. Fine. I give up. Maybe I'm getting a tiny bit defensive, but you're also being weird. Can we agree on that?"

He shrugs. "I was just trying to figure out if you're okay."

"I have three brothers, a sister, my parents, and a brother-in-law for that. Consider me sufficiently worried about, okay?"

"Okay. Got it."

"Good." Sneaking a look at his profile, I swear he looks a little hurt. Am I being too intense? After a pause, I sigh. "Um. Thanks, though. For worrying. I'm fine, but it's nice of you to care, I guess."

Joey flashes a crooked smile as he gazes over to my side of the car for a millisecond. "Sure."

Joey clears his throat. "So we missed you at the build-up this week. We've made a ton of progress."

I let my lips form a faint smile. "Oh, yeah? I'm not sure how you guys ever survived without me, to be honest."

A laugh that turns into a fake-sounding cough bursts from his mouth. "Yeah. We made it, but barely."

"Who won?"

He wrinkles his nose. "Not important."

Ha. That means Callie beat him again. I haven't talked to Callie or Jen all week, except to text them both to say I was going to Washington. It's weird, having only been in Texas a few weeks so far, but having people care about where I went.

"I bet you miss everything back home even more now." He's trying to change the subject. But I consider his statement.

I try to think of something I miss. Seconds tick by. "Actually, no. I can't think of anything I miss, other than my parents."

"And Griffin?"

"And Griffin."

It's different though. The way I miss Griffin. Not an ache so much as a memory. He's still there and we haven't quite figured things out between us, but still. The thought of him doesn't make me want to grab my bike and ride to Washington.

I try to remember how it felt when Griffin and I first started dating. We were friends for so long first, and then it was like we almost fell into a romantic relationship. Our hugs got longer, we started holding hands unironically when we walked home from school, and then he kissed me that day after the ceremony.

It was a lot like friendship, but with kissing. And I don't know if that's how it's supposed to be, or if it's a common mistake you make with best friends, thinking you should be more. Maybe one of you hopes and the other one doesn't want to let the other down. I've never thought about it before now.

Maybe Griffin really is *just* my best friend.

And suddenly, I want to test my theory.

"Joey?"

"Hmm?" His eyes slide sideways as he pulls to a careful stop at a yellow light about to turn red.

"I thought of something else I miss from back home. The food is so much better. It's impossible to get good teriyaki here."

His mouth cracks into a grin. "Fair enough."

I smile. "Also, I want to show you something."

JOEY FLAWLESSLY MANEUVERS HIS CAR INTO A PARALLEL parking spot, pulls his keys from the ignition, and turns to face me.

"You had me drive to my family's photo shop." Clearly unimpressed, his eyebrow knit close together.

I bite down a smile. "Yes. But that's not where we're going. This is only our starting point."

I throw open the car door, hop out, and gesture for Joey to do the same. "Come on, come on."

He's got to be moving slow on purpose, just to be a spoilsport. I swear my dad moved faster thirty minutes out of surgery than Joey is right now.

"Can you tell me where we're going and what we're doing? Maybe also tell me if I'm going to hate it or not?"

Okay, wow. Besides making me want to give him a sharp kick in the shin, his whining is adding nothing to this adventure.

"I get it," I tell him. "You don't like surprises and you're a boring old man. Just humor me."

Grabbing his hand, I tug him away from the car and towards the sidewalk. His fingers are stiff in my grasp until we pass Prince Prints. Then they fold into mine, gripping softly.

A tremor of warmth skips over me. With Griffin, everything feels so comfortable and easy and safe. But this.

This feels different. New and exciting and a little scary. Call me crazy, but I've always loved being scared. It's like being jolted awake with a thousand possibilities in front of you, but you don't know which to choose.

I squeeze his hand and flit my eyes to his.

Joey's smile lights up his face, bigger than I've ever seen. It sparks a wave in me, bigger than I've felt. We walk quickly because I'm setting the pace, and right before we round the corner, my heart flutters in my chest, going double its normal speed. I don't know how Joey will react. I don't know if I'm making a huge mistake, and normally I wouldn't care if I was. But my feet drag as hesitation grips me. "I brought something from home."

His eyebrows rise lazily. "Okay. You have it here?" He eyes the empty street like my belongings might be scattered across it.

"It's right here in my purse." I pat the bag strapped across me. I found it entirely by accident, while I was switching out my clothes. If Mom had seen it when she cleared my room earlier this summer, she'd definitely have confiscated it, but apparently past-me had the foresight to hide it away. Tucked in the folds of my favorite pink beanie was my last bottle of glow-in-the-dark spray paint. A memento left over from one incredibly late and hilarious night with Griffin that I made sure to put in my checked bag and then switch to my purse once I landed. Something told me I'd need to keep it handy.

I pull it out now, still half-concealed in my purse. Joey drops his hand from mine and steps backward.

"What? Put that away before someone sees, and we get arrested or something." Frantically, his hands push down on the can until it's hidden away again.

I stare at him, my stomach sinking. I should have known he'd react like this. Like everything matters so much, when in reality, having a little bit of fun is good for you. He could definitely use it. I was stupid to think I could convince him to take a risk with me. Stupid to put my off-the-cuff idea to the test.

"We're not going to get arrested." He's right about all the progress they've made. Where the lot used to be half-crumbled buildings and exposed pipe, now several almost-finished frames line the street. "We can write our names real small on something they're going to get rid of, anyway. It's just for fun."

He stands up taller, his eyes like steel. "It doesn't sound fun. We've been working on this crap all summer. Why do you do this? This tagging thing?"

I slip the can back out from my purse and push it into his chest. He clasps his hand around it before it clatters to the ground. "Why don't you try and find out for yourself."

When he does nothing, I bite my lip. How do I explain it so Joey will understand? "I guess it's nice to do something where you don't have to think for once. Like, when I'm spray painting something, it's just me and that thing, whatever it is, and all other *expectations* disappear for a second."

His eyes narrow, and I swear there's a spark of something in there. His Adam's apple bobs as he extends his hand to return the paint.

Nearly whispering, his voice is so soft as he says, "Okay, but you pick where we do it."

Giddily, I oblige. A bubble of surprise bursts to the surface and I grin widely. I wander toward the remaining wreckage and study the piles of steel siding, bricks, and wooden posts we've decided are unusable. I stop in front of one of the piles and wave him over.

"Ready?" I shake the can and he takes it, pressing so softly on the nozzle the paint comes out in a hazy mist. I guess he's got to work up to it. In the center of the wide square piece of metal I've chosen, he forms his initials: J.P. When he's done, I take the can from him and add a finishing touch. I draw a wonky heart around his name, closing the pointed end with a little loop.

Then we run. We don't stop until we reach his car, where we lean against the driver's side door, panting and out of breath but exhilarated.

"Ahh!" I double over until my hair sweeps the ground. Hand clutched over my mouth to control the loud laughter tumbling from my lips, my shoulders shake silently. Next to me, Joey watches me with round eyes and a grin plastered on his beautiful face.

I suck in a breath and grab his arms. With a little shake for emphasis, I say, "You did it. You actually had fun, and you didn't get arrested or die."

He pokes me in the ribs. "I'm still going to call you to bail me out if we get caught."

I catch his hand in mine and I don't let go. "Sounds good. Now let's get ice cream." Because really, every mildly illegal activity should be followed with dessert.

CHAPTER
Twenty Four

By the time Joey drops me off at Allison's house, it's almost dark. The sun sits low in the sky and bathes the lingering clouds in orange and pink light. I like to think my heart looks a little like that right now.

Ally calls me out on my mood as soon as the kids are firmly asleep, and I've gone upstairs to unpack. Poking her head in my room, she grins. "It took you a while to get home from the airport."

Ally is always one sneak attack ahead of me. She looks much too smug for my comfort. "Yeah. It was really surprising to see Joey there to pick me up instead of you or Justin."

She flips her hair. "I thought you two needed a little push, and I was obviously right. You look really happy. Is it because of Joey? Did you kiss?" Ally leans closer with every question.

I roll my eyes. "We didn't kiss." It's not nearly as ridiculous a question as it should be.

She pulls an exaggerated frown.

"But we did kind of hold hands."

Ally's eyes sparkle. "That's adorable, Paige. So, you like him as more than a friend, right?"

Sighing, I pull a floral dress from my suitcase and slip it onto a hanger. If she'd asked me a week ago, I'd have rather died than admit to a crush on Joey. Now...

With my back turned as I re-organize my closet, I say, "I'm

trying to figure that out." I'm trying to figure a lot out right now. Joey surprised me today by taking that spray can. Maybe he'll surprise me in other ways too.

"And things with you and Griffin are over?"

I turn, dress still in hand. I study my sister as she leans against the half-open bedroom door. The question is innocent enough coming from her, but it strikes me as suspicious. I've had an entire lifetime of other people—my parents, my siblings, my friends—pushing me to do one thing or another. But not this. It's too much.

"Are you spying for Joey? Is that what having him watch the kids is about?"

Nudging us together is fine, but asking me questions so she can run back to feed him info—that'd be disturbing. Not to mention a total betrayal.

Her eyes narrow and her mouth springs open, round and angry. "Are you serious? I would never do that, Paige."

I clench the dress in my fingers. "I'm so tired of everyone else running my life. I *know* I'm a loser compared to the rest of you, but I still get to make my own decisions. No matter what you all think of me." Mom tells me what to do and refuses to budge. Dad won't form an opinion without Mom's approval. And my sister, the only person who gets me even a portion of the time, is going behind my back to set up play dates for me. It's infuriating.

She crosses her arms and studies me. "You're not a loser. And I'm not trying to make any decision for you. Sorry if it came off like that. I assumed you had a thing for him."

I don't give into her apology so easily. "Oh yeah? It has nothing to do with the fact you've never liked Griffin?"

Ally's eyes widen. "I've never said that I don't like him."

She doesn't have to.

"You've always hated him because he's not like Justin. Not like you." I'm not even sure what I mean by that. Just that no one in the family approves of my choices, so why would they approve of who I date?

She shakes her head like she can't quite believe what she's hearing. "Paige, I don't care who you date. It's your life. Don't date someone because it's the convenient thing to do."

I arch an eyebrow as my face grows warm. "You're not trying to control me like Mom?"

"I wouldn't do that," she says again.

And she wouldn't. I know that. My feelings for Griffin and my feelings for Joey are muddling everything up. I'm stuck between two decisions that feel right for different reasons. And whatever I do, I'm going to hurt someone, and I'll end up regretting something. A sigh leaks out of me, and with it, my anger.

And maybe I'll mess up like I always manage to do.

I sniffle, sucking back tears that start to flow without warning. "I'm sorry. It's stupid. I know you wouldn't do anything like that."

The dress and the hanger are still in my hands, and I can't seem to find the brain space to hang the stupid thing on the rack, so I stand there, frozen. Tears drip down my cheeks, smearing my mascara and leaving vertical stripes through my blush and concealer.

Ally looks horrified as she lets go of the door and sweeps across the room to wrap her arms around me. She squeezes until there's not enough oxygen getting to my brain for tears to even form. When she lets go, she smooths my hair and wipes her thumbs under my eyes. My erratic heartbeat slows.

"I'm sorry," I repeat.

She waves a hand. "Stop saying that. I'm not even mad. It's my fault for being too nosy." She grabs the dress from me and hangs it in the closet.

"I don't know what to do. I'm supposed to be showing Mom and Dad that I don't need boarding school to teach me to be an obedient daughter. On top of that, Griffin and Joey both want me to be a different person. I'm one person in Seattle and another in Texas." I suck in a noisy, raspy breath. "It's like I can only make one person happy at a time, and it's never going to be me."

Ally lifts her chin. "Then you need to change the options because making yourself happy is the whole point. Don't let anyone bully you into thinking otherwise."

I tilt my head, shock plain on my face. "Did you just call Mom a bully?"

She shrugs. "Maybe I did. This boarding school thing? It's ridiculous. You broke a window, you didn't commit homicide."

I bite my lip. "It's all the same to Mom."

Our eyes meet and we both laugh behind our hands. The kids are asleep and waking them up is not an option.

She exhales. "So what are you going to do about your boy problem?"

A "boy problem" is not what I had in mind for this summer. And as crazy as it sounds, I'd trade anything to not have Griffin's or Joey's hearts on the line. No matter what I do, one of them will end up hating me, even if they pretend to be okay with my decision. And that's assuming Joey even feels something for me other than a casual friendship.

"What do you think I should do? I know you have opinions but try to be fair. Think like me."

Ally nods. "I can do that." She smooths her hands over her skirt. "Do you remember when I broke up with Tyler?"

Tyler was Ally's boyfriend from high school. They dated all four years, went to prom together, and he brought her flowers every Friday afternoon. I used to watch them walk from his car to the front door when I was supposed to be asleep just so I could catch them making out. That's also when I found out tongues are involved in kissing and swore off it forever. Until, you know, I didn't.

"You guys broke up the day after graduation."

"Yeah. I broke up with him, and he was very upset. Told me

I'd ruined his life and a lot of other dramatic things. But now we're both happy and married to other people."

I shake my head, eyes shifting sideways. "I'm not marrying anyone."

"Well, thank goodness for that. I'm just saying even if someone feels important to you right now, it doesn't mean you have to stay with them. You've got college and the rest of your life to look forward to."

I look up at her. "So you're saying I should give Joey a chance?"

She shakes her head.

"Griffin?"

Allison smiles. "What I'm *saying* is, if it's good for you, it'll happen on its own. If not, you have years and years to fall in love again. With whoever you choose."

"Don't worry about it?"

Something heavy lifts from my chest.

"Exactly. You don't have to worry, okay? You can't control how other people react. Be kind but make your choices based on how you feel."

I exhale and wrap my arms around my sister. "Thanks. I'm going to keep unpacking and then go to sleep."

She stops at the door. "Probably smart, considering Cam will be up extra early to wake you up. He missed you."

CHAPTER
Twenty Five

"Mo' mo' mo'." Mattie beams at me as he repeats his new word. I reward him with another cookie.

"Now say 'thank you.'"

In between slobbery bites, he says, "Mo' mo' mo.'"

On my lap, Cam nibbles his cookie slowly and scrolls through the pictures I took while in Washington. "Have I ever been to Wash-in-ten, Piggy?"

I ruffle his hair. "You went for Christmas last year, silly."

He leans back into me, snuggling close. "Are you going back to Wash-in-ten again, or are you going to stay here?"

I wiggle my fingers across his belly until he giggles and squirms away. "I'm going to stay here the whole rest of the summer, and then I'll go back to Washington. But I'll come visit whenever you want."

Cam cups my face in his small hands. "I'll miss you," he says, his bottom lip quivering.

I smile at him. His eyes are bright and on the verge of tears, hair sticking straight up in the front and chocolate smeared along one cheek. The image of perfect, infallible love.

If only it were always so easy to love someone.

"I'll miss you too. But, like I said, we'll visit each other lots."

As long as I'm not banished to boarding school. As long as I'm not sick like Dad. Maybe I should cross my fingers behind my back to avoid straight-out lying to my nephew. Somehow, I don't think that'd make up for it.

I press my cheek to his. "I promise."

Mattie coos in agreement and rubs the slobbered-on part of his cookie along his highchair tray.

The front door opens, and I call toward it, "Hey Ally! You're right on time for cookies."

A boy's voice answers. "Cookies? Sweet."

I turn so quickly I almost throw Cam off my lap. "Joey?"

He appears around the corner, hands up in surrender. "Sorry. Allison said I could let myself in when I got here."

Ally. Of course. Very subtle, sis. After our talk, she still couldn't resist one more stab at playing matchmaker. Even though I'm annoyed she didn't think it was a nice idea to warn me he'd be stopping by, little butterflies flutter in my belly. "Oh. So what are you up to?"

He raises an eyebrow. "She didn't tell you?"

I slowly shake my head, a blush creeping up my face. It's awkward to admit I do not understand what he's talking about, and he gives me a look like I'm lying.

Joey turns his head and points at Cam. "Do you know where we're going?"

Cam shrugs and throws his hands up. "I don't know anything!"

We all laugh, even baby Mattie.

Joey sighs, tucking his hands in his pockets. "I thought we were all going to the park. Your sister said you could use some help walking both of them down there, so I offered."

The park?

Oh.

OH.

That park. The one we flirtatiously dubbed the make-out park when we were feeling much braver with the thousand miles between us.

I raise an eyebrow, open my mouth, and shut it. Looking at

Cam and Mattie and *not* Joey, I say, "What do you guys think? Should we go to the park?"

They both munch their cookies, and no one cries, so I guess that's a yes.

After I show Joey the clunky stroller in the garage and I fill the boys' sippy cups with water, I strap on sandals and head down the street to the park.

It's a quiet walk. One part of me wants to joke about the texts and relieve some tension. Or expectation. But really, he can't expect us to kiss in the corner while the kids play, right?

Please let that not be what he's hoping for.

"I didn't pick the park," he says, right as I'm unbuckling the kids from the stroller.

I clear my throat. "Oh. Okay. I mean—that's good to know."

Relaxing my shoulders, I focus all my attention on Mattie gripping my finger and wobbling his way toward the play structure. Cam bypasses all of us and makes a beeline for the tallest slide—a green one that spirals on the way down. As he disappears inside of it, his whoops echo off the sides, muffled but still loud enough for everyone playing to turn and watch as he catapults to the mulch underneath.

"I did it!" He runs to Joey and me and hugs our knees in turn before circling us and running back to the slide.

"Wow." Joey's mouth makes an O as he watches Cam zoom across the playground.

I stifle a laugh. "Yeah." Cam's energy is never-ending and awe-inspiring to everyone who meets him.

Mattie whines and tugs on my finger as he babbles and points with his free hand toward the swing set. I ruffle his hair. "Good idea, buddy."

Strapping Mattie into a swing, I train my eyes on Joey, who leans against a tree next to the play structure. His eyes roam back and forth, following Cam's path of destruction. His insane sense of responsibility can be annoying, but moments like this make it less so. I'm not sure I could count on Griffin to not lose

Cam, or at least to not get distracted and give up on tracking him down for a while.

Mattie and I stay at the swing set until the muscles in my arms twinge in spots I didn't even know could hurt. I wave a sore arm at Joey until he notices, then I wince and wait for him to wrangle Cam. They meet us at the swing set, stroller in tow, and we work together to strap the kids in. Almost the same second we move, their eyes slip closed and their heads roll to the side.

Joey and I make another quick, quiet walk back home. Seamlessly, I roll the stroller in through the garage, over the step to the kitchen, and into the dark silent hallway, where I park it. I've done it so many times this summer that now I'm a pro.

"Think they'll keep sleeping?" Joey stuffs his hands in his pockets.

"They did play pretty hard."

He raises an eyebrow. "I always thought people were exaggerating when they said kids have endless energy, but it's true."

I quirk my mouth, looking toward the hallway. "Well, almost endless."

Smiling, he pulls his hands from his shorts to run them through his hair. "So, um, maybe I should teach you to play Mario for when I'm not around."

My heart thumps double-time. Do I want him to stay? Why are my hands suddenly clammy? It's just Joey Prince. Nothing to sweat over. But he tilts his head as he waits for an answer, his brown eyes big and warm, and for some reason, my tongue is too dry to speak.

I shake my head slightly, trying to rid myself of the sudden case of boy flu that's come over me. This isn't me. I'm not flustered around guys. I'm rarely flustered, period.

Ugh.

"I know how to play Super Mario for your information." I grab a set of game controllers from the drawer in the coffee table and set them on the couch.

An easy smile slides over his lips and he jumps onto the cushion next to me. "The new one?"

I roll my eyes until they practically touch the back of my head. "I'm pretty sure they're all the same. You've played one Super Mario, you've played them all."

He shoots me a look out of the corner of his eyes and hands me a controller. "Prepare to be proven wrong."

We focus so hard on the controllers that my thumb might be jammed and his tongue sticks out of the side of his mouth in absent concentration. It's nothing like the Mario I played when I was younger, and I'm very, very, very confused. I will never admit that he's right, but I needed a tutorial badly. I'm kind of excited to show off my inkling of knowledge the next time Cam wants to play video games and Joey isn't here to be the expert.

My controller slips from my hands at the same time Joey raises his in triumph. "What do you think?"

I'm thinking a lot of things. One, Joey Prince *was* cute until he started gloating. And two, I'm naturally lousy at video games, but they're still fun. "I think if you celebrate any louder, you're going to wake up the kids."

He shrinks down, sliding his back along the couch. "Sorry."

We both reach for the same controller and our hands bump. He tugs back on his cord. "One more round to even things up."

"You're already beating me pretty bad. Take the win and run before I start getting lucky." I reach for the controller again and his fingers brush mine.

My eyes blink downward. His slide across our frozen hands. Slowly, carefully, he grabs my hand, turns it palm up, and laces his fingers with mine.

If I move too quickly, will I scare him away? Touching Joey like this feels so tenuous, so fragile. But it also feels right and good and solid. I barely even worry about my sweaty, sticky palms. Letting my body sink back into the couch, I say, "Thanks for coming to the park today."

He chuckles. "I think we have to thank your sister since you didn't know we were going to the park. I couldn't tell what you were thinking."

I bite my lip, hesitation stalling me. "I was a little worried you thought we were going to the park to make-out. With the kids there. And everyone else."

He hits his free palm on his forehead, making a satisfying *smack* sound. "Ugh. I am really bad at flirting. Just—please forget that text, okay? It was so stupid."

Giddy, I shake my head. "I'll never, ever forget it. And the park will always be the make-out park to me. There's no going back on that."

His voice is close to my ear when he says, "So if I want to kiss you, do I have to wait until we're at the park?"

I'm suddenly hyperaware of my chest, rising and falling with each breath. As well as the exact amount of space between his face and mine.

"Yep. Sorry, those are the rules." My voice cracks at the last second.

He tightens his fingers around mine. "Got it. Rules are important."

Something pangs inside my chest as the heat radiating from his body lessens when he leans back onto his own cushion. What's wrong with me?

"Piggy? I'm stuck. I'm stuck!" Cam's panic reverberates from the hallway as he wakes up from his nap. Inevitably Mattie's cries echo Cam's.

I stand and Joey drops my hand. He stands across from me. "I should probably get home." Hesitantly, he steps closer and pulls one arm around me. It's such a quick, weird hug I barely have time to react. Then he disappears down the hall.

CHAPTER
Twenty Six

"Just wanted to check in with you, Paige. How are my sweet grandchildren? How are Justin and Allison?"

I pick up the book balanced on my leg and set it on top of a leaning stack of still-warm dresses. "They're all great, Mom. They went to the zoo again without me. I kind of forgot to do laundry for a few weeks and now I have nothing to wear. So it's my laundry day." I try not to grumble as I admit this.

"Well, it's probably for the best. You must be exhausted after all the time you've been spending rebuilding those businesses downtown."

I've spent so much time at the build-up this week I'm getting honest-to-goodness callouses between each of my fingers. I've been put in charge of a building that used to be a Laundromat but resembled a pile of bricks when I first saw it. We've already rebuilt two-thirds of the frame, and as much as I hate to admit it, I *like* working hard. As flat out exhausted as I feel afterward, there's also a sense of accomplishment that I've never gotten before.

"Well, it would have been fun to go, but, like I said, it was kind of a laundry emergency."

Never mind that Mom doesn't ask how *I'm* doing. She only cares about an update on my service project. If she wants to check up on everyone else, she should call them. For the record, I'm not doing well. Not that Mom will ask, or care.

"You should wash your clothes every other day. Every three days at most."

"I know, Mom." I pinch the bridge of my nose.

"Well, I was just calling to check on you."

Check on me? More like make sure I'm still playing by the rules. It's so typical. Nothing is actually about me, is it? Not even the reason I'm in Texas. I'm only here because Dad got sick, and they needed an excuse to get me out of the way. Not because I broke into one measly house.

"I'm good. I miss you guys."

Tsk. The click of her tongue sounds into the phone. "Aw. We miss you too. I wanted to let you know Dad is struggling with his health. His appetite isn't where it should be.. He's going to go see the surgeon tomorrow to make sure everything's looking good still."

Everything slows. "I thought..."

The closest thing to me is the hand towel I used to scrub toothpaste from my pajama shirt before I threw it in the washer. I snatch it up and squeeze my hands around it, the pressure grounding me.

Mom interrupts and I can almost picture her palm facing me, head tilted in patient sympathy. "It's normal to have a few setbacks, even after surgery. We're doing the due diligence, that's all."

"He's okay?" My voice is small and babyish, but all I care about is the fact that I *need* to hear her confirm Dad's alright.

"He's great. He's just having some trouble adjusting, I bet. Don't worry about him, okay?"

I nod vigorously into the phone. "Okay. I love you. Tell Dad I love him too."

"We love you. Talk soon."

I hang up and stretch my hands behind me, the low rumble of the dryer filling my head. Breathing deeply, I suck in air and release it until the anxiety from Mom's scare passes.

I have to run to the bathroom, and it feels like I have the stomach flu times one hundred. Stomachache doesn't cover what's happening to me.

My phone chimes.

Want to walk to the park with me?

Heat courses over my face.

There's no way to excuse it this time. We both know exactly what an invitation to the park means. And oh boy, do I need a distraction. My fingers trip over themselves as I type.

Meet you there in 10.

Only one load of clothes is in the dryer, and they're half-dry at best. I pilfer through them until I find my yellow cotton dress and slip it on. It'll dry in the summer sun, I bet. I use the bathroom, pop a handful of Tylenol, and brush my teeth twice, just to be safe.

I hold my breath and count.

One.

Two.

Three.

Pulling the front door open, I march outside.

By the time I'm at the park in just a few minutes' walk, my dress is dry and warm and stiff. Glancing around, there's no one else. I must have beaten Joey, even with my clothing emergency. My stomach even feels a tiny bit better. Good enough that I can walk without limping. It's already into the afternoon and the sun is blazing hot. I haven't checked the weather, but going on feel alone, I'd say it's one million degrees outside. I touch a plastic slide as I brush past it and it leaves my fingers red and sore like I've stuck them in an oven. No one's bringing kids here today, and for good reason.

My phone chimes, and I pull it from my purse pocket, squinting against the bright glare to read the message.

I'm past the picnic tables.

Turning, I spot a cluster of picnic tables behind the play

structure, and behind those, a woodsy trail. Joey leans against a shaded tree, surrounded by taller oaks, his hands stuffed in the front pockets of his shorts. He lifts his head in recognition.

Feeling suddenly shy, I wave. I suck in my cheeks and force myself forward. He's watching me the entire time, grinning goofily like I've never seen before.

It's half-endearing and half-terrifying. It's never a good idea to go into this kind of thing with high expectations. I learned that the hard way when I kissed Tate Thompson after an entire year of flirting in freshman biology, only to immediately gag on his tuna fish breath and for him to never speak to me again. I never could figure out what I did to scare him off that was worse than reeking of tuna.

Joey meets me the last part of the way, greeting me with a quick hug. Gesturing to the shaded path in front of us, he asks, "Want to go for a walk?"

"I walked over here."

His mouth twitches and I swear he concentrates hard for a second on *not* rolling his eyes at my attempt at humor. "Okay. Another walk then?"

I slip my hand into his. I expected it to be sweaty, at least clammy, but it's sturdy and warm, and it sends a little tingle through my stomach.

Sweat drips down the small of my back as we walk slowly along the trail, dry branches cracking under our feet. I tuck a piece of hair behind my ear, untuck it, then tuck it again.

"I wanted to show you this." In front of us is a grassy field filled with wildflowers of every color. Purple, pink, yellow, orange, blue. And they're literally *wild*. Instead of obeying the rules like flowers you'd see in a garden center, the stems snaggle in between each other. The petals overlap and reach sideways and upward and across until, if you squint, all you'd see is a blur of rainbow pastels among the green-yellow grass.

"This is so pretty."

He stares at the flowers, his lips barely moving. "Yeah. They kind of remind me of you. They're wild and free and they make me happy. Like you."

And I *know* it's cheesy, but it's Joey. He's not just saying some line. His mouth is firm, and his fingers press against mine.

My cheeks puff up with a repressed smile. "Thanks."

He leans back, his eyes suddenly grim. "We don't have to actually kiss, you know. I know we've been joking about it, but you're still getting over Griffin. We don't have to do anything."

I close my eyes and breathe. The air is a perfume of wildflowers, grass, and dirt. Joey's fingers unlace from mine and pull away. A jolt of disappointment crashes through me.

"I'm over him," I say. I'm over him enough to feel like wanting this isn't a betrayal of some kind. Maybe I've felt differently about Griffin for a long time. Maybe our breakup wasn't just because of my leaving.

Whatever it is, I'm not torn between the two of them anymore. Maybe I never really was.

It's Joey. And he's standing in front of me, *not* kissing me.

Tilting my head to the side, I step closer to him. He looks up, his eyes still cautious. If this were the beginning of the summer and we were this close, I'd give him a verbal smackdown and he'd roll his eyes and walk away.

But not now.

Now he watches my face like he'd watch a cat that's sometimes cute, sometimes rabid.

Cautiously. And like he wants to touch me.

I reach for both of his hands. We swing our clasped hands, pulling each other closer as we do.

"I'm glad," he whispers, his nose almost touching mine.

I smirk. "Me too."

My mouth brushes his, and we both hold our breath. Then his head ducks down and our lips press together softly.

As soft as flower petals at first, and then, with a rush in my chest, he guides me backward until I hit something solid. Eyes still closed, the tree bark against my back brings me back for just a second. I blink up into his face, at brown eyes that smile and hair that swoops over his forehead at an angle.

I curve my mouth into a smile as his lips press into mine again and the wildflowers over his shoulder fade into a pastel sea.

CHAPTER

Twenty Seven

I kissed Joey Prince.

And it was a really good kiss. Not one of those first kisses where you instantly wish you could go back to before the kiss, to where it was better wondering what it'd be like to do it.

No.

This was the kind of kiss I felt in my toes, and when I press my fingers to my lips, it feels like it's still there. I pull up his number on my phone and stare at it. My freshly showered hair drips down the polka dot dress I just put on.

I should probably say something. The problem is, there's nothing to say that doesn't sound completely stupid. And texting him first thing the morning for the first time after we kissed could be seen as—what? Needy? Clingy? Crazy?

Probably all those things.

The weird thing is, I never thought I'd want to kiss him. Now I can't stop thinking about doing it again.

I sigh and flop backward across my bed. Maybe if I say something normal and not kiss-related, it won't count against me. I never had this problem when I was dating Griffin. When I wanted to talk to him, I did. When I wanted to ignore him, I hid from his calls. But this feels different. With Griffin, I didn't have to *do* anything because he was always right there.

Joey challenges me. He frustrates me.

I roll off my bed and slip my shoes on. Downstairs is quiet and empty, and a scribbled note on the counter tells me they all went to the grocery store.

And I bet I know where Joey is.

On my bike, I steel my shoulders and make a mental list of conversation topics. We could talk about our group losing to Callie. That's always a good way to get him on a long rant, but not necessarily the vibe I want to put out. I could talk to him about Cam, but even though my nephew adores Joey, it feels a little ridiculous to bring him up every time we meet.

I stroll into Prince Prints with a bunch of subpar ideas and a false cheery smile painted on. It doesn't take me long to spot him. He's in the far corner of the store, near the back where he helped me find stationery one hundred years ago. He's there talking to two girls around our age, and they're staring at him with the intensity of a hawk that's just spotted a baby bunny.

But Joey's *my* baby bunny, and no way am I going to stand here while they flirt with him. I don't feel bad about interrupting, because it's not like they're customers. They're in here for one reason and one reason alone.

Sidling up to Joey, I bump him with my shoulder. "Hey."

He turns, eyes wide and mouth already split into a smile. "Hey. What are you doing here?" The way he asks reminds me of yesterday when his hands touched mine and his kiss made me feel warm all over. Suddenly I wish we were alone.

One girl narrows her eyes at me and nudges her friend. Her bright red lipstick drops into a pouty half-circle when Joey leans his head close to mine and whispers, "This will be quick. Give me a minute."

I step off to the side. A faint smirk slips its way onto my lips.

Joey points to the small selection of cameras the store has on display, then gestures to the rest of the store. The girls laugh, nod, and prance away.

Good riddance.

Once they leave, Joey wraps an arm around my shoulder and squeezes. "I'm really happy to see you."

Oh, wow.

My heart hammers in my chest and my neck prickles. I'm happy too. It's crazy, but I really am. "Me too," I tell him, feeling light. "So what did those girls want? Your phone number?"

He lets out a short laugh and shrugs. "They said they're interested in photography. I told them I don't know much about it." His voice takes on that same bitter edge it sometimes does when he talks about working at the store. Honestly, I don't understand it. We're in high school. None of our job options are amazing, but at least he's making money.

If I hadn't gotten shipped off here, I probably would have found a job somewhere local. Maybe even at the sandwich shop. It's not like I want to make sandwiches for the rest of my life, but a summer of warm bread and extra money doesn't sound awful.

"You really hate it here, huh?"

He grunts.

"It's my dad. He's so set on me making the exact same choices as him: major in finance, attend business school, manage the store. Maybe even help him *franchise*." He spits out the word "franchise" like it's venomous. Rubbing a thumb across his forehead, he sighs. "Knowing that's what he wants for me makes every day here feel like one big trap."

I remember Joey saying he doesn't know what he wants to do with his life. We shouldn't have to have it all figured out yet. College isn't even for two more years—forever away. But even so, out of anyone our age, I would have expected Joey to have some sort of plan.

"Sorry." I have little else to offer than that.

A man sweeps across the store, his short blond hair combed stiffly to the side and a Prince Prints polo tucked tightly into his khaki pants. Joey's eyes follow his movements, and if I didn't already suspect it, the way Joey's mouth tightens lets me know who he is.

"That's your dad?"

Joey nods. "You want to meet him?"

I start to stammer out that that's the complete opposite of what I want, but Joey's already waving his arms, shouting across the busy store. "Dad! A customer." He points his finger above my head, like a tracking beacon for his dad to follow. "A customer's the only way to get his attention," he tells me.

Joey's dad glances up and hurries toward us. He plants his hands on his hips, a cheerful smile brightening his face. If I don't think too hard about it, he looks a lot like Joey, minus the hair and skin color. File that away in things I should most definitely never say out loud. "Hi there. How can I help you today?"

Joey sucks in his cheeks. "Dad. This is Paige. She's staying with the Woods, remember?"

His dad cocks his head, a wave of understanding dawning on him. He looks me over carefully. "Oh yes, of course. How are you, Paige? We love doing business with your sister. She's one of our favorite customers."

I smile and Joey makes a face like he's trying to not breathe. "I'm good. Ally's good too. I stopped by to say hi to Joey."

As soon as his name leaves my mouth, Joey's mouth quirks and his dad's eyes pop. He goes from a friendly sales pitch to a somber dismissal in one smooth move. "Well, we appreciate you stopping by. We'll see you later. And be sure to say hello to your sister."

I hesitate and my eyes rove to Joey, hoping he'll give me some sort of cue. He stares at the floor. "Sure. I'll do that."

Joey's dad doesn't move. He nods at me, his jaw set. "Maybe my Joey will learn something about hard work from your family, since he refuses to do anything around here."

"Okay, Dad. She gets it. I'm worthless." Joey's voice takes on a gruffness I never would have expected from him. Especially toward his own dad.

Mr. Prince waves a hand impatiently. "Her sister owns a photography business. She's an entrepreneur. That's more than you can say, son."

What a weird thing to say to a sixteen-year-old boy. The energy between Joey and his dad sizzles, leaving me feeling like I'm stuck in a lightning storm. Part of me wishes I could back out of the store slowly, leaving Joey on his own. But that would obviously make me a crappy *whatever* I am to him, so I stand my ground.

Carefully, I say, "Joey would make an excellent teacher someday. He's great with kids and he's amazing at getting people to listen to him.." It comes to me in a flash, but it's true. Joey would be great at a lot of things. Why doesn't his dad see that?

His dad looks twice at me. He nods and appears to consider. "It'd be nice to see him do something he actually cares about."

Ouch.

Joey scowls but he grabs my hand tightly. "I'm taking a break." He drags me from the store, his dad's eyes on us the entire time.

Once we're outside, I reach for his arm. "Joey, wait. Are you okay?"

He still won't look at me, either from embarrassment or anger. Maybe a little of both. I can't blame him. Parents can be harsh.

"I'm fine," he says, his voice shaky. His eyes meet mine, and I see he's not.

I pull him along the sidewalk until we reach the bakery. I could find it blindfolded by the smell alone. It's bread and sugar and yeast and warmth all rolled into one tiny storefront. My mouth waters the second we walk inside and the full power of the scent hits me. Joey inhales and sighs, a hint of relaxation wafting over him.

"I knew I liked you for a reason," he says, teasing as I stare open-mouthed at the rows and rows of baked goods.

I jab him in the side with a sharp elbow and point to a row of chocolate éclairs. "Pretty sure I could eat ten of those."

A bright voice calls from behind the counter. "Not even *I* can do that. But you're more than welcome to try." The lady I once saw handing Joey a paper bag of donuts straightens her flour-dusted apron and flashes a pleased smile. To Joey she says, "I'll throw in a free donut since you brought a new customer."

His smile spreads slowly. At the sight of it, dimples and all, my heart gallops and my fingers tingle in his hand that's tangled with mine.

He's *so* cute.

Lips quirked in my direction, he shrugs. "Thanks, May. I guess we'll take ten eclairs and one donut."

I whip my head toward him, eyes wide. "No! I was *joking*."

He and the baker exchange an amused glance. "I'm pretty sure you weren't. Plus, who says they're all for you? I'm pretty good at eating pastries, too, you know."

Before I can further protest, he pulls a leather wallet from his back pocket and hands over a card. May winks at me as she bags up our goodies. She even adds an extra donut, sending Joey into a spiral of laughter.

We opt to eat outside, mostly because I'm scared of the looks the other customers will give us when we unpack our outrageous meal for two. And selfishly because being alone with Joey is my new guilty pleasure.

Seated across from each other at a tiny iron table in the warm morning sun, everything feels cozy and easy. I hope Joey forgets about his dad and the whole store fiasco. He deserves better than that.

"I'm glad you came by this morning," he says through a mouthful of éclair, cream bursting out one of the sides.

Leaning forward, I let out a happy sigh. "Me too. But sorry for making things awkward with your dad. I shouldn't have said anything."

"No. I'm glad you did. And it's cool what you said about me being a teacher. I'd probably like doing something like that."

"I bet you would." I lean across the table. "And your dad is wrong. About you not caring. Just because you don't want to do the same thing as him, it doesn't mean you're some worthless employee. You're allowed to be different from him."

Joey chews thoughtfully. He picks up a napkin and wipes melted chocolate from his fingertips. "I don't know how to tell him I hate the idea of growing up into a version of him. It seems too harsh to say out loud. So, I just..." He shrugs. "I get all passive aggressive. Which is probably worse."

I bite into another warm éclair to hide my smirk. "Get it over with and tell him. I bet it will be better for your relationship in the long run. Maybe if you tell him it's only the store you hate, it will feel like a win."

Joey points an éclair at me. "You don't know my dad."

"He reminds me of my mom." Mom's not as outspoken as Joey's dad was back at Prince Prints, but she's just as disappointed in me.

Joey taps his éclair against mine. "To disappointed parents."

I sit up taller. "To disappointed parents."

CHAPTER
Twenty Eight

Ding.

Joey looks up from the register. I smile at him and continue pretending to leaf through the stationery. His dad is out of town and reluctantly left Joey in charge. Not that Joey is thrilled about that.

But it's kind of fun to watch him work. And every few minutes I catch him sneaking glances at me. I volunteered to keep him company because Ally had no shoots today and took the kids to a play date across town, leaving me free to follow Joey around the store.

Ding.

Ding.

Ding.

My text notification goes off in rapid succession, which can only mean one thing. Joey raises an eyebrow and leans forward, elbow pressed against the laminate top of the counter. "Aren't you going to look at all of those messages?"

Gritting my teeth, I pull out my phone. Sure enough, my entire screen is swallowed in message notifications from my family group thread. I hold my breath and scroll back, starting from the beginning.

Ted: *Saw Griffin today and he said you broke up with him again. Harsh.*

I tip my head back, dizzy. I could kill him for starting a

gossip chain when I thought something was seriously wrong with Dad.

Peter: *What he actually said is that you mutually broke up, but we read between the lines.*

Ted: *And the tears.*

Mom: *I hope you're being kind to him, Paige. That boy really cares about you.*

Dad: *How do I opt-out of these messages?*

Smoothing my pale pink skirt, I sit on the stool next to Joey and begin to type quickly into my phone's keyboard.

Peter and Ted, stay out of my business! Griffin is still my friend, and I'm not dating....

I start to type the word "anyone" right as a shadow eclipses my phone. I press backspace, blanking out everything I've typed. Hugging my phone to my chest, I clear my throat.

"Are you spying on me?"

Joey nods, nonplussed. "Kind of. Are you talking to your family about me?"

I sigh, dropping my phone to my lap. Rubbing a thumb along my temple, I say, "I'm trying to curb the family gossip. What should I tell them?"

"Hmm." He slides a finger along his jawline, pretending to be in deep thought. "Start by telling them how responsible I am, and end by telling them I'm ruggedly handsome."

Snorting, I clap a hand over my mouth. "Ruggedly handsome? What does that even mean?"

He stops rubbing his chin. "I don't know. I read it somewhere."

Giggling, I pretend to type it in my phone until his head pops over my shoulder again. "You're not really saying that, are you?"

"Yeah, why?"

Throwing his hands up, he groans. "Now your family will think I'm dumb."

I wave my phone in his face, my text box blank. "I didn't

send anything. And you're not dumb. You're *ruggedly handsome*." I pat his face as he scowls.

Ding.

Ding.

More incoming messages mean my brothers have figured out a new angle to torture me. I look at my phone and read quickly until my breathing turns into one big long groan.

Gavin: *Paige, you don't need to worry about dating right now. Focus on being young.*

I'd send him a big eye roll emoji if I could.

Ted: *Yeah, Gavin. Kids these days, am I right?*

Allison: *Leave Paige alone. And leave Griffin alone, too.*

Mom responds with a smiley face. Not directed toward me, obviously.

Hands shaking, I back away from the phone. I need to cool off before replying.

"You're not going to respond? You just got like, a lot of messages." Joey nods toward my phone.

"My siblings are just as bad as my parents sometimes. It's like having three sets of parents instead of one. You don't know how lucky you are."

Joey fiddles with the buttons on the cash register, poking them one by one with his pointer finger. "I used to wish I had an older brother. Someone cooler than me to help with stuff." He says it shyly, his head ducked.

I click my tongue. "Trust me on this one. You're better off. I mean, sure, my brothers and my sister have always been there for me, but that's the thing. They're *always there*."

"Yeah. I can see how that would get old."

"It does. But they can be cool sometimes. Like Allison letting me stay with her this summer and not being a control freak about it. She's actually given me a lot of space."

"A lot of time with me, I think you mean."

My cheeks warm. "That too."

I wiggle the phone in front of his face. "So what should I say? Are you ruggedly handsome?"

He rolls his eyes. "If you can't come up with anything better, it's probably best not to say anything."

I nudge him with my elbow. For the split second I'm close to him, I breathe in the scent of soap and something else. Maybe cookies. Covering the screen with a cupped palm, I turn away and type.

Joey doesn't lean over me this time. Instead he pokes at the buttons on the cash register with a blank-faced determination, tallying up the total for the day. When I'm done, I slide him my phone, open to the message I've just sent.

Paige: *I'm kind of hanging out with someone else this summer. He's nephew-approved, and he bakes me cookies.*

Joey's mouth twitches, darting up at the corners, and his eyes zero in on mine. I slip my hand in his, warm and sure in the moment.

CHAPTER
Twenty Nine

A blur of red, orange, and yellow whirs past my head. Against my better judgment, I dive after it. Sharp edges of concrete collide with my legs and arms as I tumble to the ground, scraping several inches past where the stack of wires lands.

Callie moves past me. "You're okay, Paige. Shake it off. Shake it off."

Easier said than done. Out of the corner of my eye, I see Joey watching me from across the cul-de-sac. He won't embarrass me by coming over to help me up, but my cheeks still sting from my lack of athletic ability so prominently on display.

Ben grimaces. "Sorry. That was my bad! I thought you'd catch them if I tossed them right to you."

Oh well. I'm good at other things. Like, according to my sister, being brave and adventurous.

After Joey and Callie take turns chewing Ben out, we all meet for bottles of cold water and bananas that someone's mom dropped off. Because of everyone's misaligned schedules, we're working late into the afternoon and it's at least twice as hot as in the morning. Which means I'm sweating twice as much.

I've always secretly hated bananas, but I stuff the entire thing in my mouth and chew until it's squishy enough to swallow.

Jen watches in horror. "That's disgusting."

I shrug, smiling through cheeks stuffed with banana. Gulping, I say, "This is my skill. Maybe it's not as impressive as some talents, but..."

"But nothing." Joey's voice interrupts us, and I twirl to find him stifling a laugh. "Your banana eating skill is one of my favorite things about you.

I hand him a banana and a water bottle. "Thank you. I like to think it's part of why my team won." I may not play a big part in our winning streak, but I'm still entitled to bragging rights.

Joey's mouth turns downward into an exaggerated pout. He puts a hand to his chest like I've wounded him. "Hey. No gloating. I was sticking up for you."

"You're right. Sorry. We should have at least tied after all the work you did today." I put an arm around his waist.

Jen wrinkles her nose and Callie fake coughs into the crook of her elbow. Joey smiles down at me and wraps an arm around me, too. Our friends stare at us.

Callie points. "Aw. Look how cute they are." I laugh at the confused look on Jen's face. Callie notices too and says, "What? You don't think they make a cute couple?"

Jen swivels her eyes between Joey and me. "Why did no one tell me about this?"

Callie shakes her head. "I did."

Jen frowns. "I thought you were joking."

Joey's arm drops from my shoulders as he reaches forward to touch Jen's arm. "Wait. Are you mad?"

She scrunches up her face. "I mean, yeah. A little. I'm happy y'all finally got together, but it sucks no one even thought to tell me."

Callie mutters, "Except I *did*."

Jen huffs. "I told you that doesn't count because it was said in passing and I completely thought it was a joke."

I gesture to Jen. "I'm really sorry you're upset. We only told Callie because she wouldn't stop asking. It kind of just happened, so it's not like anyone else knows."

Jen shrugs. "Yeah. That's fine. I get it." Callie grimaces

behind Jen's back. Joey and I stand beside each other, careful not to touch. Jen rubs her head between her palms. "Okay. Sorry. It's honestly not a big deal. I'm happy for you." She smiles at Joey and me but avoids Callie's eyes.

Joey runs his fingers through his bangs. "Paige and I are headed over to her sister's house, so I guess we'll see y'all later." Still aware of the girls watching us, we walk with some space between us.

In the car, I finally exhale. "That was awkward."

He nods. "Yeah. Jen's kind of sensitive like that. I forgot to say anything, I guess..." Scratching at his arm, he pauses and clears his throat.

I blink. Am I supposed to say something else? Was *I* supposed to tell Jen? I thought since they've been friends so much longer, everyone would find out organically. It never occurred to me that we had to make an announcement about the fact we kissed.

Shifting my eyes, I watch Joey as he stares straight ahead. "What?"

He shifts a little in his seat, one hand on the steering wheel while the other hovers in the air. "It's just—well, what are we?"

I suck in a breath. *Oh.* We've barely started this—whatever it is. Why do we have to give it a name? Forcing out a shaky laugh, I say, "We're friends. And we've kissed. Why does it have to be anything else?"

One of his eyebrows slowly propels upward. "So, you think we're friends with benefits or something?" His tone is one octave away from accusing, and I hate it. It makes my mouth taste sour.

I shake my head slowly. I did not wake up today prepared for this conversation. "Well, you're not my boyfriend. We've only kissed a few times. What do you expect?"

His eyes go wide and his shoulders stiffen. He starts the car and drives, saying nothing else. The inside of the car is sticky with silence.

All my annoyance is completely zapped. I lost it, and now

everything is heavy and wrong. Quietly, I say, "I'm sorry. I don't think we're friends with benefits. But I also don't know what we are yet. The title doesn't matter that much to me."

A muscle in his jaw twitches as he mulls over my apology. "I'm sorry too." Rubbing a palm over the steering wheel, he looks over at me. "Does that mean you're still dating Griffin, though?"

"I'm *not* dating Griffin. I already told you that." I lean closer. "I'm only dating you. But I want to take things slow. I'm not good at that normally, but it's what I need right now." The banana I stuffed in my face a few minutes ago sloshes around in my stomach.

"I'm good with that. As long as you're not being shady."

Is he serious? "Shady? Is that what you think of me?"

Breaking into a smile, he laughs, eyes big. "I'm just joking!"

Not funny. Especially considering no one in my family trusts me anymore. I grumble, "I don't think it's funny."

We stop in front of Allison's house. He turns in his seat to face me and his hand reaches for mine. "It's funny because you're the opposite of shady. I was trying to make you laugh during an awkward situation, but obviously it backfired."

I smirk. "It definitely backfired. But I might be a little sensitive."

Or a lot.

But I tuck my hair behind my ear, smile, and lace my fingers with his. "So, we're good?"

"Of course we are. As long as we're clear that I like you. And I'm *only* dating you. And I'm going to keep coming up with excuses to see you every day, as long as you're okay with that."

A fluttering in my chest answers before I can ask myself if it all feels like too much. I angle my head and press my lips to his. He smiles against my mouth.

"I'm very okay with it."

We're fine. So I don't understand why, when I get out of the car, my stomach gurgles like I'm nervous or hungry when I'm neither.

I also don't understand why, when I take a step forward, my legs wobble and my skin flushes hot and then cold. Suddenly my world tilts sideways, and I blink my eyes open to see an up-close and personal view of blades of grass. Joey's voice hovers somewhere over my head, bodyless and wrong sounding. Ally screams—or maybe it's Mom. I drop my head back down onto the grass pillow, letting my eyes close all the way.

CHAPTER THIRTY

I have a dream that I'm visiting Dad in the hospital. He's got a zillion wires taped to his body, and he's skeletal, just bones and skin. But when I open my heavy eyes, it's me lying in the hospital, not Dad.

And then I remember that Ally drove me here last night after I passed out on her front lawn. The doctor asked me lots of questions about my symptoms and I tried to answer them as best as I could before falling asleep. I think they put pain medication in the IV sticking out of my right arm. Whatever it is, it's making everything blur at the edges and my tongue feel like a heavy slug living in my mouth.

"Are you awake, Paige?"

A woman I swear I've never seen before smiles down at me. Judging by the clipboard she holds and the scrubs she's wearing, she's my doctor. Her nametag reads *Doctor Abebe*.

I nod and scoot myself up onto an elbow.

"Great," she says, smile lines crinkling into her cheeks. "We're going to let you go home later today. Your sister just left, but she should be back soon. We've done some blood work based on samples we got last night, and we couldn't find anything wrong except for a slightly lowered iron count and an elevated white blood count. Not enough to be too concerned. But given your family history, we've scheduled you for a colonoscopy next week, just to be sure."

My brain buzzes. I open my mouth, but it's heavy and dry inside. "So," I creak, "I'm probably fine?"

She frowns and taps a pen on her clipboard. "Nothing showed up during our initial tests, but the colonoscopy will give us a much clearer picture. Are you feeling any better?"

I bob my head so quickly it nearly snaps off my neck. "I feel a ton better. I think I was just tired. Maybe I had a 24-hour flu or something."

The doctor opens and closes her mouth and then smiles flawlessly again. "Maybe so. We'll get you checked out of here in the next few hours and then you can go home and rest."

I smile at her out of the room and then collapse onto my pancake-flat pillow. First step: get out of here. Second: do whatever it takes to avoid that colonoscopy. If I have to will myself into good health, so be it. Because I'm too young. Because I'm scared. Because I don't want to be sick, and so I won't be.

The door opens and my heart hammers in my chest. Joey's face spreads into a slow, wary grin. Directly behind him is Jen, followed by Callie. And behind them is a grandmotherly nurse carrying a domed plate of food on a plastic tray. "Hungry for lunch?" she calls as she sets the tray on top of a rolling cart next to my bed.

I thank her and turn to my friends. "This is embarrassing," I tell them, peeking under the lid at a bowl of limp macaroni and cheese and a cup of applesauce.

Callie cocks an eyebrow. "Which part? Us or the food?"

I laugh. "Neither. I meant *me*. Only I could pass out and land myself in the hospital over *nothing*." I emphasize the word to make sure they understand how perfectly fine I am right now. Not. Sick.

They exchange a funny look, and I pick up my plastic fork and take a huge bite of macaroni to prove it to them.

"I don't think I'd call this nothing," Joey says, voice soft. He's looking at me like I'm something breakable, like he doesn't want to get too close or I might pass out again. Like my worst nightmare come to life. I don't want to be the vulnerable one.

I swallow. "I know. Sorry you had to see that. I bet it was scary. But I really am better now. The doctor said it could have just been a weird flu thing."

"Okay..." His throat bobs, but he steps a little closer to my bed. "Do you need anything?"

A. k. a. he needs an excuse to escape. I twist my lips like I'm thinking really hard. "I heard they have pudding here somewhere, but they obviously didn't bring me any. Think you can find it?"

He nods fervently. "Yeah, definitely."

Callie skips after him, shooting me a thumbs up. "I'll help you look, Joey."

Jen stays behind, twisting her hands behind her back.

After they close the door, I look at her. "So what's up?"

Jen makes a low humming noise. "I feel so bad about the way I acted. I was just surprised to find out about you and Joey." She looks away.

Oh.

I take another bite loaded with fluorescent orange noodles. "I'm really sorry about not telling you. I wasn't sure it was my place, since Joey and Callie have known you for a lot longer. I should have said something, though." I brush unruly hair from my face.

"No, you don't have to apologize. I don't want it to be awkward, you know?" Her voice is tight. It oozes with awkwardness.

"Awkward?" I nibble a tiny bite of cheesy noodles, slurping the salty flavor off the edge of my fork.

She sighs into her hands. "Yeah, I mean, I'm sure Callie told you, but I used to have a crush on Joey." Before I can react, Jen rushes on. "Butitwasalongtimeago."

I twirl the plastic fork along the sides of the bowl. "So you don't like him that way anymore?"

"I don't like him like that," she confirms.

"You swear you'd tell me if you did?"

There's a pause where I think she's about to cry or something. I grit my teeth. What do I do?

Her voice is light. "I'm so over that crush, I promise. I'd tell you if I wasn't. Not sure I'd tell Callie though, because she has such a big mouth." We both laugh. "So, we're good? I already talked to Joey, and he was so dumb about the whole thing. I think he wanted to get the conversation over the second it started."

I smile. "We're good. I'm glad you told me."

"Me too. By the way—you should have seen Joey last night. He was *so* freaked out about you being sick. He likes you so much. I've never seen him this into a girl before."

"You don't think all this will scare him away?"

She shakes her head. "What? No. He's obsessed with you. He was panicking the entire way to the hospital that you'd hate him because of some conversation you had right before you passed out. If anything, he's scared of losing you."

Oh no.

"I'll talk to him." The promise is both for her and me.

When Callie and Joey come back, each of them carrying an armful of vanilla and chocolate pudding cups, Callie announces that she and Jen have somewhere to be. Jen winks and I pretend to believe them.

Joey hands me a plastic spoon and unwraps one for himself. He scoots a metal chair right next to my bed, and I sit up and open a chocolate pudding. "We need to talk," I say when I finish it, licking the last of my pudding from the underside of the spoon.

On the table near my bed, my phone vibrates. I'm sure it's Mom. Ally texted that she's been calling nonstop ever since I checked in. I'll have to call her back eventually, but not right now.

Joey's eyes go big. "We do?"

"It's nothing bad. I want to apologize for scaring you last night. It had nothing to do with me being stressed about our conversation. I like you. A lot. This being sick thing is just a freak accident." I offer him my most convincing, wide-eyed-innocent smile.

"Promise?" His jaw relaxes as he reaches over and threads his fingers through mine.

I squeeze his hand. "I promise. I'm definitely okay now."

CHAPTER
Thirty One

The first thing I do once I'm busted out of the hospital is lie on the couch with Cam snuggled next to me. He strokes my arm over and over again, asking if I'm 'kay. Which I am. I'll always be okay around my nephews—they're the best.

The next thing I do is a thousand times less fun. I return Mom's phone calls. She and Dad insist on a video call so they can see for themselves that I'm not near death. I check myself out in my phone camera and give my cheeks a quick pinch, just in case they notice that I *am* a little paler than normal.

I call Mom's number, but Dad answers. "Paige?" he says in a breathy voice. And because I'm already looking for it, I see how wan his face looks. Maybe it's the lighting.

I flash him a smile. "Hi Daddy. I'm calling to prove that I'm healthy. Is Mom there?"

His eyes circle every inch of my face, but apparently, he doesn't find anything to worry about because he nods and calls my mom over. She moves way too close to the screen and takes up the entire thing. "Paige, baby, how are you feeling? You scared us, you know. I thought Allison was playing some bad practical joke when she told us she'd just driven you to the hospital."

"It was a weird fluke. The doctor said nothing came up on the tests."

Dad reappears over her shoulder. "Ally said you have a

colonoscopy scheduled for next week. Let me know if you need any tips since I'm something of an expert."

I pity-smile for him. We say *I love yous* and Mom makes me swear to update her again tomorrow.

I hang up, suck in some much-needed air, and call Griffin. For the first time in forever, he doesn't answer, so I leave a rare voicemail and make sure to sound super upbeat in case Mom asks him if he's heard from me.

And then, finally, I text Joey. I need some fun in my life.

I RUN MY HANDS OVER THE CLOUDED SCREEN IN FRONT OF ME. Leaning back onto the plastic padded seat attached to the game, I reach for the handlebars. They're tacky and cold under my grip. It's been three days since I was released, and this is the first time I've been able to convince everyone that I'm truly *fine*. My knees are a bit wobbly, my stomach gurgles loudly, but I'm not admitting that to anyone and thankfully, no one seems too concerned anymore.

The arcade was *not exactly* what I had in mind when I envisioned all the fun I'd have outside of the hospital. But being with Joey is, so I don't care.

Joey raises an eyebrow. "You ready?"

I squeeze the handlebars. "Go!"

I twist my body and stare at the graphic of a motorcycle on the screen in front of me. Joey's motorcycle zips past mine. Out of the corner of my eye, I catch the ghost of a triumphant smile.

Oh no. He's not going to win this easily.

I squeeze down on the gas pedal on the handlebars and ram my body sideways. The corresponding motorcycle on the lit screen turns and revs sharply. I inch closer to Joey's bike. At the last second, I pull into the handlebar until my fingers ache.

Victory. My motorcycle passes his just as they both round the finish line, mine barely but firmly in first place.

Joey gasps. "What just happened?!"

I giggle, lightheaded. "What happened," I say, shifting to face him, "is I beat you fair and square."

His eyes flash, and without warning, he dismounts from his motorcycle and moves toward me. His arms slide around my waist, lifting me up and onto the ground. He tilts his mouth close to my ear, whispering, "I've never been more attracted to you."

"Then congratulations," I say, my cheeks warming. I pretend to push him away. "You're officially the world's biggest nerd."

Hands held up in defeat, he grins. "I'm good with that."

"So..." I lean back against the motorcycle. "We've played most of the games. What else should we do?"

Joey smirks. "I have another game."

He whips his phone from his pocket and holds it up too close to his face. Standing on my toes, I attempt to peer over his shoulder at the screen. "What are you looking at?"

"It's part of the game, and therefore a secret." He tucks the phone flat against his chest.

"I'm not so sure about this game."

"Trust me. You'll love it."

Whenever someone asks you to trust them like this, it never turns out how you hope. Dread pulls at me as Joey's eyes scan his phone and a line forms between his eyebrows.

"Maybe we better race again. It sounds safer than whatever you have in mind."

He laughs, throwing his head back. "I have some questions for you."

I point to his phone. "You have questions on there? Since when?"

His mouth quirks into a funny shape, all hesitation and something else. "It doesn't matter. Are you going to provide answers?"

This seems suspicious. I don't have a list of questions for Joey on my phone. I don't have a list of questions for anyone—

anywhere. I'd be hard-pressed to think up questions even if I met Beyonce in this arcade right here, right now. Has he been jotting down questions every time we talk?

"Okaaaay. Do *I* get to ask you questions, too?"

Joey nods. "Of course. I always play fair."

Is there anything I'd even ask him? And what could he want to ask me? I haven't kept any secrets, but maybe he has. Maybe this is all leading up to him telling me something I don't know about him. Who knows, maybe this is an elaborate way to say he wants to stop hanging out, stop this. Whatever *this* is.

Even though my gut clenches, I let my arms swing casually by my sides. "Okay. Let's do it."

He leans his back against the motorcycle so we're facing each other just a few feet apart. "Cool. First question—why did you hate me so much when we first met?"

My eyes widen. *Wow.* I was hoping for funny questions about my favorite ice cream flavor, not hard-hitting stuff I don't even have the answer to. I chew on the inside of my cheek. The not-so-easy to say answer is this: I hated everyone when I got to Old Oak. I was miserable with myself, and Joey was one more thing in the way of going home. Now I'm ashamed of that girl. That might mean I've actually changed, just like Mom wanted. Or it might just mean that I've fallen hard for Joey Prince, despite our differences. "Can I pass?"

"No way. Not unless I get a pass, too."

I nod. "You get one."

Joey ducks his head. He sighs loudly. "Okay. Next question— what is the weirdest thing you have in your purse?" He points to the purse perpetually slung at my side, eyes wide as if this question is *very* serious.

"I always have a book. That's not weird, though."

Joey's eyebrow cocks. "I've noticed that, actually. They always have people kissing on the cover."

"So? What's wrong with that?"

He shrugs. "Nothing."

I wrinkle my nose. My turn, I guess. I toss my ponytail over one shoulder and smile carefully, sucking in a steadying breath. "Okay. What makes you think I hated you?"

"I liked you right away. Since the first time we talked. So I watched you a lot, and I could tell you didn't like me. At all."

I rear back, unable to hide my shock. "What?"

He nods. "Yeah. You were cute and funny. I mean, I know you didn't like me right away, but I felt like..." Joey's brows meet. "Why are you staring at me like that?"

I press my lips together. I'm staring because I'm sure Joey and I mutually hated each other from the beginning. There's no way I'd ever have guessed he liked me, especially that first day. "You called me a liar and tried interrogating me!" The memory of the interaction still irritates me when I think of it. And then it makes me laugh a little.

"I was just doing my job. And I don't think I called you a liar..."

"Ugh. You made me so mad. I thought you were cute too, but you're right—I kind of didn't like you." His mouth twists, and I step closer to squeeze his hand. "Sorry. If it makes you feel better, I don't hate you now."

He squeezes my hand back. "Well, I was hoping, but it's good to hear you say it."

My eyes find his lips, only inches away from mine. My heartbeat thuds in my ears. From across the room, a chorus of voices boos as a group of tween boys dressed in baseball uniforms watch their friend lose at one of the games. Stepping back, I tug on his hand. "Let's go somewhere else."

In the car, I stretch my legs over his lap, taking up the entire front seat. He leans forward, fingers gently resting on my ankles. "I don't hate you," I say again. The words are a hoarse whisper in the privacy of his car.

His hair falls out of place, covering his eyes completely. I scoot closer and brush it back. My fingers skip downward to trace the edges of his jaw. He stays silent, watching me in that careful way of his. Something flutters in my chest, dipping into my stomach and stretching to my throat, where it sticks.

"I like you, Joey."

His lips curve and his arms reach for me. I half-crawl to him and settle on his lap. His hands circle my waist, and I dip my head to his.

Mouth on mine, he whispers against my lips, "I like you, Paige."

I breathe into him, inhaling everything about him. "Like" isn't enough of a word, but there's time left to say so. For now, I pull myself closer.

CHAPTER
THIRTY TWO

Joey walks me up the driveway and kisses me once more, his forehead resting against mine. We just spent three hours together, but it still feels too soon to say goodbye.

Ally's silhouette looms in the crack of the slightly open door. Her lingering is awkward, but maybe she's spying for Mom. Or at least pretending to so she can say she didn't leave me completely unsupervised with a boy.

When Joey's car disappears down the street, I pull the door open the rest of the way, hands on my hips to confront Allison.

She's not smiling, but she's not frowning either. Her face is pinched and red, and for once, her hair is not perfect. It's frizzy and piled on top of her head in a messy half-hearted knot.

"Ally?" My voice sounds strange in the late evening air. Like it's out of place and I'm just now noticing how badly it doesn't fit in.

She waves her arms for me to come inside. Shutting the door behind us, she staggers against it, her arms hugging her middle protectively.

"What's wrong?" Even as the words choke from my mouth, I know.

"It's Dad. He's dying."

Dying. She gasps the last word before sliding to the ground and rolling into a ball, wracked with sobs.

Carefully, I tip-toe to her and sit on the floor with my back against the door.

Fat, silent tears slide down my cheeks, onto my shirt.

My dad.

Our dad.

Dying.

My arms circle my knees as I hiccup through my sobs. Allison's hand reaches for mine, and we stay that way for an undetermined amount of time. Maybe a minute, maybe hours. Because grief doesn't run on clocks; grief is a measure all its own.

"What happened?" My voice is raspy. My throat is so dry I'm surprised I'm able to form words.

Allison straightens, crossing her ankles delicately in front of her. She sucks in a huge breath. "Infection, I guess. He wasn't feeling well, so he went back to see the surgeon. It was supposed to be a check-up, but they kept him overnight to watch him. Things got worse from there, and they weren't able to catch it quickly enough. Most of the damage was already done, and the infection was in his bloodstream before Dad even went in for the appointment."

Chin wobbling, I stare at my sister.

She squeezes my hand. "They don't think he'll hang on for much longer."

"So we're going home to see him?"

She pushes herself to her feet. "Justin's packing upstairs with the kids. Our flight's in six hours, at midnight. So pack quickly and meet us down here at nine-thirty, okay?"

I stand on unsteady legs. My heart thuds dully in my chest. Why does it feel like my entire world is collapsing when earlier today I was happier than I've felt all year?

I THROW THINGS INTO MY SUITCASE WITHOUT EVEN LOOKING. For all I know, I could pack three skirts and no shirts. I count out enough clean underwear and grab my blow dryer, cord tangled around it. I sit on the edge of my bed, head in my hands, eyes swollen and nose still runny.

My phone sits on the floor where I dropped it as soon as I walked into my room and pressed the door shut behind me. The screen lights up once, twice.

Half-crawling toward it, I read the messages. One from Mom in a group text updating us on Dad.

No change. Still sleeping and very unstable.

A tremor passes through me. This can't be real. People don't just die suddenly like this. Dad was fine. He was great. I was there taking care of him only a week ago. The doctors must be wrong. Mom's overreacting again, being overprotective as usual. And then another part of me curls up in terror. Will I die too?

I force that part of me back.

We'll probably fly all the way home and Dad will be awake, rolling his eyes behind Mom's back as she tells us how "near-death" he is.

The second text is from Joey.

Can I see you tomorrow?

Tomorrow I'll be in Seattle, sleeping in my own bed. Tomorrow I'll be with my dad.

Rage burns bright, blurring my line of sight as I type back.

How about tonight?

Almost immediately, he responds with a question mark.

I'll meet you outside in five minutes. I toss my phone onto the bed without waiting to see his answer. Wiping my eyes, I glide down the stairs and out the front door.

☙

AFTER HE PICKS ME UP, I LET JOEY DRIVE IN SILENCE UNTIL WE park. In the downtown parking lot Joey drums his fingers on the middle console in the darkened car. "I don't think this is a very good idea."

I turn steely eyes on him, my chin pointed. "Why?"

He shakes his head slowly. "Are you feeling sick again?"

I glare in answer.

"You seem upset. Do you want to talk and get ice cream? We can drive around for a while."

Ice cream isn't going to fix this. And talking is the last thing I want. I need to do something. Anything but sit around and *feel*.

I pull the door handle and step out of the car. A few seconds later, Joey joins me. "Let's not do this, Paige." His voice comes from behind me while I forge on ahead, toward the construction site.

From my bag I pull a new bottle of spray paint, one I bought in a moment of weakness last week. I pop off the lid and shake it. I bounce with the motion, letting my entire body help me in the task. The more I move, the better.

"Paige—"

I slip an arm around his waist and stand on my toes. Reaching up to his cheek, I press my lips against his warm skin. He sighs, leaning into me.

Then I step back and spray. Angry midnight black paint shoots out of the nozzle, covering the brick wall to the side of us. I swoop letters across the red, spelling out the first thing that comes to mind. *SHIT.*

It's all gone to shit. My entire world.

"Hey, stop! What are you doing?" Joey steps in front of me, almost getting himself sprayed with paint in the process. I turn the can downward at the last second and a few specks land on his sneakers, peppering the white laces.

I smirk. "Just having fun, remember?" Extending the can to him, I raise an eyebrow, adrenaline coursing through me. "Help me."

His eyes grow even wider. "What's wrong with you? You know this wall connects to my parents' store, right? And the rest of it we've been working on all summer. So have our friends."

Gazing at the wall, I see he's right. It's technically also the backside of Prince Prints, but whatever I paint will be cleaned up whenever we finish building up the other shops. So someone will have to scrub the wall a little. Big deal.

"It's not gonna be permanent. It's only a little paint, Joey."

He's no fun when he's like this. This serious version of him that annoyed the crap out of me when I first got here. The rush I felt drains away. With a last burst of fury, I send a spray of thick paint over the front door of the Laundromat, sending dripping black paint over the shiny new doorframe.

"Paige!" His voice contorts with confusion and sadness. "You worked so hard on that."

The words slice through me. They urge me to *stop* and *think* and *feel*. The look on his face tells me he doesn't understand. No one understands. And as much as I stop and think and feel, it will never be right. I hate it.

"You suck. You know that, right?" I aim the spray paint at him, finger hovering over the nozzle. I'm not really going to do it, but he doesn't know that.

He shakes his head like I'm some lunatic he doesn't even know.

Maybe I am.

"Okay. Can you tell me what's going on? Earlier today was so great. And now..."

He blinks at me. "I have no idea what's happening right now."

I line my mouth with a callous smile, eyes like daggers pointed at Joey. I don't know anything either. I just want to act without all the questions. I don't want someone checking up on my every move. Right now, I don't want anything. "I want you to go away. You're boring right now."

His head wobbles backward, as if he's been hit by an invisible weapon. "What?"

I wave the paint can around wildly in the air, screaming, "Go away! Go!"

On the outside I'm raving wild, fueled by anger. Inside, I'm a shell. So empty, nothing even hurts.

I'm just a girl manically splashing paint on walls. Screaming at a guy she actually likes. Desperately trying to ignore the fact that she might never see her dad again. And all of it—every last detail—is my fault.

Joey narrows his eyes with a look of hurt that speaks more than any words could. Palms stretched out in front of him, he takes a step backward. Then another. And another.

He's leaving me. He turns and walks the rest of the way across the parking lot to his car and slowly escapes my line of sight.

Too wild, too sick, too young. I'm too much to deal with, even for him.

Where anger was, tears spring up, and I double over in instant agony.

But it's just me. Alone.

CHAPTER
Thirty Three

Poke, poke, poke.

Cam's finger jabs into my side as he bounces up and down in his seat.

"Look out the window! Look!"

I turn my head and gaze at the moonlight encasing the plane. We're inside a cloud right now. The thought should make me smile. Or feel something other than the dull throbbing in my head.

"Wow, Cammy. So cool." I turn away from the window and cross my arms tight across my chest.

Sitting by Cam and entertaining him on the flight is my way of trying to apologize for sneaking out and having to call a horrified Allison for a ride home so we wouldn't miss our plane.

If it weren't for the reason we're flying home, I'm sure she'd be shooting me dirty glances and working on a real good come-to-Jesus speech this very second. But no one's thinking about punishments. We're all crossing our fingers and toes that Dad's still hanging on by the time we get there. So we can say goodbye.

The lump in my throat blocks me from breathing correctly. Every breath is heavy and wrong and hard. It's impossible to sit here and do *nothing*. Mom is in the hospital watching Dad, who's sicker than he's ever been, and I'm on a plane with no way to help. Maybe I'll be this sick soon too.

Maybe they'll be glad.

Maybe that's why they sent me away in the first place.

After all, I am the family screw-up.

Cam pokes me again, but I brush his hand away. "Here. Watch the movie and eat your snacks. I'm going to sleep for a minute."

His lips pucker and pull down. Ally broke down and gave him a lollipop after he cried his way through the airport and the sugar seems to keep him wired. Aunt Piggy doesn't brush him off like this. I'm supposed to be fun, not boring and strict like the adults.

I gnaw on the inside of my cheek. "Sorry. Let's play cards."

He claps his hands and wiggles his body, huffing and puffing, until he reaches the miniature *Cars* backpack under his seat. He hands me the Go Fish deck, and I deal. Behind us, Mattie screeches and kicks the back of my seat. He's always sweet, but the plane ride is too long for him to sit still without going crazy.

When we finally land, I grab a sleeping Mattie from Justin as we are herded through the aisle to get off the plane. We silently wait for our ride, an Uber that drops us off at home.

Everyone's here.

Almost everyone.

The twins, Gavin and his wife Sarah, and Mom huddle together, forming a tight circle in the living room. One that we join and turn into a tight oval. The kids weave in and out, not aware we're trying to block out the rest of the world. Mom's eyes are a water feature that never turns off, and she dabs at them with an endless supply of tissues.

The drive to the hospital is slower than any drive in the history of automobiles. Gavin drives over the speed limit, and my knuckles still turn white, gripping the side of my seat, urging the car to move faster.

We're running out of time.

DAD IS PALE AND DIMINISHED UNDER THE STIFF WHITE hospital sheets. Covered in wires, he's smaller than I've ever seen him.

It's like he's already gone.

Allison chokes out a sob and buries her head against Justin's chest while he rubs circles on her back. The twins stand close together. Gavin's arm is slung protectively around Mom's shoulders, Sarah's hand clasping his free one. The little boys are at home asleep. Our elderly neighbor volunteered to sit with them while we were gone.

And I'm by myself.

Arms at my sides, I squeeze into myself. It'd be pretty nice to disappear right now. And no one would even notice. We're all wrapped up in our grief, and as usual, I'm the extra. Not seen, not needed, not even wanted.

A nurse comes in, breaking the sore silence. She lets us know visiting time is over, and only two guests may stay, given Dad's condition. I drift from the room, not bothering to see who'll stay with Mom. Everyone quickly follows me, including Gavin, who I figured would be the one to stay with her.

Peter, the last one out, clicks the door closed behind him and leans against it. He lifts his chin and faces Gavin. "You weren't planning on telling anyone else?" His whisper is like a scream.

Ted glances at me and I lift my eyebrows. I have no idea what this is about.

Ally steps close to them. "What's going on, guys?"

Peter jabs his finger in Gavin's chest, poking hard enough to bruise his collarbone. "He knew Dad was going to die, and he kept it a secret because he's an *ass.*"

Gavin's eyes narrow to slits as he steps backward. Sarah wraps an arm around his waist. "Don't say that," she says, blue eyes watery.

Ally touches a hand to her heart. "Did you know something, Gavin?"

Gavin blinks for a long time. "Mom told me. After Dad's

surgery, the doctor said it was risky because he was already weak, and his immune system was all messed up." He's still whispering, but the volume of his words washes over us.

Peter points at Gavin again, but words don't come. Ted claps a hand on his shoulder, and Peter sags backward.

I curve my fingernails into my palm until the stinging snaps me back. "It doesn't matter." What does fighting accomplish? It's too late to argue over who kept a secret and why.

Gavin half-nods. "Mom asked me to not tell anyone. I guess she hoped he would get better and it wouldn't matter."

It's so typical. Gavin's always kept secrets, and Mom has always trusted him the most. We stand there in a silent group for another moment. Then Sarah squeezes Gavin tight, and he goes back inside the hospital room. Peter, Ted, and Sarah walk down the hall single file.

Ally taps my shoulder. "We're heading back to the house to get the boys from the babysitter. Want to ride with us?"

I train my eyes on the white speckled tile at my feet. "I'm going to sit in the waiting room for a little bit. I kind of want to be alone." It's a lie. But what's another lie in this family?

Allison nods, her lips pressed tight. Justin pats my head as they pass by, leaving me standing alone. My eyes glaze over as I drift toward the waiting room. I suddenly *don't* want to be by myself for another second. I want someone or something that can drown all these emotions until I don't have to do anything other than breathe.

I fumble for my phone and lean against the sharp white wall, then I press call.

Griffin's shiny red car pulls through the front loop outside the hospital, and I hurry toward him, my flats slapping the pavement. I shouldn't leave—who knows how much longer Dad has? But I can't stay here another second.

As soon as I'm in the passenger seat, Griffin leans over to wrap his arms around me. I tolerate it for only half-a-second before shimmying away to buckle my seat belt. "Take me anywhere."

He drives obediently, though his hand slides across the divide to mine. I cling to it like a lost child. I barely register the piles of McDonald's wrappers under my feet. Wringing his fingers, I tuck my feet under my body and lean my head back against my head-rest. I let my eyes close. My stomach twists with more than emotional turmoil, and I do my best to push it back. Hold it off. I'm not sick. Not sick.

With a gentle shake, Griffin gets my attention to let me know we've arrived, but it's somewhere I don't recognize.

"Where are we?"

He gazes at me sideways, his voice gentle. "It's a new spot I found."

I look around the car for the usual spray bottles and art supplies but see none. Irritation courses through me. "You didn't bring anything?"

He shakes his head, looking wary. "I came straight to the hospital when you called."

Sniffing, I hug my arms against my chest. I follow him out of the car and to the beginning of a trailhead. The sign marking it advertises a beginner's 1.5-mile hike. Without waiting for Griffin, I set out toward the trail, putting each foot in front of the other with steady determination.

"It's pretty, huh?" From behind me, Griffin tries to engage in conversation, but I clench my jaw and keep moving.

After a moment, the crunch of his footsteps behind mine halts, and I whirl around. I swear, if he disappeared into the woods to pee without telling me, I'm going to scream.

But he's not in the woods. A few feet back is a carved wooden bench, and he's sitting there, back hunched. I didn't notice him stop walking.

Sighing, I double back and fold myself down beside him. "Your stamina has really gone downhill in the past few months," I tease, my throat tight.

He fiddles with a leaf, twirling the thin brown stem between two fingers. His eyes don't meet mine. Something about his mouth, usually perked up with a smirk or a laugh, looks so sad. He's changed too, and I'm responsible. It's been hard on him, me being gone. Not just physically gone, but far away mentally too. With the boarding school threat and Dad and my new life in Washington for the summer, I've barely given a thought to what Griffin has done with his time.

I lower my head onto his shoulder, and he stiffens. "Griff." Mumbling into his arm, I say, "I'm sorry for being a jerk. I just don't know what I'm supposed to be doing right now. Dad is…"

I'm angry and confused and numb. Too many emotions to hold inside one body. Too many thoughts to keep bottled up, but my throat all but collapses around my words, swallowing them whole. Choked sobs pour out of me, and my shoulders shake with the release of pent-up grief. At some point Griffin's arms wrap tightly around me, and he holds me while I smear snot all over his shirt. "You can talk to me. I'm here whenever you need to." He rubs a palm across my back while I hiccup into my hand.

"He's going to die, Griffin. My dad is going to die, and it's my fault." Somehow Griffin's presence convinces me to confess.

His hand stops. Grabbing my face in his palms, he turns my head to face him. Blue eyes burning into mine, he shakes his head carefully. "No."

I hiccup again, tears welling up in my reddened, blurry eyes.

"It's not your fault that your dad is sick. You didn't do anything wrong."

Voice small, I say, "But I made this past year stressful for him, and that could have made him sicker."

It's my secret fear. Living in the back of my head, too awful to speak out loud, all summer long. My stomach clenches as I finally release my shameful truth. It churns with the words, threatening to make me sick all over the trail.

Dad is dying because of me. And now, to pay for my mistakes, I'm sick too.

"He missed you. He told me."

Griffin plucks a new leaf and twists it in his fingers, eyes focused on a sprawling oak directly in front of us.

I suck in a breath. "He told you?"

He nods. "Yeah, one of the times I came over this summer. I said I was checking on your parents, but I missed you. It felt more like you there than anywhere else, you know?" He rubs the back of his neck, ears pink. "I know it's stupid."

It isn't, though. The thought buoys me out of my self-depre-cation for a moment as I bring Griffin's hand to my cheek and hug it against my face. "That's really nice of you, Griff. And I missed him too. I missed all of you."

He shrugs. "Well, he told me once that he was never that mad about us getting in trouble. He told me a story about doing something similar when he was in high school. Except, you know, he didn't get caught, so it was less epic."

Only Griffin could find a way to make this about how cool he is. I slap his knee. I'm equal parts touched and confused about him visiting my parents while I'm away. Things aren't easy for Griffin at home with his dad's flakiness and his mom being so busy. I used to ease the sting of that for him. Honestly, it was probably the only perk of being with me.

Rubbing the spot, he glances down at me, eyes hooded. "You missed me, for real?"

My lips slide into an easy smile, despite how unhappy I am. "Are you seriously asking that? What do you think?" It cracks my heart in two he has to ask.

He smirks. His body angles toward mine so our knees touch. I draw closer to him, inching forward in a dangerous game of chicken. He slides even closer.

It's easy to do what I do next. I stand, pulling him up with me. My arms loop around his neck and my chest pushes against his. Staggering backward, Griffin stops against a tree trunk. He tilts his head back, lifting an eyebrow. "Paige?"

I shake my head, brushing the question away. "Just kiss me. I want this." I whisper in his ear so he can't tell when my voice cracks through the words.

His lips are soft on mine. Familiar and easy. My brain shuts off and we kiss until I need air and my lips start to feel chapped.

When my eyes blink open for a second, a different boy against a different tree flashes through my mind. And it's the same, but it's different. Joey may hate me now, but this is as close to cheating as it gets because my heart knows when I'm lying, even if no one else does. And I'm not that person.

I taste sawdust. Every inch of my skin stings with a crawling feeling I'm desperate to itch away. I feel dirty. Cheap.

Pulling away, I take several steps backward. Griffin's eyes slide open lazily, one side of his mouth curving into a grin.

My stomach twists.

He reaches for me again. He whispers to me, "I'm so sorry about your dad. I wish I had something better to say. I don't know how to help."

I cross my arms against my chest and stare at the sticks and pebbles under my feet. "You're a good friend."

He blinks at me, comprehension clear on his face. "But just a friend."

I turn to look him in the eyes. Through my wet lashes, I see him squaring his jaw, fighting to pretend he isn't crushed. Crushing Griffin is the last thing I want to do.

"You're my best friend. But that's all. I—I shouldn't have kissed you."

"We can't be just friends. That's not how this works." He chokes out a bitter laugh.

"We've been just friends all summer."

He rests his forehead in his open palm. "Not to me."

I inch forward to touch his arm. "I'm sorry."

He doesn't pull away, but he doesn't touch me back either. He freezes, ignoring my hand and my apology. And that hurts more than anything else.

G riffin and I don't do awkward. Even when things were
hard, like when we first broke up, we laughed our way
through it and pretended everything was fine. But the
ride home is uncomfortable. Griffin's silence speaks accusations
I can practically taste, but he won't spit them out.

At the end of my driveway I wait, hand paused on the car
door handle. Maybe he'll say something to me now. Maybe I
should apologize again.

Griffin's head doesn't move from its stationary spot facing
straight ahead. His eyes look through the windshield like he's
taking his driving test for the first time and he's too terrified to
blink, much less move his eyes from the cars ahead of him.

I'm so awful, he'd rather stare at empty air than tell me
goodbye.

I swallow, looking over at him one last time, before I exit the
car and close the door behind me.

By the time I reach the front door and look back, he's
already halfway down the street, tires squealing as he speeds past
my neighbor's house. They'll be sure to complain about it
tomorrow morning.

Mom's not there when I wander into the living room, but
everyone else is. Seeing me look around, Allison nods her head
toward the bedrooms. "She's napping before she goes back to the
hospital."

Justin adds, "We had to drag her home. She hasn't slept in over twenty-four hours."

My brothers' mouths form three identical grim lines. Every one of us in this room has aged years since just yesterday. I guess your dad dying will do that to you. Before I can think of anything to say, Allison opens her mouth again. "The boys are sleeping right next to your room, so try to be quiet if you sneak out tonight, okay?"

My mouth drops as her words slice through me. Justin narrows his eyes and glares at her silently. She shrugs and throws her hands up. "I'm just letting her know. It won't be long before she's running off to be with Griffin again. And the kids need sleep."

There's something deeply personal about the way she says Griffin's name. I search my siblings' faces for a show of support, but magically all of them are now absorbed in their phones and won't meet my eyes.

"Why do you care? What's it to you who I'm with?"

It isn't the point, and we both know it, but it's a hell of a lot better than fighting about what she's really getting at. Than admitting how terrified and guilty I am.

A plastic smile appears on her lips. "I honestly couldn't care less. It's really awful what you're doing to both of those boys, and you don't even care that you're using them."

My eyes burn with angry tears, hot and sudden. "I'm not using them." My hands form tight fists at my sides.

Allison blows air from her lips, a mocking sound. "What do you call it when you kiss two guys in one week?"

I stare back at her, dizzy, as shame washes over me. It doesn't even matter how she knows that, because she's right. I'm awful.

Justin places a hand on her wrist, but she throws it off. She's still getting warmed up. "Joey's mom called me right before we left because you vandalized their shop and didn't even bother telling anyone. He cleaned it up on his own, or else we would have probably had to pay for it. They might have pressed charges if he hadn't stood up for you."

I blink, blink, blink. Joey cleaned up my spray paint, even after I chased him off and ruined everything. It should make me happy to know he doesn't completely hate me, but every part of my brain is numb. Too many emotions ebb and flow, and I reject all of them. They're worthless, every single one.

"Sound familiar?" Allison nods, more to herself than anyone else. "You can't just go around using people to get out of trouble. It's cruel. And I've been dealing with all this while flying home to visit Dad for the last time ever. But you don't care. You won't even say anything because you don't care about anyone else."

In a snap, her harsh tone turns quieter, until it dissolves into crying. Without missing a beat, Justin pulls her head into his lap. He shoots me one last reproachful look, and my heart sinks.

I run to my bedroom and cry myself to sleep.

MY HAIR STICKS STIFFLY TO MY DRY LIPS AS I ATTEMPT TO PRY my eyes open. Everything is dark and disorienting, so I can't figure out why Gavin's trying to talk to me when it's clearly not morning.

"He's gone, Paige. Mom called. Dad passed just a minute ago."

If I were to drop my head back onto my pillow and force my eyes shut, I could pretend this is a nightmare. The worst bad dream ever.

"We're all going to the hospital to be with her. Are you coming?"

My never-ending guilt, the fight with Ally, the fact that maybe I really have been using everyone to get what I want all this time—none of it matters anymore.

Because Dad's dead, and it's my fault.

I find the energy to say, "Yes. I'm coming."

Gavin disappears from my doorway, presumably to give me some privacy as I crawl from bed and throw on a wrinkled National Honor Society t-shirt and the short cotton shorts Callie gave me at the first build-up day. Padding out to the van in the driveway with the rest of my siblings is surreal. Like we're all back home together, heading to church or to get ice cream or to watch Ally win a soccer game.

Instead we're going to see Dad at the hospital, but he's not really there.

As we drive, insects hum to provide the only sound in the heavy quiet.

"I think Dad used to say something about different kinds of heaven. Like, people go where they're going to be happiest." I look around at my siblings.

It's silent. Maybe everyone's still too mad at me to speak. I close my eyes again and try to block out the tiny part of me that cares what they think.

"You're right." Ally's voice sends me swaying in my seat, eager to find balance with her. "He said we go where we're best suited. He told me once he'd like to go to a version of heaven where he could be with his family. With all of us." She pauses. "I've always thought that was really nice."

My lip wobbles. Next to me, Peter loops an arm through mine, nudging me softly. "That sounds like Dad. He was like, the quintessential family man." Ted's voice rumbles through me.

I nod, even though no one can see. Dad loved all of us. Griffin's admission comes to mind, and through some miracle—Dad, is that you? —I find myself believing what he said about Dad not blaming me, not being angry. He missed me. Simple as that.

Now I miss him in the form of a hole carving its way through the center of my heart. In a way that pulls and tugs and jabs at me. The last time I saw him he was asleep, but alive. Now, he's just a body.

Maybe he's still asleep. Maybe everyone's got it wrong.

I dig my nails into my palm and stare out the darkened window into the night until we reach the hospital.

After a crowded elevator ride, we move through the fluorescent-lit halls, up the silent creaky elevator, around the fifth floor to Dad's room. All in something stronger than silence. That feeling of being alone, no matter how many other people you're surrounded by.

Mom's slumped in a chair near the window, her eyes closed. How is she asleep? There's exhaustion, and then there's this. But as I creep nearer, I see her eyes are actually glued shut with moisture, tears leaking from her eyes and staining the front of her pink floral shirt. Her hair is rumpled and greasy and frozen sobs wrack her body.

Sinking to my knees, I wrap my arms around her waist. I bury my head in her lap, and she grabs around my neck, nearly choking me, like I'm the only visible lifeline and she's seconds from drowning.

"Mom," I whisper into her legs as she strokes my hair.

"I know. I know," she whispers back.

After a little while, I stand up. I sniff and find my eyes are too dry for more crying. My siblings circle around the bed where Dad's body lies. They stare down at him, but I train my eyes on their faces, not his.

I can't look at him. My hands shake before I'm even close to looking at him.

Mom leans her head back against her chair again as she lets loose a shuddering sigh. "The nurses are waiting for us to say our goodbyes before they take him."

Take him?

Suddenly my head is light, and my knees buckle where I'm kneeling. I fall back, landing on my butt on the hard, white tile. My breaths come too hard and fast.

Allison rushes to my side and pulls me up by my wrists. I stand, lean against her, my chest heaving unsteadily.

"They're going to take him?" My lip quivers as I ask the unfathomable.

She nods swiftly. "They have to, Paige. So if you want to say goodbye, do it now."

I'll never *want* to say goodbye to Dad. I'll never want to leave him. Or to see him without really seeing *him*. It's unthinkable. But if there's a chance, I'll regret it someday...

I clasp my hands in front of my chin and nod. "Okay."

Stumbling toward the bed, I force myself to focus on his hair. Dad always liked his hair better than any other part of himself. He was so proud to never have a receding hairline like a lot of his friends, and he always said he'd have a full head of hair when he was a great-grandfather, and if he didn't, he'd wear a wig. He thought it was a pretty funny joke.

My mouth doesn't even twitch at the memory. I'll probably never laugh at another thing again. How can I? Dad was the funny one in the family. And the easygoing one. Without him, we'll be something else entirely. Not the same group we've always been, forever without our leader.

The lightheadedness comes rushing back the second my gaze lands on his closed eyes. They're artificially closed and not at all what he looks like when he's sleeping. I used to sneak into Mom and Dad's room when I was younger and scared in the middle of the night, and Dad's eyes would be squinted shut, almost like he was pretending to be asleep, and his mouth was always half-open, a trail of soft snores cascading out.

Now he's too still, too peaceful. He was always warm and full of life, and this—

My hands shake by my sides.

"Goodbye, Dad." I'm not talking to the body on the bed, but to Dad, wherever he is now.

"I hope you're in your own heaven with lots of good food and basketball games running nonstop with an endless supply of LA-Z Boy chairs."

Behind me, the twins snort and sniffle.

I close my eyes and step backward. I don't want to look at this not-Dad a second longer than I have to.

Everyone else takes their turns. Mom stands from her chair and presses a button on the hospital bed. A second later, a nurse opens the door and Mom tells her we're done with the body.

That's just how she says it, too. The body.

She doesn't feel like it's Dad either, I guess.

We all circle Mom and we walk to the parking lot and load into the van. None of us will be able to sleep, but we go home anyway. After someone dies, apparently you have to pretend at just about everything. Goodbyes, sleeping. What else?

CHAPTER
Thirty Six

After the funeral, Griffin comes up to me and wraps his arms around me. I melt into him a second longer than I should. Because it's easy, and because I'm exhausted. He still feels safe, even after what has happened between us.

But things are still different because after he hugs me, he walks across the church to his mom, puts his arm carefully around her, and they leave.

Even if I weren't numb, I don't think I'd care that much. I love Griffin like I love my own brothers. I want him to be happy. Especially after I hurt him. Intentional or not, he doesn't deserve that.

On the ride home, Allison and Justin are quieter than usual. I'm in the back with the little boys, careful not to even breathe too loud as they both nap in their seats. Justin and Ally usually whisper between themselves up front, but they say nothing. Instead, they look at each other meaningfully, occasionally glancing backward at me. I close my eyes and ignore them.

Finally Ally turns around to whisper, "So, what do you think, Paige? We're leaving tomorrow morning. Are you coming with us, or do you want to stay?"

I chew on my lip. I guess I could stay? With everything else going on, plans for the remaining few weeks of summer never crossed my mind.

I shake my head slowly. "What do you think Mom wants?"

Ally's mouth twists. "Honestly? I'm not sure she's thought of it either. She's a mess right now, so maybe you could gently ask her what she's thinking."

At home, I find Mom in her room and sit on the end of her bed. She's tucked in under the covers and her face is red. It's always red now.

"Paige," she rasps, attempting a ghost of a smile.

I reach over and squeeze her hand. "Mom. I'm so sorry. I know you loved Dad so much."

She nods and her eyes well up again.

"Ally said I should ask you about this summer, about what I should do..." I bite my lip.

Mom blinks. "It's up to you. Gavin and Sarah are staying for the rest of the month, so I won't be alone." She sniffles as if the thought of being alone just occurred to her. "What do you want to do, Paige?"

It's strange having a choice after being exiled without a say in the matter. With Griffin and me and how we left things, I'm not sure who I have left in Seattle, except Mom. And Mom is so wrapped up inside her own grief, who knows when she'll come out. Or when she does, if she'll care that I'm here or not.

And Allison and Justin are asking me to go back.

My chest rises as I inhale deeply and lift my head. "Well, I do have half my clothes at their house. And everyone there might wonder why I disappeared." I lift my lips into a smile. The muscles twitch from the strain. "Maybe I'll go to Texas and see out the summer, if that's okay with you."

Mom smiles more fully now. "I think that's a good idea. You seem happy there."

A spark of happiness floats in my belly, warming me and waking up the cold parts that stopped working when Dad got sick.

AN HOUR AFTER WE GET HOME FROM THE AIRPORT, CALLIE shows up in her traditional uniform. Her jersey is so long not even a hint of her short shorts peek through. Allison raises her eyebrows the second she thinks Callie can't see as I'm sliding past to the front porch.

"I heard about your dad. I'm so sorry." Callie throws her arms around me, stunning me a little. I've never really thought of her as the hugging type. But I've learned death brings out many surprises in people, and it's never easy to predict what they'll be.

I hug her back quickly, then pull away. "Thanks. It's okay."

That's something I'm supposed to say. Because if I don't, if I admit I'm devastated, that I can't sleep, that crying is a more constant state than not, people give me a very specific look. It's a look that says, "Oh you poor lost baby" and "This is so awkward, what do I say now?" A mixture of the two is the worst of all, and I'm not emotionally prepared for any of that, so I lie and suck back impending tears at any mention of Dad.

"How's the build-up? I hear you're still kicking Joey's butt."

Her eyes roll into the back of her head. "Are you kidding me? Of course I am. I'm twice as fast as he is. Most of the work is done now. We just need to paint."

I haven't heard a word from Joey since the night I yelled at him like a lunatic and he drove away from me in the parking lot. I figured even if he heard about the funeral, he didn't want to talk to me, period. And I can't blame him. The way I treated him was equally, if not more messed up, than what I did to Griffin. "I'm not sure I'm going to be there anymore. No one but you and Jen wants to see me."

Callie raises an incredulous brow. "You might have broken Joey's heart, but I guarantee he'll still want to see you. You should come, even if it's just to say hi to everyone. We've all been worried about you."

Heartbroken? I don't think so. "Maybe I will," I say. "But it wasn't like that with Joey and me. No broken hearts."

She laughs under her breath like I'm too ridiculous to take seriously.

I purse my lips. "I'm serious. We kissed a few times. It was nice, but we're obviously *very* different."

"Whatever. That's not what he said." Her eyes narrow knowingly. But what could she know that I don't?

"You do the same thing with Kevin, don't you?"

"We're talking about you and Joey." She folds her arms against her chest, one of her cheeks sucked in tight.

"I don't want to talk about Joey. Tell me about Ben's party last weekend."

Callie gives me one last meaningful stare before launching into a story about Ben's cousin who came to stay for the weekend and instantly fell in love with both Jen and Callie. Apparently, he was a slime ball, and they narrowly avoided him the entire night. Ben had to be the one to tell him neither of them was interested, resulting in his cousin storming off into the woods and getting himself lost enough the state troopers organized a search party.

I nod at all the right parts. When she's done, I say, "That's crazy." I pause. "Where was Kevin?"

Wrinkling her nose, she says, "He was there too. I hung out with Jen the whole time, though."

Interesting.

She slugs my arm. "Come to our ultimate Frisbee game next week. It's our last big thing before school starts. Everyone from the build-up comes to celebrate, and I get to kick Joey's butt one last time. Talk to Joey, okay? You can't avoid him for the rest of the summer."

Funny. That's exactly what I plan on doing.

CHAPTER
Thirty Seven

The calendar behind Ally's desk says it's Wednesday, August 14.

Standing alone in the too-bright afternoon glare coming from the big bay window, I laugh drily to myself.

I was supposed to change. I was supposed to do something big, something amazing, to show my parents how wrong they were about me.

Instead, I did nothing, and Dad died. My eyes fill with tears —a reflex so common I barely even notice.

"I bet your friends miss you." Ally stands in the doorway of her office, a stack of manila envelopes in her hands.

Sniffling, I shrug. "Are those new pictures?"

She walks to me, handing over one of the envelopes. I carefully unhook the metal tab at the top and slide the contents out.

My heart twists and leaps. I grab the picture on top of the stack, placing my fingers gingerly on its edges. Bringing it close to my face, I swallow as I gaze at a candid shot of Joey and me. "When...?"

Ally smiles softly. "I came home one day, and you two were sitting on the couch, so into that game you were playing, you didn't even notice me. I snapped a few pictures and snuck back out."

In the picture, Joey and I look sideways at each other. Our eyes crinkle at the edges as we laugh over whatever challenge we were trying to beat on Mario. The wide, toothy smile stretched across my face is nearly unrecognizable. Was I really that happy just a few weeks ago?

My eyes burn. I don't know if I'm crying over Joey, or me, or Dad.

Maybe all of us.

"Ally, did I kill Dad?"

A sharp intake of breath whooshes over me as her arms wrap around my back. "Of course you didn't. Dad was already sick.."

"But they sent me here because I made him sicker. That's why they wanted me to go to boarding school. Because Mom knew I'd end up stressing Dad out so much he'd die." I nearly choke on the words. On the truth.

Ally's hands cup my shoulders. Her words pour out with urgency. "Listen to me, Paige. You didn't do anything wrong. Mom and Dad love you. And forget about boarding school. You're not going away, okay?"

I inhale into her neck, and she strokes my hair like I've seen her do with Cam and Mattie when they're close to nap time. She did the same thing when I was a little girl. It's easy to believe her. It's easy to accept her consoling words and let go of the soul-slicing pain, at least a little.

I exhale. "I think I'm sick too. I think I'm sick like Dad was. Can you help me make a doctor's appointment?"

⚘

ALLY HOLDS MY HAND AND MOM SMILES AT ME FROM MY phone screen where it's propped up against my hospital tray.

"Dad would be so proud of you." Tears shine in her eyes, visible even over the grainy video call.

I nod, unable to say much due to a vicious mixture of frog-in-my-throat and groggy post-surgery brain. I spent the entire day yesterday drinking clear liquids and forcing myself to down an unpleasant laxative drink that promised to taste *just like a milk-*

shake. It did not. But the colonoscopy is over, and now all that's left is to hear what the doctor has to say.

I'm jittery and sweaty and my brain is muddled. But I'm also a little bit proud of myself. This thing I've been running from all summer is here. And there's nothing I can do to change whether or not I have Crohn's. It has nothing to do with how brave I am or how fun I am or if I'm a screw-up or not. Dad lived his life with this disease, and he was an amazing person—the best.

When my doctor comes in and flashes me a small smile, I recognize from my time visiting Dad in the hospital, I know. Ally squeezes my hand because she knows too.

"Well," Doctor Abebe says, "the bad news is that you definitely have Crohn's disease. We saw a lot of inflammation and ulcers along your colon that are consistent with the disease. Given the way you've been feeling and your father's struggle, we can safely say that you have it as well."

At her diagnosis, I expect my heart to sink or for tears to flow. But I'm strangely calm. And so are Ally and Mom. I nod. "Okay." I can deal with the diagnosis. I can deal with it if it means I'll feel better soon. A weight lifts off me from the stress of wondering, the stress of hiding and keeping it a secret.

Doctor Abebe smiles again, and this time it's more genuine. "The good news is that with diet and the right medication, you'll feel a great deal better. We'll get you started right away."

That sounds good. It sounds more than good. I squeeze my eyes shut for a second and imagine Dad hugging me tight. Mom's right—he would be proud of me.

O n my way to the Frisbee game, I half-step off my bike before gripping the handlebars and deciding to rush back home before anyone notices me. At least my legs are only wobbly thanks to a case of nerves and nothing else this time.

"Paige is back!" Jen's bubbly voice cuts through my indecision, forcing me to stay. Callie's team gathers around me, filling me in on our past victories. Some guys from Joey's team wander over to say hi, but I don't see Joey himself.

Not that I'm looking for him.

When I came to Frisbee, regardless of the awkwardness that surrounds Joey and me, I told myself I'd be polite but distant, if I talk to him at all.

Now that I'm here, I'm shaky and unconfident.

What if he confronts me in front of everyone? What if he tells them how I treated him? Or about what I did to his parents' store with the spray paint?

What if he says I broke his heart?

My own chest pangs as I think of what Callie said. She's being dramatic, that's the only explanation. Breaking someone's heart requires more than a few weeks of hanging out. It's what happens when you've been dating for years and one of you cheats on the other.

That's clearly not what happened with us.

Someone tosses Callie a Frisbee, and she holds it in the air, instantly commanding everyone's attention. "Let's play!" She waves the Frisbee with a cocky smile and jogs toward one side of the field right before a voice interrupts her.

"Not so fast. We start first this time, remember? And we said we'd pick teams to even things up." Joey lifts his chin in the air. He wears an intense look that he has so often it's his default expression.

Callie drops her arm holding the Frisbee and shrugs a shoulder. She looks bored. "Whatever makes you feel better."

I try so hard to make myself invisible, I end up stumbling over a foot of the guy I'm hiding behind. With an *oomph,* I twist to the ground, my hands behind my butt as I crash to the grass.

"Are you okay?" The guy I tripped over reaches a hand out to pull me up at the same moment Joey bounds forward to grab me by the wrist and heave me to my feet.

His fingers circling my wrist, he pulls me along into the center of all the players. "Found my first pick," he says, his voice light.

My skin prickles against his. For some reason my brain can't possibly fathom, he doesn't let go of my hand right away, and we stand there holding hands in front of all our friends. Callie and Jen smirk happily on the other side of the group.

I snatch my hand away and plant it on my hip.

I'm here to play Frisbee, period. And whatever show Joey's trying to put on right now doesn't change things. We're not together. We might not even be friends after how mean I was to him.

Friends don't force each other to do things they don't want to. And friends don't cut the other one out for something they didn't do. I don't deserve Joey in my life.

Joey steps back and surveys the rest of the people, waiting his turn as Callie makes her first pick, which is Jen.

It gives me a chance to stare at Joey because everyone else watches as he and Callie choose their teams. Now that I've seen

Joey again, it's like my eyes never want to *stop* drinking him in. His hair is cut shorter than it was the last time I saw him, but he keeps running his hands through it like it's still there covering his eyes.

I bite back a smile, because I shouldn't be allowed to smile about anything Joey related.

Not even if it's this cute.

The rest of the Frisbee game goes the same as things like this always go- me running at a snail's pace along the outskirts of the field as everyone else chases after the Frisbee. Callie's team wins, but Joey just shakes his head good-naturedly and congratulates her.

I guess he's given up on ever beating her at a game. Everyone leaves after that until it's only Callie, Jen, Joey, and me. I'm showing Jen pictures I took back home in Washington while Callie and Joey are arguing about a basketball game that was on TV.

Jen looks at her phone and frowns. "Crap. We have to go, Cal."

Callie narrows her eyes. "Huh?"

Stabbing her finger at her phone, Jen says slowly, "It's time to go. Right now."

Callie's eyes widen and her mouth forms an O. "Oh. Right."

She shifts her gaze between Joey and me. "We have to go... somewhere. See y'all later."

They're so painfully obvious, it takes all my self-control to not slap my face into my open palm. Behind Joey's back, they both turn and shoot me an enthusiastic thumbs up. I hope they know something I don't.

Joey squints at me. "Need a ride home?"

My heart leaps in my chest, skipping a beat as I grin wildly. I clear my throat to curb any emotion from creeping into my voice. "Sure. That'd be nice."

It's just a five-minute drive. It means nothing. He's probably just being polite.

Joey walks straight to my bike and picks it up. I unlatch the back of his unlocked 4Runner and together we slide it inside the trunk. Sitting in the passenger side of his car is the most comfortable I've felt in days. It's like taking a deep breath and letting it go and your whole body sinks into itself and there's nothing left to worry about.

Which is stupid.

There's a ton to worry about. Especially with Joey and me. I do not understand where we stand. And even if we're still friends, what's the point when I can count the time I have left in Texas in days?

Still, some closure would be nice.

I start small. "You got a haircut."

One hand goes automatically to his bangs. He winces. "Yeah. You think it looks stupid, don't you?"

I shoot him a sideways look. "I didn't say that."

He bobs his head, dimples showing. "You didn't have to. I can read you pretty well now. Your voice gets all cracky when you're uncomfortable."

A small wave of heat blooms over my ears. "I think it's nice. I do miss your swoop, though."

Raising an eyebrow, he angles his head. "*Swoop?* Is that what you called it?"

I bite my lip to keep from laughing.

He shrugs. "I can grow *the swoop* back for you. Don't worry."

For me. The sound of that phrase coming from him sends a wave of giddiness straight through my knees. I lean my head against the headrest. I grip the door handle until my fingers sting with the pressure.

"Joey—I'm really sorry."

The moment the apology leaves my mouth, all the emotions I've held in come spilling out. Fat tears slide down my cheeks and my lips tremble with lost control. I suck in a breath that turns into a rasping sound.

Without missing a beat, Joey maneuvers the car to the side of the road just outside the entrance to Allison's neighborhood. He turns off the car and climbs out, crossing to the passenger side. Pulling open my door, he takes both of my trembling hands in his and helps me out onto the tall dead grass.

"I'm the one who should say sorry. The minute I found out about your dad, I should have been there for you." He clenches his fingers against my palms, his voice catching. "I wanted to call you so many times when you were gone last week. I just didn't have the words to say how awful I feel for not knowing."

I shake my head. "I could have told you." A bitter laugh ekes out. "Instead, I bullied you into vandalizing your parents' store. And Ally told me you cleaned it up and got in trouble. You shouldn't have done that." His hand brushes my hair, smoothing it into place. His eyes find mine and steady me. "I should have done more than that."

His hand hangs in the air before inching closer to my face. It settles on my cheek, tickling it softly. "I should have realized how bad you were hurting. I'm sorry I didn't figure that out sooner. I feel stupid. Plus, you've been sick."

It's still hard to accept that I was and am sick. It feels like a weakness to admit it, but Ally says that's my own neurosis. "I actually went to the hospital again."

Joey's eyes go big and I hold up a hand.

"I have Crohn's like my dad. But I'm feeling optimistic. Mine is a mild case, and the doctor said I should start feeling a lot better as long as I take these giant pills she gave me."

"Wow. I know that's gotta be hard to come to terms with. I feel even more stupid now. We've spent so much time together, and I never suspected you were sick before you passed out on me."

I sniff and give him a wry smile. He's so nice. I don't deserve his sympathy, not after everything. "I hid it well, I guess. And I'm the stupid one. I kissed Griffin while I was at home. He was there, and I needed to just be in control of something and do something stupid. Again. I always do that, and I hate it, but I do." I swallow. I expect him to step away from me, or yell, or drive off and leave me here alone.

Instead, he dips his head. "Do you love him?"

Swiping my eyes with the back of my hand, I nod. "Yeah, I do. I love him like I love the rest of my family. It took me a while to come to terms with it. I was pretty crappy to him."

Joey lifts his eyes to mine. "So you're not together?"

Together? Didn't he hear me say Griffin is basically my brother?

I let out a short huff. "We're *very* not together. But I kissed him, and I know *you and I* are not together like that, but we kissed, so I thought I should tell you. It didn't mean anything, if that helps."

Joey's mouth stretches out into a long, thoughtful line. "You didn't have to tell me that, you know. I was a jerk to you, and I never even asked you to be my girlfriend. You can kiss whoever you want."

Oh.

For some crazy reason, him being so cool about all of this leaves me a little deflated. Not that I'm hoping for a green-eyed monster, but a little jealousy wouldn't hurt. After all, I did kiss my ex-boyfriend a few days after Joey and I kissed.

"Thank you," I tell him. Stepping closer, I slowly, slowly, slowly pull my arms around his neck.

Joey's eyes widen. He holds his arms in front of his body and steps back. Like I'm poisonous. He ducks his head. "I just need some time to think."

Wordlessly, I nod. My chest pulls tight, and I bite my lip to stop more tears. We get back in the car, and even though things should feel better now, they're still wrong. Too bad I have no one to blame but myself.

CHAPTER
Thirty Nine

My hand hovers in the air near the door. I don't want to do this. Because if I knock and I say what I came to say, and Joey still doesn't forgive me...

I'm out of options.

But if I don't do this, things might never get better. And then I'll never forgive myself.

Squaring my shoulders, I lift my knuckles to the door and knock. After a few seconds, the door swings open just as the butterflies in my stomach threaten to engulf me. At least it's not stomach pains though. The medicine works just as well as the doctor promised.

Joey's mom stares back at me, smiling like she already knows who I am. She looks exactly like her picture from the Prince Prints counter. Her hair is swept back into a sleek black bun on top of her head. She tilts her head, face expectant.

I lick my lips. "Um. Hi. Is J-Joey home?" Dang it. Why do I trip over his name like a guilty little kid?

His mom leans forward slightly, shaking her head. "I'm sorry. He isn't. I'll tell him you came by though, Paige. I know he misses you." She grins at me with a set of pearly white teeth offset by cherry-red lipstick.

Shifting the bag slung across my shoulder, I bite my lip. "That's okay," I say in a rush. "I'm actually here to talk to you and your husband, if you don't mind."

She frowns a little, but ushers me inside just the same.

I don't know what I was expecting the inside of their house to look like, but it's so different from Ally's, I gasp. Instead of sleek lines in monochromatic designs, warm colors bleed from every corner. That they have almost as many framed pictures decorating their walls as Ally does shouldn't surprise me, given their store. As I turn, I take in the yellow piano pushed against one wall and the turquoise Persian rug lining the hall.

Joey's mom's eyes trail over mine. Finally she says, "Do you want to sit?" She gestures to a cushy brown leather couch in the center of the room.

Joey's dad sits quietly on one side of it, his eyebrows arched severely in my direction. As Joey's mom lowers herself next to him, he lifts a hand from his tablet. "Hello there."

I perch on the edge of the couch on the opposite end. In theory, talking to them should be easy. I only have one thing to say, and I can spit it out quickly and run home in shame if I need to. Still, apologizing always sucks. And I don't like the idea of them hating me.

Before I can speak, his mom leans forward, eyes big. "We were so sorry to hear about your dad. How is your family doing?"

Mr. Prince doesn't meet my eyes when he mentions Dad. Joey's mentioned he doesn't like to talk about feelings, so maybe he's afraid I'll cry.

I cross and uncross my ankles, running a hand on the cool, smooth surface under me. "We're okay. My mom is having the hardest time, I think. She's seeing a therapist though, so I think that will help."

They both keep sympathetic smiles trained on me. But this isn't right. As messed up as I am over Dad, I didn't come here so they could offer me words of comfort.

I suck in a breath. "I need to apologize for the graffiti. I wasn't thinking clearly that night, but I shouldn't have done it. Even if it wasn't your store..." My teeth find my lip as I try to steady myself. "It was very, very wrong, and I'm so sorry."

Surprisingly, Mr. Prince speaks. "Joey explained the situation to us after he cleaned the wall." His voice goes deeper for a moment and his eyes shine with pride. He should be proud of Joey. Joey deserves that.

"It was sweet of you to come over and apologize," his mom says. She reaches her hand across the couch and finds mine hidden in my lap. She squeezes it with soft, gentle fingers before letting go.

I expected anger or indifference, but not this. Not easy forgiveness. My eyes burn, and I bury my face quickly in the shoulder of my shirt.

"Thank you," I choke out. I look both of them in the eyes, and I find they seem to forgive me. If only it were that easy with Joey. My heart clenches with the thought as I stand.

"Still, I'd like to do something to make it up to you. Maybe I could work for free at the store? I have a few weeks left before I go home, and Ally and Justin said I can use the rest of the time to help out with whatever you need."

Mr. Prince stands. "We have a job for you."

Mrs. Prince's eyes narrow at her husband, but she says nothing. I'm glad. I deserve whatever he's about to ask of me. I cross my arms over my chest as he points to the front door.

He stops at a closet near the front door, opens it, and pulls out a pair of pale blue rubber gloves and a metal hand shovel. "I've been busy with the store, and the weeds in our yard have grown out of control."

Mrs. Prince's hands go to her hips, and she looks like she's about to argue. Before she can say anything, I grab the supplies. "I'm great at weeding," I say with a smile.

Despite the stifling morning heat and the itchy grass on my bare knees, it's easier to breathe than it has been in days. Mom went through a gardening phase back when I was twelve, and the two of us spent all spring and summer desperate to keep our scraggly plants alive. At the end of the season, all we were left with was a brown withered graveyard in a patch of messy dirt. I was good at weeding the plants, just not remembering to water them.

Footsteps crunch along the driveway behind me, and I turn in time for Joey to notice me as well. I grit my teeth as his eyes meet mine. His stare is blank and unreadable.

"What are you doing?"

I brush hair from my face. "I'm pulling weeds." Sweat drips from the small of my back down my skirt, and my fingers itch to rub it away.

"Pulling weeds?" The words come from somewhere else, far away and small. The thunder of my heartbeat in my ears drowns out everything else. Joey's mouth quirks as he uses his toe to nudge a pile of thorny weeds to my left. "Um, why?"

I stand, sighing. "Because I asked your dad to let me do something. Because I wanted to apologize." I gesture to the gardening tools and weeds piled at my feet. "And this is what he wanted."

Joey shakes his head slowly, eyes big. "You shouldn't have to do anything. This is crazy."

My lips curve. "The yard isn't bad. I hear they have a pretty good grass guy."

His hands hover over his nonexistent swoop. "My parents would never say that," he mutters. "They think my lawn mowing is 'sloppy.'"

I shrug. "That's just what I heard."

Before I can think of something else to say, he steps toward me, his words spilling out. "I'm sorry I said I needed to think. I was jealous, and it was stupid of me to avoid you these past few days after everything you've been through."

I reach my shaking hands around him, and we hug for so long my chest grows warm. His skin burns under my hands through his thin t-shirt. "You have nothing to apologize for. I'm the one who made massive mistakes. And now the summer is almost over. I was awful to you."

His fingers brush my hips, causing me to suck in a breath. "You weren't awful. Please stop apologizing."

I laugh drily. "Only if you promise to stop, too."

"Okay." Joey's voice rumbles against my hair where his chin rests.

I exhale against his chest. Into his shirt I say, "Can we just start over? Pretend this summer never happened?"

Joey's grasp on my waist loosens, and my gut clenches. But instead of pushing away from me, his hands find my face. Gently, his fingers brush my cheeks, tracing my chin and my lips. I drag my eyes to his.

"I don't want to pretend it didn't happen. It was all worth it."

Holding my breath, I raise an eyebrow. "All of it?"

Joey lifts a shoulder, smirking. "Okay, maybe not all of it. We both messed up, but I'm done thinking. I miss you."

"I miss you, too."

Hands still cupping my face, he pulls me toward him until his lips cover mine. My mouth and my hands and my heart all breathe a giant sigh of relief. Because at this moment, it's like remembering something I've been trying to forget. Kissing Joey is so perfect I can't imagine ever having *not* kissed him. My lips press harder into his and my hands dig into the fabric of his shirt. We kiss until we have no other choice than to come up for air.

I bury another smile into his chest, squeezing my eyes shut for one more second. I feel his lips press a kiss on the top of my head before he loosens his grip on me. Sucking in a shuddering breath, I step back.

He kneels on the grass. His hands tug at the tall weeds, and we work that way, side by side, until all the weeds are gone, and his dad pulls us inside for lemonade and chocolate chip cookies and awkward stares.

CHAPTER
Fourty

"**P**iggy, you're going too slow."

Cam pokes my arm and drapes his bare feet over my legs as I press buttons on the game controller. I have no idea what I'm doing.

But I have to beat Joey. If only to make my five-year-old nephew proud.

Allison puts her hands on her hips and taps her high heel against the wood. She does a good job of pretending to be annoyed with us. But not even Mattie is fooled. He waddles straight toward her and strangles her leg while screaming a high-pitched squeal.

She bends to pick him up and then collapses down with him on her lap.

"How'd they turn out?" Joey sets his controller down, only to have it immediately snatched up by a certain dark-haired copycat.

Allison grins. "You'll have to wait and see, but I think everyone's going to be really happy."

As a favor to the Prince family, and a semi-bribe after the whole vandalism debacle, she offered to take some pictures for the store's online ads. Joey confided in me that his dad in particular was pretty nervous about having his picture taken. But Ally's able to get good pictures of screaming babies and easily distracted puppies. Middle-aged dads with camera fright are nothing. Still, it's good to hear what should have gone well in theory actually worked out.

And it's nice that Joey and his dad are sharing their feelings now. It gives Joey the perfect opportunity to confess that he's not so excited about working in the store. And for his dad to confess that he had his doubts all along. Who knows? Maybe Joey will be a teacher someday.

"Do you want to talk in private?" Ally looks pointedly around the room and then at me.

I frown. "I think I'm fine. Unless you want to gossip about Joey."

He tickles me in the ribs, and I catch his hand and squeeze it in mine. Cam sees and wrinkles his little nose in either confusion or disgust. Maybe a little of both.

Allison nods briskly, like that's what she was expecting me to say. "Okay. So I wanted to do this while Justin was here, but he's working late again. We've been talking a lot about this summer."

Dread settles in my chest, heavy and thick. I don't want to think about the end of summer. Not when it means leaving some of my favorite people on the planet. Not when leaving means going back to a nearly empty house full of memories of Dad.

Beside me, Joey goes still. We've deliberately avoided any discussion of what happens after. As far as we're concerned, there is no after. Just us together right now.

But logically, I know in my heart it will be hard as a long-distance couple. Especially when I don't know when I'll be in Texas next.

More than any of that, Washington doesn't feel like home anymore. Not after this summer in Texas. Not after Dad. And not after the way I've changed. I'm not the same Paige that arrived at the beginning of June, sweaty and hopeless and mad at my parents and the world. I've come to terms with a lot, starting with my place in the world and ending with my health.

Allison tucks hair behind her ear and steadies her shoulders. "We want to ask if you'd like to stay here for the school year. You can go to school here and you wouldn't have to nanny the kids or anything."

My mouth goes dry, and I can't say anything.

She rushes on. "I know you love Washington, but Mom is in a really difficult place right now, and I think she needs some time to herself to grieve while she's on this weird life-crisis cruise. It might be healthier for you to have more support around you. And you could have that here with us..." Trailing off, she offers a weak smile.

My heart pounds in my ears. Mom called last night to tell us her plans to leave next week for a cruise to South America. Ally already promised to fly to Seattle to stay with me while Mom's gone. And I could hear it in Mom's voice. The rush of relief and the lilt of happiness at not having to worry about me. So I bit back all my fears until she hung up, saying she needed to shop for a new swimsuit.

But now Ally's offering me something I never even dared mention. It's all I can do to not crush Ally as I leap across the couch and wrap my arms around her.

"But what about Mom? She'd be alone after her cruise..." Mom's face at the hospital and the funeral and after isn't the face of someone who should live alone. No matter how much she distracts herself with cruises and new clothes.

Ally nods. "Justin and I invited her to live here once she's back. And you know Mom, she was totally against it at first, but at the end of the conversation she seemed like she was considering it. Especially if it means she can help with your doctor's appointments and keep track of your health."

"All of us here?" I can't picture it, but the idea makes me smile.

Ally laughs. "Right? So, what do you think?"

"I would love that so much."

I get to stay.

It's like a dream come true, but I never thought to dream it because it seemed so impossible. My heart pounds and my head spins from breathlessness.

Pulling myself off my sister, I step back. "Okay. So, what are the rules?"

Ally shrugs. "There are no conditions to you staying here, Paige. We *want* you here. Just don't burn down the house and we'll be fine."

"Nothing?"

She tilts her head. "Maybe we should get you in an art class so you aren't tempted to tag our house. Because rumor is, you're actually pretty good at that."

Joey slips me a guilty look. "That could be cool," I tell Ally, and my mouth splits into a huge grin.

Cam jumps up and down on the couch cushions like he's on a trampoline. "Whee! Piggy's staying forever." Ally scoops him up and hugs him.

Joey pulls me close and pushes his lips softly against my cheek.

I exhale and settle in for a long round of Super Mario with my favorite people in the entire world. We've got time.

ACKNOWLEDGMENTS

This book was inspired in part by my own dealings with chronic disease, and so, in a weird way, I guess I have my own dysfunctional body to thank for the inspiration. In all seriousness, I owe a great deal to M.B. Dalto and Laynie Bynum for rescuing my manuscript from their slush pile and seeing the potential in my story. Sword and Silk is such a fun group to be a part of and I feel so lucky to have the two of them handle my words. Thank you to Jennia for her editing. She saw through the fluff and helped me cut my story down to its final, shiny form. A big thank you to Lucy Rhodes for her gorgeous cover art. She gave me something that perfectly sets the tone for Paige's story.

My friends who read this book in its earlier and much rougher form: Jordan Green, Brielle Porter, Britney Brouwer, Jessica Hall, thank you. Writing without supportive friends would be lonely and their feedback helps more than I can say.

Thank you to my parents and my in-laws who cheer on my writing endeavors with enthusiasm even though the world of publishing is hard to explain. I'm lucky to have them.

A million thanks to my husband Mark for being an excellent sounding board and always supporting my dreams. And to my kids, Bennett, Silas, Nolan, Drew, and Vivian– thank you for putting up with writer-mom brain and loving me just the same.

ABOUT THE AUTHOR

Haleigh Wenger is a Young Adult author and avid romance reader. She graduated with a B.A. in Communications from Brigham Young University in 2009. She is a lifelong fan of Young Adult novels, starting with Sarah Dessen and Judy Blume and now spanning a wide variety of authors such as Sandhya Menon, Morgan Matson, and Jenn Bennett. When not writing or reading, Haleigh is chasing her four young kids or baking cookies. Find out more at HaleighWenger.com

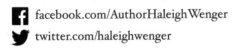

facebook.com/AuthorHaleighWenger
twitter.com/haleighwenger

When her Opa dies right before summer break, all Claire has left is a sand-sculpting contest application with her name on it and the lingering question of why Opa filled it out in the first place.

Joining forces with local teen, Foster, they take on the contest and salvage the Summer of Art. But Foster has a secret that threatens to ruin everything: he's homeless and hiding from an abusive brother.

When someone close to Claire spills Foster's secret, they're both forced to choose between love and familial obligation. If Claire can't break through long-held beliefs and prove family is more than shared DNA, she could permanently lose Foster and a chance at the sand contest to honor Opa.

A SPECIAL THANK YOU TO OUR KICKSTARTER BACKERS FROM SWORD AND SILK BOOKS

Alexa James, Mary Beth Case, Jasmine, Morgan, Elayorna, Brynn, Lane R, Rhiannon Raphael, Sara Collins, Tabitha Clancy, Erica L Frank, Jen Schultz, Tao Neuendorffer, Kyle "kaz409" Kelly, Patrick Lofgren, Rebecca Fischer, Bridh Blanchard, William Spreadbury, Wm Chamberlainq, Adam Bertocci, Susan Hamm, Paula Rosenberg, Morgan Rider, Elizabeth Sargent, Greg Jayson, Jamie Kramer, Karen Gemin, Jonathan Rice, Bonnie Lechner, Katherine Pocock, Mary Anne Hinkle, Marlena Frank, Melissa Goldman, Stacy Psaros, Meghan Sommers, Marisa Greenfield, Anne-Sophie Sicotte, S. L. Puma, Jenn Thresher, Caley, Jim Cox, Kris McCormick, Jamie Provencher, Melody Hall, Ara James, Leigh W. Stuart, Sarah Lampkin, Stuart Chaplin, Amanda Le, Rae Alley, Arec Rain, Megan Van Dyke, Hannah Clement, Kathleen MacKinnon, Paul Senatillaka, Christine Kayser, Jennifer Crymes, Christa McDonald, Debra Goelz, Amber Hodges, Thuy M Nguyen, Jess Scott, Ella Burt, Sarah Ziemer, Mel Young, and Claire Jenkins.

NEXT FROM SWORD AND SILK BOOKS

Coming October 2021
The Almost Queen
By: Alys Murray

Coming December 2021
Mind Like a Diamond
By: Amanda Pavlov

Coming February 2022
Unravel
By: Amelia Loken

CPSIA information can be obtained
at www.ICGtesting.com
Printed in the USA
LVHW081631030821
694428LV00017B/129

9 781736 430033